MANON LESCAUT

ANTOINE-FRANÇOIS PRÉVOST (1697–1763) was born in Hesdin in northern France. He was educated by the Jesuits but, after various escapades and absences, it was as a Benedictine that he was finally ordained. He was sent to Paris, where he combined monastic life with a successful debut as a novelist, publishing the first two volumes of his fictional *Mémoires d'un homme de qualité* in 1728. Faced that same year with arrest, following a dispute with his order, he fled to London, found work as a tutor, and moved in literary circles. Dismissed in 1730 for a secret engagement with his employer's daughter, he sought refuge in Holland. The final volumes of the *Mémoires d'un homme de qualité*, which included the original version of *Manon Lescaut*, were published there in 1731. Bankruptcy and a ruinous love affair drove him, accompanied by his mistress, back to England, where he started a periodical, *Le Pour et Contre* (1733–40), designed to introduce French readers to the English social and cultural scene. After a brush with the law in London, he returned to Paris. Reconciled with his religious order but as ever short of money, he embarked on a third long memoir-novel, *Le Doyen de Killerine*, and published his *Histoire d'une Grecque moderne*. In 1741 further trouble with the authorities again drove him into exile. Permitted to return to France and parted from his mistress, he spent the last twenty years of his life in relative tranquillity, maintaining a prodigious output of histories, journalism, translations from the English, and fiction, including the revised version of *Manon Lescaut*. Although he is remembered today chiefly for his two short novels, *Manon Lescaut* and *L'Histoire d'une Grecque moderne*, his contemporaries admired, above all, *Cleveland* (1731–9), which, with his translation of Richardson's *Clarissa*, exercised considerable influence on the course of the novel in France.

ANGELA SCHOLAR has worked as a translator and teacher of literature, following postgraduate study of Renaissance French poetry. She is the translator of Rousseau's *Confessions* for Oxford World's Classics.

OXFORD WORLD'S CLASSICS

*For over 100 years Oxford World's Classics have brought
readers closer to the world's great literature. Now with over 700
titles—from the 4,000-year-old myths of Mesopotamia to the
twentieth century's greatest novels—the series makes available
lesser-known as well as celebrated writing.*

*The pocket-sized hardbacks of the early years contained
introductions by Virginia Woolf, T. S. Eliot, Graham Greene,
and other literary figures which enriched the experience of reading.
Today the series is recognized for its fine scholarship and
reliability in texts that span world literature, drama and poetry,
religion, philosophy and politics. Each edition includes perceptive
commentary and essential background information to meet the
changing needs of readers.*

OXFORD WORLD'S CLASSICS

——

ABBÉ PRÉVOST

The Story of the Chevalier Des Grieux and Manon Lescaut

——

Translated with an Introduction and Notes by
ANGELA SCHOLAR

OXFORD
UNIVERSITY PRESS

OXFORD

UNIVERSITY PRESS

Great Clarendon Street, Oxford OX2 6DP

Oxford University Press is a department of the University of Oxford.
It furthers the University's objective of excellence in research, scholarship,
and education by publishing worldwide in

Oxford New York

Auckland Bangkok Buenos Aires Cape Town Chennai
Dar es Salaam Delhi Hong Kong Istanbul Karachi Kolkata
Kuala Lumpur Madrid Melbourne Mexico City Mumbai Nairobi
São Paulo Shanghai Taipei Tokyo Toronto

Oxford is a registered trade mark of Oxford University Press
in the UK and in certain other countries

Published in the United States
by Oxford University Press Inc., New York

First published as an Oxford World's Classics paperback 2004
Reissued 2008

British Library Cataloguing in Publication Data

Data available

ISBN 978-0-19-955492-8

14

Typeset in Ehrhardt
by RefineCatch Limited, Bungay, Suffolk
Printed in Great Britain by
Clays Ltd, Elcograf S.p.A.

CONTENTS

INTRODUCTION

Manon Lescaut—a story of passion and betrayal, of lovers divided by social difference and destroyed by fate—has moved from modest origins to become one of the great love stories. Composed rapidly, probably early in 1731, it appears at first sight to be accessory, the work of a moment, written in the margins of Prévost's more serious novels. Indeed, it was offered to the public in the first instance as an appendix, literally, to his own highly successful series of fictional *Memoirs and Adventures of a Man of Quality*. Within two years, however, it was also being published as an independent story; since when it has moved steadily centre-stage in public affection and critical esteem, to become Prévost's best-known work.

Manon too—the metaphor is appropriate—has moved centre-stage. The original title of the appended episode was *The Story of the Chevalier Des Grieux and Manon Lescaut*. But by the time of its first appearance in France in 1733, which was also that of its first appearance as a novel in its own right, Montesquieu was already referring to it by the abbreviated title *Manon Lescaut*, which soon afterwards began to appear on title-pages, and by which it has been known ever since.

Prévost: Life and Art

The young Prévost emerges, even from a brief outline of his life (for which, see the Chronology, below), as a somewhat ambivalent character: on the one hand there are his merits and achievements as the son of a highly respectable family, as a model pupil and talented novice; and on the other, his defections, disappearances, entanglements, and conflicts with authority. His own contemporaries were not slow to point out these evasions, one of them noting that:

Having been a soldier, then a Jesuit, a soldier for a second time and again a Jesuit, he made himself a soldier once again, then an officer, a Benedictine and at last either a Protestant or a Gallican, I doubt if he himself knows which . . . Finding it difficult to live out his own romances in his Order, he had the kindness to retreat to England, whence he was banished for practising them too much. He then took himself to Holland . . . [where] he has

had the honour of becoming bankrupt and of letting himself be kidnapped
by a young girl or woman . . . This author takes the name sometimes of
M. Prévost, sometimes that of M. d'Exiles . . . according to his needs.[1]

Small wonder, this same writer implies, that such a writer, for all his
evident literary taste and talent, should have come up with so
'ignoble' a story—*Manon*—as that which occupies the last volume of
the *Memoirs of a Man of Quality*.

Manon Lescaut is the story of a *coup de foudre*, of the fatal passion
of a young man for a girl he meets in an inn yard and with whom, in
order to save her from the convent, he elopes; of their difficulties in
making ends meet in Paris, of the wealthy lovers she takes to remedy
this situation, and of the deceits they practise against these lovers,
which lead them into crime, imprisonment, and finally exile. But
what earned this 'abominable'[2]—and immediately highly successful—book its notoriety (unsold copies were seized some three
months after its publication in France) was not only that it painted
vice and dissipation as insufficiently horrifying, but also that it portrayed 'people of standing' as acting unworthily: for Des Grieux is an
aristocrat, a young man of the highest rank, character, and prospects
who ruins himself for a courtesan and, worse still, justifies so blatant
a betrayal of his class by asserting not only the irresistible power of
sexual passion but the claims of sentiment over those of social
convention.

So compelling a story—or so many readers have thought—could
only be true, either autobiographical or confessional. The search for
the 'real' Manon has often proved irresistible; while Prévost's own
equivocations on the relationship between his life and his art, not to
mention his adoption of the poignant alias 'M. d'Exiles', make it
tempting to view Des Grieux as yet another alter ego.

Prévost and Des Grieux are, after all, of much the same age and
origin. Born in northern France of respectable (in Des Grieux's case,
noble) stock, both of them lose their mothers before they reach
maturity, have strained relations with strict and conventional fathers,
are educated by the Jesuits, show early academic promise, and hesitate between careers in the Church and the military. They mix in
Parisian society at all levels, enter into unwise emotional entangle-

---

[1] *Histoire du Chevalier des Grieux et de Manon Lescaut*, ed. F. Deloffre and R. Picard
(Paris: Classiques Garnier, Dunod, 1995), 278–9.

[2] Ibid., p. clxix.

ments, come up against the law, run away from the monastery and into debt, are indeed continually on the run, disappearing, or fleeing into exile. And both show, when called to account, a marked talent for self-justification and, above all, a gift for storytelling.

Nevertheless, all attempts to find the genesis of *Manon Lescaut* in Prévost's own life have failed; nor has an original of Manon been traced. Lenki Eckhard, with whom Prévost fell passionately in love in Holland, who all but ruined him by her extravagance, and who shared several years of wandering and insecurity with him, is the most likely model. But it was only several months after finishing the manuscript that Prévost met Lenki. As so often, life imitates art: 'Whatever one writes', said Oscar Wilde, 'comes to pass.'

Perhaps this truth holds good, too, for the last twenty years of Prévost's life, which find him parted from Lenki, reconciled with the authorities of Church and State, and—in imitation of the life of rural tranquillity imagined by the imprisoned Des Grieux—settled comfortably in various modest country retreats, enjoying the company of a few chosen friends and a considerable reputation as a writer. He further enhanced this with a prodigious production of journalism, history, translation, and fiction, including the revised version of *Manon Lescaut* (1753). 'Sooner or later,' he concluded, 'sensible people acquire a taste for solitude . . . In short, I am the happiest of men.'[3]

Manon Lescaut: *Aspects of the Novel*

Manon's story is told by her lover Des Grieux. But we owe its preservation to the intermediary of M. de Renoncour, man of quality and author of the seven volumes of *Memoirs*, of which this story occupies the last. In its opening pages M. de Renoncour relates two chance encounters he has with Des Grieux, the first at the inn at Pacy, just before Des Grieux embarks with Manon for America. M. de Renoncour relates the sympathy the sight of the young man arouses in him ('I have never seen a livelier image of grief'), based not only on class feeling ('one can tell at first glance, a man of birth and education'), but also on the apprehension of a shared sensibility ('I discerned . . . in all his movements so refined and so noble an air

[3] Ibid., p. lxxii.

that I instinctively felt disposed to wish him well'). So affected is he
by the young man's demeanour that he intervenes to help him, lending him money and support, and so earning, on the occasion of their
second meeting in Calais some nine months later, the narration
of the story the young man delivers, 'with the best grace in the
world'.

These introductory pages are themselves prefaced by a 'Foreword
to the Reader', added at the somewhat later point, we infer, when
M. de Renoncour is preparing his *Memoirs* for publication. Here he
paints a very different picture of the young man. The instinctive
sympathy he had felt for him during both their encounters has been
replaced, in the course of the intervening period, by moral outrage.
Des Grieux has become 'a terrible example of the power of the
passions'. His talents and merits have been wasted. He is, at best, 'an
ambiguous character, a mixture of virtues and vices, a perpetual
contrast between good impulses and bad actions'.

Such ambivalence is arresting, but not implausible. Des Grieux's
story, however eloquently told, is so scandalous (as its banning soon
after publication in France confirmed) that M. de Renoncour, with a
social position as well as a reputation as a respectable man of letters
to maintain, clearly thinks it prudent to offer it to the public as a
terrible warning of how not to behave, and so absolve himself in
advance of the charge of portraying an illicit passion as attractive
and, still worse, of seeming, by his own sympathetic response to it, to
plead its cause. Whereas, in the story that is to follow, Des Grieux
claims sexual passion as the greatest happiness known to man, M. de
Renoncour, in his Foreword, is careful to show him as refusing
legitimate happiness in favour of the misfortunes to which such a
passion must inevitably lead; and whereas Des Grieux presents his
passion for Manon as both unconquerable and involuntary—the
work of fate—M. de Renoncour insists that he had chosen his path,
and all its attendant misfortunes, 'voluntarily'.

This is, after all, standard practice in the eighteenth century, when
editorial claims of edifying intentions were customarily used to
legitimize fictions of a more or less dubious nature. There remains,
however, another and more interesting explanation of M. de
Renoncour's change of mind about Des Grieux: that he has had
time, while preparing his *Memoirs* for publication, to reflect on the
manner in which Des Grieux presents his story of fatal attraction,

and to suspect that beneath the 'good grace' of his narrative there lies a degree of bad faith: that it is his duty, in short, at the risk of unsettling his readers, to warn them against too complicit a sympathy with the ambiguous narrator of an ambiguous tale. In other words, M. de Renoncour, by his double introduction to Des Grieux's story, suggests two ways of reading it: we can either, as he himself initially does, succumb to the charm of its lucid and compelling eloquence; or we can read it dispassionately, noting its contradictions and inconsistencies.

As well as a certain ambiguity of response, the two narrators share a gift for storytelling. After his preliminary warning, M. de Renoncour provides Des Grieux's story with a dramatic and poignant opening scene in Pacy—the crowds converging on the wretched inn, the steaming horses, the chained prostitutes, the pale and desolate young man, the old woman wringing her hands. And when, two years later, he again catches sight of Des Grieux in Calais, even paler than before and, moreover, alone, M. de Renoncour cannot wait to hear his tale, thus setting an example to the reader who, drawn into the story by the suspense he has created, cannot wait to hear it either.

Manon Lescaut is one of the great Parisian novels, evoking the city with verve and precision, although it arrives at this end by very different means from those used in, say, Balzac's *Old Goriot* or Henry James's *The Ambassadors*. Its young heroes encounter a range of Parisian types: wealthy financiers, monks, gaolers, guardsmen, hired ruffians, innkeepers, gamblers, prostitutes, servants, policemen, and justices. We even get a glimpse of the circle of dissipated young aristocrats whom Des Grieux cites as models for his own misconduct. The places where these characters meet, as well as their movements around the city, can be traced minutely: there are scenes in the Jardin du Luxembourg, the seminary of Saint-Sulpice, the Palais-Royal, the Comédie-Française; Des Grieux waits in a carriage at the gate to the Tuileries, or frets in a coffee-house on the Pont Saint-Michel. There is little description of people and places, however, and not a vestige of local colour. We are told only what we need to know in order to follow Des Grieux's story. The city is evoked simply by naming its streets and sites, or by the mention of a turn of a path in the Jardin du Luxembourg, recorded for no other reason than that it ensures privacy. We are told nothing of the scene at the theatre, except Des Grieux's mingling with the crowds and his

anxious gaze as he scans the boxes, hoping to find Manon and young
G... M...; nor anything of the gaming-house, whose elegance of dress
and décor, the trickery of some and the ruin of others, is conjured up
by the flick of Des Grieux's lace cuff as he corrects the anomalies of
fortune.

Such details are chosen not for their visual impact—although they
may have this effect—so much as for their psychological, social, or
moral implications. The lovers rejoice in Paris—Manon in its pleasures, Des Grieux in his freedom to roam its streets. It is their natural
habitat. It is also an ally, a conspirator in their schemes for making a
fortune, whether by card-sharping or sexual manipulation; and,
when they are on the run, it becomes a threat, a party to their
destruction, a symbol of the forces they must either conform to or be
destroyed by. Paris, in other words, is a deeply ambivalent presence
in the novel.

Poetic realism, as we might call it, informs Prévost's account of
Louisiana too. If the town of New Orleans itself is rendered accur-
ately enough (see p. 133 and note), this is because the reality of the
place accords with the role it plays in Manon's and Des Grieux's
story. The rows of miserable mud huts that greet them on their
arrival, while they seem at first sight the image of social rejection—
and perhaps remain so for Manon—offer the possibility of a society
very different from that of the Old World. Indeed, they are briefly
'transformed to gold' by Manon's apparent conversion to fidelity
and the lovers' joint conversion to social respectability. But when this
New World shows itself, with the threatened appropriation of
Manon, more brutally patriarchal even than the old, the town offers
them no cover. The hostile sandy wastes into which the lovers flee, in
contrast to the relative realism with which New Orleans is drawn,
bear no relation to the actual environs of the town: in their barren
emptiness, they are purely symbolic.

A similar blend of realism and poetic realism characterizes the
treatment of historical and chronological time in the novel. *Manon
Lescaut*, written in 1731, is set in the recent past. Certain verifiable
events are alluded to—the establishment of a gaming-house in the
Hôtel de Translylvanie in 1713, for example; the death of Louis XIV
in 1715; the deportation of prostitutes to Louisiana in 1719–20. But
these fixed points do not always coincide with the internal chronology of the novel. The story takes place over five years, but which

five precisely? According to the time-scheme established by M. de Renoncour in the opening pages of the novel, his first meeting with Des Grieux takes place early in 1715, some six months before the death of Louis XIV, and the second towards the end of 1716, in which case the action of the novel takes place between 1712 and 1716. But we know from contemporary evidence that the Louisiana deportations happened only in 1719 and 1720, and that New Orleans, named after the Regent, was not founded until 1718. So that, if we accept that Manon cannot have been deported before 1719, then the novel's action must take place between 1717 and 1722. The latter chronology has generally been accepted by literary historians, but some prefer the former, since it places the story in the last years of Louis XIV's authoritarian regime, rather than during the overtly permissive Regency that followed. The anguish felt by Des Grieux, torn between duty to his family and passion for a low-born girl, is the more acute, the argument runs, if the old structures of authority represented by his father, although already undermined by a rising tide of permissiveness, are still in place.

The internal chronology of the novel is handled with care. Particular attention is paid to establishing the period of time—some nine months—that elapses between Manon's death and Des Grieux's meeting with M. de Renoncour in Calais: a period short enough for Des Grieux to relive the emotions of the past without any lessening of their intensity, and long enough for him to feel it is time he came to terms with them—a period of suspense in other words, between a past that haunts him and a future that is obscure. Where there is a lapse in the internal chronology of the novel (see p. 115 and note), this suggests that, concerned though Prévost is with verisimilitude, he is more interested in what we might call psychological or even tragic time: with the persistence of passion, the discontinuities that a moment can bring, joys that are brief and sorrows that are lasting.

Wherever, precisely, we prefer to place the novel, the second decade of the eighteenth century emerges, from Prévost's account, as a period of crisis in social values and the social order. Des Grieux's father is a member of the old nobility, with its code of honour, duty, and loyalty to family, class, and country, even if this code seems at times to have been reduced to a concern for the preservation of social difference and the keeping-up of appearances. As an affectionate father, and a man of the world, he is prepared to compromise himself in order to rescue his son from a misalliance; but he would never consent to it. The old aristocracy is under threat from a new breed of financiers and tax-farmers, men like M. de B... and the two MM. de G... M..., whose wealth is immense, but whose title, if they have one, is recently acquired. Des Grieux senior views them with contempt, as people 'we don't know'. His son treats them with, if anything, even more disdain. But, as Manon's lover, he is obliged to deal with them, and to experience, in the case of the older G... M..., the full force of their power and influence.

While respectful of his father's values, Des Grieux at the same time undermines them, for he too is a member of a new class, an aristocracy of the heart, an elite of people of sensibility and feeling, whose superiority to the ordinary run of men is demonstrated by the intensity of the emotions by which they are stirred. Such superior sensibility manifests itself typically through the gentler emotions of sympathy, tenderness, and pity, as well as through the sighs and tears to which they give rise; but it is not confined to them: more extravagant displays of passion, since they arise from feelings that are spontaneous and sincere, may also be the sign of a virtuous heart. Men of feeling and sentiment are, for the most part, men of birth and education too, for the principles they subscribe to—pride, a sense of honour, shame—are common to them both. M. de Renoncour, for example, is just such a man of sentiment. M. de T..., too, is 'tender and generous' and adept at trading declarations of sensibility with Des Grieux. The lower orders, in so far as they display sympathy for Des Grieux, are also allowed a measure of sensibility: Marcel is touched by the tender spectacle of Manon and Des Grieux's reunion in the Hôpital, while the gaoler in the Châtelet is 'moved by compassion for the most miserable of men'. But such people are, by virtue of their humble birth, unreliable; and Des Grieux is careful to secure their sympathy, and to mark his social difference from them, with a louis d'or. M. de Renoncour and M. de T... will prove no less unreliable, although Des Grieux never knows of the defection of the first, and seems blind to that of the second.[4] It is left to Des Grieux—but whether out of superiority of sentiment or because of a

---

[4] For a persuasive analysis of M. de T...'s ambiguous role in the novel, see *Manon Lescaut*, ed. P. Byrne (London: Bristol Classical Press, 1999), p. 149 and nn. 174, 179, 203, 241, 267, 272.

passion that borders on neurosis, the reader must decide—to live out the claims of the heart against those of social convention.

Des Grieux's schoolfriend Tiberge, although the upholder of orthodox Catholic values, also shows himself, in his exceptional tenderness for Des Grieux, to be a man of feeling. Nor is this surprising, for the cult of sensibility derives in part from seventeenth-century religious views that identified the pursuit of happiness as a fundamental human need which had to be directed to Christian ends, the passions as a motivating force in that quest, and the soul as the source of the passions.[5] But Tiberge knows, too, that the pursuit of happiness, if wrongly directed, leads not to a state of grace but to a sinful preoccupation with some all-too-human object; and he fears for Des Grieux's salvation.

Des Grieux, then, a man of honour and feeling, finds himself at odds with representatives of various other sets of values, each of them vying with the others in a society itself in a state of change. His father responds to his displays of excessive sensibility with anger, M. de Renoncour with alarm, Tiberge with anxiety, M. de G... M..., as he readjusts his wig and cravat, with vengeful incomprehension. One thing in the end, however, unites these various groups: their patriarchal elimination of Manon, a woman, and a woman, moreover, of humble birth.

Des Grieux's dealings with these characters are in large measure financial. Manon craves luxury and security and must, at all costs, and in several senses of the word, be kept. When Des Grieux is low on funds, he seeks out his father and Tiberge. M. de Renoncour, M. de T..., and Tiberge himself are always ready, fortunately, to express their superior sensibility in monetary terms. As for the financiers, they can be relied upon to provide a means of support when all else fails.

It is already clear that money performs a complex function in this novel. Scarcely alluded to in the more prestigious literary genres of the time, it is ever-present here. We learn about debts, loans, promissory notes, and inheritances. We discover how much it costs to hire a ruffian, a prostitute, or a carriage by the hour, what annual income is required if one is to keep one's own carriage, what the son of a rich financier is prepared to settle on his mistress, and how much a string of pearls is worth.

[5] *Histoire du chevalier Des Grieux et de Manon Lescaut*, ed. J. Sgard (Paris: GF-Flammarion, 1995), 35–7.

But such details always have a significance beyond themselves. Money is a measure of social standing, but also, since wealth is increasingly in the hands of a new class, of changing values: Des Grieux's father, not wealthy but an aristocrat of the old school, never mentions money; whereas M. de B..., like the tax-farmer and parvenu he is, offers Manon a payment that is to be 'in proportion to the favours received'. Des Grieux would like to emulate his father's disdain. But, impecunious and infatuated, he must learn how to calculate, bargain, borrow, scheme, even—quite improper in an aristocrat—to earn. Having rejected the only honourable professions, the Church and the military, that are open to him, he turns to gambling, card-sharping, swindling, even pimping.

If the methods by which he acquires money allow us to trace his moral decline, the way in which he justifies these methods is even more telling—of his opportunism, special pleading, and deceit. At one moment he argues from a position of aristocratic disdain: swindling a rich financier is scarcely reprehensible, certainly less so than card-sharping, because the victim of the latter is a man of honour and of his own class, whereas the former is a parvenu. At another, he adopts the arguments of the picaresque hero on the make: is it not providential, he asks himself, that the wealthy should be stupid, and the poor intelligent, so that the latter may live at the expense of the former?

But reversal and retribution, the other side of the coin, always follow. Manon and Des Grieux cheat and are cheated, swindle and are swindled, steal and are robbed, ruin and are ruined. Money, the measure of one's worldly fortune (the ambiguity of the word is richly exploited by Prévost), is also an agent of Fortune, of the malign fate that, Des Grieux protests, pursues him, and which, working through a tragic flaw in his character, destroys him.

The financial calculations that preoccupy Des Grieux find their way, too, into the language of the novel, in the form of metaphors of paying and repaying, credit and profit, borrowing, computation, and recompense. The association of money with sex is clearly indicated at the level of intrigue, where love may be bought and sold, lovers have to be kept, and sexual and financial swindling go hand in hand. But it permeates even the language through which the noblest passions are expressed: Manon in New Orleans, for example, may have contrived to 'turn everything to gold', but she knows, nevertheless, that she can 'never repay . . . even half the sorrow' she has caused Des Grieux. The interpenetration of the languages of high passion and low finance serves, if not to debase, then at least to undercut Des Grieux's tragic and heroic pretensions; and it devalues Manon, whom Des Grieux sees, from the start and increasingly, not as a person in her own right, but as a possession.

In other words, Prévost's treatment of money, realistic at the level of the narrative, takes us deep into the social, moral, and psychological fabric of the story. The same is true of a number of objects— Manon's pearls, for example, or Des Grieux's sword—that seem at first to be adjuncts to the story, props as it were, but acquire with each reappearance a greater charge of psychological and moral significance.

The carriage, too—that Parisian accessory par excellence—is at the same time a vehicle for conveying moral and psychological significance. It is so potent a symbol of wealth and status that Manon would do anything rather than dispense with it. It is also a ruinous luxury. Indeed, we can trace the lovers' progressive social and moral degradation, as they exchange a private carriage, first for a series of hired ones, then for a prison carriage, and finally, on the road to Le Havre, for a covered cart full of chained prostitutes. Carriages are a means of escape, flight, and freedom, but also of kidnapping, arrest, and imprisonment. Scenes of reunion and joy take place in them, as do scenes of anguish and parting. They are the very image of the lovers' mobile and unstable life together. Even the coachmen take on proportions beyond their social significance. And it is perhaps revealing that the only redundant detail, arguably, in this whole narrative is the information that Lescaut's landlord at the time of his murder is a coach-builder.

Manon: The Enigma

Of the woman who haunts his dreams, the poet Verlaine knows nothing, not even whether she is 'dark, fair, or auburn-haired'. Des Grieux is no more forthcoming about Manon—even though in his other works Prévost is quite prepared to describe feminine charms. Manon is evoked through abstractions and hyperbole, and almost entirely in terms, not of her own person, but of the passion and desire she excites: 'Her charms were beyond description. There was an air about her, so delicate, so sweet, so appealing—the air of Love itself. Her whole person seemed to me an enchantment' (pp. 30–1).

Des Grieux, bent on perpetuating this enchantment by shaping Manon according to the idealized image he carries in his heart, meets with resistance and, worse still, betrayal. Dismayed by the contradictions he sees in her, between her apparent good faith and her all-too-evident infidelities, he tries to resolve them by presenting her as 'a strange girl' and her actions as 'an enigma' and a source of mystery. M. de Renoncour, too, on the one occasion he catches a glimpse of Manon, puzzled by the contrast between her air of distinction and the degrading circumstances in which she finds herself, falls back on the same conclusion: that she is a woman, and therefore 'incomprehensible'.

Of Manon's inner life—her thoughts and feelings—we learn little. If we know her, it is above all as the object of Des Grieux's hopes and fears, his anxious speculation, his incomprehension. Even her words are reported.[6] In the scene of reconciliation at Saint-Sulpice, for example, which she might be said to have stage-managed, she is allowed only two sentences of direct speech. For the rest, Des Grieux speaks for her, in a form of indirect speech that tends to dissolve her separate identity into his own version of their joint story. However much she speaks subsequently, the suspicion remains that she is only allowed to do so when what she has to say will serve Des Grieux's purposes, as he seeks on the one hand to excuse what he sees as her faults and present her as worthy of his love; and on the other to blame her both for her disloyalty and for the misfortunes it plunges them into. Out of these misapprehensions and distortions is born the myth of the enigmatic Manon. The other men in the story see her differently: captivating she certainly is, but there is no mystery about her. She is a girl of humble birth who exploits her charms in order to make her way in the world. She is there to be used, and then discarded.

It is when we see her in action that Manon is able to break free, in part, from Des Grieux's control. She emerges from his narrative as enchanting, of course, but also as playful, pleasure-loving, affection-

---

[6] This is true of other characters, too, in this self-centred and self-serving narrative; but it has a particular poignancy in the case of Manon.

ate, and inventive. She is enterprising too: it is she who persuades Des Grieux to elope, finds funds to support them, organizes his kidnapping by his father's footmen, engineers the scene of reconciliation at Saint-Sulpice, the discomfiting of the Italian prince, the seduction of young G... M... under Des Grieux's very nose, and (under young G... M...'s) the dispatch of the young prostitute to take a message to Des Grieux. She takes charge of her own life, and takes on society, to the point, on one occasion, of literally wearing the trousers. She could manage very well without Des Grieux. But she prefers him, dashing if impecunious, to the financiers and wealthy parvenus who court her, and seems genuinely surprised that he should reject her simple solution to this situation: that she should live at the expense of a wealthy lover, and Des Grieux, as her favourite, at hers. For, she explains, 'fidelity is a foolish virtue', especially when times are hard, and when what really counts is the 'fidelity of the heart'.

Manon may be playful, but she is hard-headed too. She knows her place in the social system. Shrewdly, she avoids any dealings with Des Grieux's father and allies herself with the parvenus and the financiers, since she and they each have something the other wants. Her misfortune lies in falling in with, and falling in love with, a man of sensibility, who neither understands nor wishes to understand her position and motives, and who obliges her to live out a role she is unable and unwilling to fill.

Some readers see their relationship less in terms of mutual attraction and incomprehension, than as a power-struggle, in which Manon prevails in the earlier episodes, but is bound to lose in the end to Des Grieux, who enjoys not only the obvious advantages of class, gender, and status, but the ability to exploit language too. While Des Grieux complains that Tiberge 'assassinates' him with sermonizing, his own eloquence is much more lethal: as Manon's lover, he tyrannizes her with tirades, verbal assaults, manipulations, and emotional outbursts; while as her narrator, he tells her story to his own advantage, and scarcely allows her even to speak her own lines. When she does find a voice, it is increasingly to ape his rhetoric and say what he wants to hear, as when, in New Orleans, she delivers a speech of high-flown remorse at her own ingratitude towards him (pp. 134–5). The change she undergoes in the New World, on this view, is not so much a conversion as a capitulation. She dies, the victim of rhetorical as well as of social and sexual manipulation.[7]

Des Grieux: Obsession and Persuasion

'Le style est l'homme même', as Buffon famously said: 'the style reveals the man'; and, indeed, the young man who emerges from Des Grieux's story—charming, refined, specious, equivocal, both troubled and troubling—is indistinguishable for the reader from the manner in which he has told it. And this in spite of the fact that there are two Des Grieux, the narrator and the younger self whose tale he tells. The narrative perspective moves seamlessly between these viewpoints, so much so that we soon perceive that the preoccupations of the younger self are for the most part endorsed by the older. While both are ready, disarmingly, to concede the error of Des Grieux's youthful ways, at the same time they subtly shift the burden of responsibility elsewhere: chance is blamed or malign fate, cruel necessity or the irresistible power of passion. The fault, Des Grieux constantly asserts, lies not in himself but in his stars, aided and abetted by human agency, the demands of a mistress, the heartlessness of a father, the bad example of the times, and the avarice of financiers or gendarmes. The Des Grieux whom M. de Renoncour meets in Calais is a sadder rather than a wiser man.

The words with which Des Grieux introduces his story are already revealing. 'I want you to know', he says to Renoncour, 'not only my misfortunes and my sufferings, but also my transgressions and my most shameful weaknesses. I feel certain that, while condemning me, you will be unable to keep from pitying me.' What looks at first sight like a confession of past misconduct is converted, discreetly, into an apology.[8] The style of the narrative that follows— lucid, flowing, economical—is no less calculated a form of persuasion. Just enough detail is given to enlist readers' interest in a young man's pursuit of love and happiness and, as this quest becomes both more obsessive and more criminal, to persuade them to suspend judgement as well as disbelief. The pace of the narrative

---

[7] For a powerful analysis of these and other themes, see Naomi Segal's *The Unintended Reader: Feminism and 'Manon Lescaut'* (Cambridge, 1986).

[8] For an excellent analysis of Des Grieux's rhetorical manipulation of the reader in general, and of his use of this device in particular, see Byrne's edition, pp. xix–xxvii, and p. 118 n. 29.

communicates not only Des Grieux's pursuit of Manon but also—for he aspires to the status of a tragic hero—that of his own pursuit by a fate inexorably bent on his destruction. This rhythm never falters, even when Des Grieux's pursuit of Manon takes him into the inner world of thoughts and feelings. Transports of love, jealousy, or anger, the anguished analysis of behaviour or feelings, these are related with the same relentless eloquence as the external events that resist or facilitate passion.

It is in the inn yard at Amiens, under the impulse of dawning love, that Des Grieux first becomes aware of his powers of persuasion. Well trained by the Jesuits, he soon begins to practise equivocation. The rhetorical skills he goes on to acquire at the seminary of Saint-Sulpice bear fruit in the hypocrisy he practises at Saint-Lazare; while his increasing awareness of the ambiguous nature of language—of which his exchanges with Manon on the question of fidelity are only the most painful example—enables him, in a virtuoso display of sophistry, to debate religious and profane love, at the expense of the former, with Tiberge.

The infinite flexibility of language also serves him well on the many occasions when, in order to elicit sympathy or a loan—whether from his father, Tiberge, the Father Superior, M. de T..., the ship's captain, or the Governor of New Orleans—he retells his story. Not only is he careful to tell it, each time, only 'in part', so as to present it 'in the most favourable light' possible, but he adopts on every occasion the register best suited to his audience and the needs of the moment. With M. de Renoncour he uses the language of sensibility; with his father, that of honour and filial duty, tinged with aristocratic hauteur; with M. de T..., a young man very like himself, he uses both registers—honour and sensibility—but adds a dash of gallantry. The happy 'turn of phrase' that so moves his father depends, in other words, not simply on his selecting the appropriate register, but on knowing when to slip from one to the other.

We know that Des Grieux has acquired this skill from his interview with Manon at Saint-Sulpice, where he declares love through a 'profane mingling of amorous and theological expressions' (p. 33). The languages of religion, astrology, and Racinian tragedy each provide him with a ready resource on which to draw, but are often used in combination, particularly in his manipulations of Manon. We find side by side, for example, seductions that subvert Church teaching

('You are too adorable for a mere created being'), flattery that exploits astrological determinism ('I can read my destiny in your lovely eyes'), and reproaches that echo the elevated diction of seventeenth-century theatre ('the pain of your betrayal has pierced me to the heart'). Des Grieux also knows when to distinguish them. Thus, although he constantly presents himself as the victim of supernatural forces, this is done in popular or astrological terms, through references to Fortune, the gods, malign destiny, or an evil star. Providence is invoked only to be praised, while Heaven is inveighed against only when he feels himself to be on unimpeachable ground, as when he laments that it has frustrated his pious hopes of marrying Manon.

In his debate with Tiberge about the relative merits of sacred and profane love, which occupies the centre of the novel, Des Grieux again exploits the ambiguity of religious language so as to subvert its values. He constructs an argument in favour of human passion by offering a comparison between himself, as Manon's lover, and the Christian martyr who aspires, in spite of the sufferings that torment him, to a 'perfect felicity' beyond his woes. Tiberge angrily rejects this argument as 'a wretched sophism, born of impiety and irreligion', to which Des Grieux replies, with characteristic evasiveness, by denying that he is endorsing the only inference that can be drawn from it, that human passion is a greater good than the love of God. Des Grieux ends with an apparent concession to Tiberge, designed to make his friend believe him ready to renounce his passion for Manon, while at the same time denying any such possibility, on the Jansenist ground that God's grace, and therefore the power to resist temptation, has been withheld from him—'What aid would I not need, in order to forget Manon and her charms!'[9] (The argument is specious—the belief that one is not among the elect does not absolve one from the responsibility not to sin—and it is opportunistic, calculated to persuade Tiberge that his friend is a victim of religious confusion, a Jansenist rather than a reprobate.

Jansenist views on grace and salvation were opposed by the powerful Jesuit order, with its different and more optimistic view of the individual's capacity to resist sin. Far from being 'another of our Jansenists', Des Grieux is quite prepared to borrow from Jesuit ways of thinking when they offer him a convenient means of self-

---

[9] For Jansenism, see note to p. 65.

justification: he not only practises equivocation (p. 17 and note), he also makes use of a Jesuitical 'morality of intention', whereby an act, whatever its results, is judged good or bad according to its intention. This doctrine provides the lovers with a pretext for their behaviour viewed in general terms: for how could a young woman of such artless sincerity and a young man of such honourable instincts be capable of malice in any form? And specifically, it allows Des Grieux to argue that he is innocent of the death of the prison porter he has shot, since he did not intend to kill him—an outcome for which he nevertheless blames both the Father Superior, who asked for the porter's assistance in arresting Des Grieux, and Manon's brother, who gave Des Grieux a loaded pistol.

It is puzzling that a narrator who lays such store by winning the sympathy of his audience should so often draw attention to the mechanisms by which he tries to achieve this. Is this another example of Des Grieux's habit of disarming the reader by conceding, in advance, his own errors and weaknesses? Or does he simply, in his readiness to resort to, and to reveal, every self-exculpatory device that offers itself, overplay his hand—becoming in the process a 'terrible example' of self-defeating rhetoric? Or is this, finally, one of the 'difficultés vaincues' that Sade saw in *Manon Lescaut*, whereby Prévost persuades the reader to experience the story on two levels simultaneously, condemning Des Grieux for his misdemeanours and manipulations, while at the same time succumbing to the compelling charm of his narrative?

Precursors

Prévost had a classical education, trained for the priesthood, wrote a dictionary, and was steeped in French literature. He not only knew English literature too, but through his translations, especially of Richardson, popularized it in France. Echoes of all this may be heard in *Manon*.[10] But the book has particularly close links with two kinds of contemporary prose fiction, the memoir-novel and the short story; and it asserts its uniqueness by playing them off against each other.

---

[10] For Prévost's translations, see the Chronology. Although Prévost's major debt in *Manon* is to French writers, certain phrases he uses recall recent English works, Aphra Behn's *Oroonoko* (*c.*1688), for example, as well as Richardson's *Clarissa*, which he translated just before revising *Manon*.

These genres owed their popularity to their relative realism. Towards the end of the seventeenth century readers, tired of long pastoral or heroic romances, had begun to demand stories that either were true or purported to be so. Genuine memoirs were popular, but so too were various types of fiction whose form would support claims of authenticity: the epistolary novel (as in Richardson's *Pamela*); the fictional memoir (Defoe's *Robinson Crusoe*); the historical novel (Mme de Lafayette's *La Princesse de Clèves*); and the short story. Short stories appear in two forms: within the memoir-novel, as interpolated life-stories told to its author by someone he meets on his travels (the first six volumes of the *Memoirs of a Man of Quality* contain many of these); and in collections of stories, of a kind associated particularly at that time with the name of Robert Challe, and belonging to the tradition established with Boccaccio and, in France, with the *Heptameron* of Marguerite de Navarre, in which each member of a group of friends tells a story, often autobiographical, which is then commented on by the company at large.

Most eighteenth-century readers, while they enjoyed realism and demanded verisimilitude, recognized the claims of 'truth' made by these works to be purely fictional. However, authors continued to make them because of the benefits they conferred on the novel in general. The novel had long been held to be inferior to the great classical genres of epic and tragedy—at best frivolous, and at worst seductive and dangerous lies. But if prose narratives could claim to be genuine, or at any rate true-to-life, their status would be enhanced; not only were they not lies, but they acquired, by virtue of their truth, the force of an edifying moral example.

For all its supposed authenticity, the interpolated story shared the relatively elevated tone and style of its host memoir. Challe's collection of seven 'true stories' (in *Les Illustres françaises*, republished eight times between 1713 and 1731) featured, by contrast, characters drawn from bourgeois or humble backgrounds who are nevertheless treated with the seriousness usually reserved for the characters of nobler genres. They relate, with an economy and sobriety often tinged with despair, their own stories of doomed or tragic love. In one of them a young man is driven by his 'fatal star' into an imprudent alliance with the 'idol of his heart'. He is kidnapped by his father, while she is packed off to the Hôpital, where she dies. The matter and manner of these stories, the realism of their often Parisian settings, even the form of title they favour ('Histoire de M. des Frans et de Silvie') are instantly recognizable to any reader of *Manon Lescaut*.

In spite of his evident admiration for Challe, however, Prévost immediately declares his independence from him by affording the story of Manon the protection of the memoir-novel. When he came to revise *Manon* for independent publication in 1753, he could have easily removed it from this framework, but did not do so. In other words, Prévost claims the short story *and* the memoir-novel as precursors to *Manon* in order to deviate from both. Des Grieux, refined, melancholy, and introspective, like the heroes of Prévost's memoir-novels, is cast among the social realities and obliged to live at the pace of Challe's less elevated characters. And where Challe's narrative sobriety remains demotic and sometimes a little flat, Des Grieux retains, along with his title—and however ambiguous these qualities are—a nobility of expression and a grandeur of gesture that are the legacy of the memoir-novel.

Manon *and the Theatre*

Voltaire regretted that Prévost did not write for the theatre, 'for . . . the language of the passions is his natural language'. Another contemporary, agreeing, pointed out too that in Prévost's fiction 'all the conditions of drama are fulfilled'.[11]

In spite of this, *Manon* does not transfer easily to the stage. Manon and Des Grieux, however, are avid theatregoers, to the point of parodying Racine; while allusions to dramatic technique, both explicit and implicit, abound. Des Grieux constantly presents his story in terms of a spectacle, in which the characters play their various roles, suffer reversals, stage scenes, and finally meet with some catastrophe or denouement. Action is related with the terseness of a stage-direction—'The carriage door was open. They climbed in.'—punctuated by anxious soliloquies and histrionic or lyrical speeches. Gesture and glance—the lovers at supper on either side of the candle, Manon kneeling by Des Grieux's chair—are arrested in tableaux, even if the drama of such scenes, often, is expressive of nothing so much as the mutual incomprehension of the lovers.

---

[11] Deloffre–Picard edition, p. clxxv.

But is the drama thus enacted a tragedy or a comedy? The scene of the lovers' first encounter in the inn yard at Amiens is ambiguous: its rehearsal of the great theme of Molière's *École des Femmes*—'For it must be confessed, love is a great teacher'—would set the stage for a comedy, were it not for Des Grieux's retrospective inclusion in the scene of his 'evil star already in its ascendant and drawing me to my ruin'. Increasingly, he insists on viewing his own predicament in terms of the classic tragic conflict between duty and passion, and this passion as the tragic flaw through which fate, bent on his destruction, brings about his ruin. Some readers remain unpersuaded. Des Grieux's story, the argument runs, lacks an essential ingredient of tragedy, that of necessity. The lovers could have extricated themselves from their difficulties in New Orleans. They had done so before in similar circumstances. The denouement is engineered by Des Grieux and imposed on Manon, who would be much better cast in a comedy but who, accepting at last her role as the object of a tragic passion, obliges, as it were, by dying.[12]

Besides, although Des Grieux often speaks the language of Racinian tragedy, until the last scenes of the novel this pose is precarious, even—perhaps especially—when he is staging a scene of high drama. On several such occasions Des Grieux as narrator cannot resist including a detail, a stage-direction as it were, that redresses the balance in favour of comedy—that for example of his hat falling to one side and his cane to the other,[13] as he flings himself tragically into a chair during his interview with the young prostitute (p. 88), or old G... M... adjusting his wig and cravat after Des Grieux's violent attack on him (pp. 59–60). Such moments remind the reader that the man visibly beside himself with passion is a figure of classical comedy rather than of tragedy.

These scenes are part of a highly structured plot. A classical five-act pattern may even be discerned, itself ambiguous as between tragedy and comedy. An expository act at Pacy is balanced by a denouement in New Orleans, where Des Grieux's happiness at last seems assured, then is destroyed by a last repetition of a recurrent

---

[12] For a discussion of the extent to which Des Grieux is responsible for Manon's death, see J. I. Donohue, 'The Death of Manon: A Literary Inquest', *L'Esprit Créateur*, 12 (1972), 129–46.

[13] Lovelace expresses his despair through a similar gesture (Richardson, *Clarissa*, Letter 480).

pattern. The three intervening acts, all set in Paris, trace, with variations, this same sequence. In each a new beginning and a period of happiness is overturned by Manon's defection to a new rival, and ends with an imprisonment. Moreover, with each recurrence the knot about Des Grieux tightens: in his attempt to keep Manon, he becomes increasingly enmeshed in crime. 'How have I become so wicked?' he asks at one point. His own answer, constantly rehearsed for the reader, points to tragic forces beyond his control. The economy of the plot, however, its repetitions and recurrences, suggests an answer informed rather by traditional comedy: that obsessive or incorrigible characters who pursue some *idée fixe* will continually find themselves worsted.

Patterns of reversal, as well as those of repetition, are part of the stock in trade of comedy. In *Manon*, as in any comedy, lovers quarrel and make up, old men make fools of themselves over young girls, fathers compete with their sons, servants ape their masters, tables are turned, dupers duped. While complimenting himself on painting old G... M...'s portrait as a complaisant dupe 'to the life', Des Grieux is in fact painting his own. He cheats old G... M... out of his night with Manon and is cheated out of his; he has young G... M... arrested and held prisoner and is himself arrested and imprisoned.

Parallels and contrasts between characters, too, are the stuff of comedy and, at the same time, psychologically and morally revealing. Tiberge is Des Grieux's wise mentor, Manon's brother Lescaut, his evil genius. Des Grieux, who both needs Lescaut and despises him as low-class, opportunistic, and unscrupulous, is obliged to pose as his little brother, and perhaps has more in common with him than with his own—exemplary—brother. When Lescaut is murdered M. de T... takes over as Des Grieux's ill-adviser, although Des Grieux never suspects this. Des Grieux encounters even more surrogate fathers than he does brothers. He benefits from the leniency not only of his own father but of the Father Superior, the Lieutenant of Police, M. de Renoncour, the captain of the ship, the Governor of New Orleans, even, once his ruffled pride is soothed, M. de G... M... He deceives and exploits them, but returns to them in the last paragraph of the book. After all, he is a son of the aristocracy, a 'fils de famille'. Manon is a woman of humble birth, a mere 'fille', and an inconvenient one. They combine to eliminate her; and Des Grieux, who secured his release from prison through the two fathers by remaining silent about Manon, is not without complicity in the plot.

Few witnesses of this 'sad comedy' speak up for Manon, except the old woman who emerges from the inn at Pacy where the prostitutes stand in chains, wringing her hands and crying that 'here was a barbarous thing, a thing to make you weep with horror and pity'. Horror and pity, the tragic emotions. The old woman does not know that she is quoting Aristotle. But she knows what a tragedy is, at least in popular terms, and that it is to be found in the inn-yards and on the roads of contemporary France.

In *Manon* Prévost weaves together into a compelling and coherent whole a variety of styles and tones—the restrained sobriety of the memoir-novel and the picaresque restlessness of contemporary prose realism, the ineluctable course of tragedy and the cheerful recurrences of comedy. The narrative voice that is thus created is at once unified and complex, the voice of a definitively ambiguous narrator, caught between a traumatic past he is constantly reliving and a future full of uncertainty. Will the telling of Des Grieux's tale to the man of quality act as a form of exorcism? Will Des Grieux, as both M. de Renoncour and Prévost himself have done, seek solace in retirement and writing? Or will he be forever accosting some new stranger with the words 'I was seventeen years old...'?

Manon Lescaut: *Afterlife*

Prévost's early readers reacted to his scandalous story with a very eighteenth-century mixture of moralizing and sensibility, combined with a taste for paradox. Des Grieux and Manon, said Montesquieu, are, respectively 'a scoundrel and a whore'; but so artful a portrayal does Prévost give of their mutual tenderness that the reader is seduced into forgiving even so flagrant an instance of immorality. By the 1790s, by which time *Manon* was somewhat neglected, the Marquis de Sade wondered whether this 'delicious work', a triumph of the art of the *difficulté vaincue*, is not, for its profound study of the human heart, 'our best novel'.

While Des Grieux sees himself as a hero of Racinian tragedy—an Oreste, pursued both by fate and the furies of love—we must look for his spiritual successors among the troubled, ambivalent, introspective first-person narrators of the early Romantic period, with their blend of eighteenth- and nineteenth-century sensibility. Constant's *Adolphe* (1816) offers the best example, but later there is Fromentin's *Dominique* (1862), as well as, in a somewhat different vein, Mérimée's *Carmen* (1845). The young Stendhal devoured Prévost in secret; and although the hero of *Le Rouge et le Noir* (1831), Julien Sorel, unlike Des Grieux, does not narrate his own story, and is survived by his lovers, he too hesitates between the military and the ecclesiastical life, and is a consummate hypocrite. He even goes to a performance of Scribe's 'ballet-pantomime', based on Prévost's novel.

The year of Julien's visit to the theatre, 1830, marks the beginning of *Manon*'s meteoric, if posthumous, rise to fame and fortune. The novel was reprinted almost annually for the rest of the century. There were already two stage versions, and there would be others, including a 'vaudeville' and, irresistibly, a 'cry from the heart, in three acts, without entr'actes'. More significantly, however, the poet Alfred Musset published an oriental tale in verse, *Namouna* (1832), in which Manon was celebrated as 'an astonishing sphinx, a true siren, a thrice feminine heart', words which were later to be incorporated into the libretto of Massenet's opera *Manon*. Thus, almost at a stroke of the pen, Prévost's slip of a girl of common birth, witty and fun-loving, streetwise rather than mysterious, acquired the status of a myth, that of the *femme fatale*, the bewitching temptress, seductive as a siren, enigmatic as a sphinx. More than forty years later, Dumas *fils* was still under her spell: 'you are sensuality, you are instinct, you are pleasure, the eternal temptation of man.'

Carmen—sexually provocative, defiantly unfaithful—is the most striking example of this type, especially as presented in Bizet's opera of 1875. Other writers have preferred another variant of the archetype: that of the courtesan reclaimed for virtue and constancy by love, to the point where—conveniently—she sacrifices herself for the young man she has led astray. Hugo's popular play about a kind-hearted prostitute, *Marion Delorme* (1831), was followed by the most successful example of this genre, Dumas *fils*' *La Dame aux Camélias*, first a novel and then, in 1852, a play, whose heroine Marguerite makes explicit her kinship with Manon by keeping a copy of her story by her bed, even though she regrets her hard-heartedness. The two texts interweave at the level of opera, too: Verdi's version of

Dumas's play, *La Traviata* (1853), owes much to *Manon*, a debt which Massenet's librettist later reclaimed by borrowing, in his turn, from the libretto of Verdi's opera.

Of the operas based on *Manon* itself, Auber's opéra-comique *Manon Lescaut* (1856) offers a somewhat bland version of the original. Massenet's *Manon* of 1884 and Puccini's *Manon Lescaut* of 1893, although influenced by the Romantic perception of Manon as a femme fatale, represent a more serious attempt to return to Prévost's story. While these operas are responsive to its drama, however, they necessarily simplify its contradictions and ironies, its sombre—or comic—twists and turns. Manon's three infidelities, which in the novel mark stages in Des Grieux's moral and social decline, are reduced to one, so that Manon appears as regretfully rather than wilfully faithless, and a mere victim of men rather than a courtesan who could, were it not for her weakness for Des Grieux, conquer society.

Manon has continued to influence works in the post-Romantic period, from Kipling's novel *The Light that Failed* (1890) to Billy Wilder's film *Irma la Douce* (1965), about a prostitute with a heart of gold. Hans Werner Henze's opera *Boulevard Solitude* (1952) follows Henri-Georges Clouzot's slightly earlier film *Manon* (1949) in setting Prévost's story in 1940s France. These two reworkings of the story, like—although in a very different way—Kenneth MacMillan's ballet *Manon* (1974), to music by Massenet, are arguably more faithful to the spirit of Prévost's novel than many nineteenth-century versions.

NOTE ON THE TEXT

Of the numerous editions of *Manon Lescaut* to appear during Prévost's lifetime, two have the authority of his close involvement: the original edition of 1731 (*Mémoires Et Avantures D'un Homme De Qualité Qui s'est retiré du monde, Tome Septième, A Amsterdam, Aux dépens de la Compagnie MDCCXXXI*); and a new version of 1753, published independently of the *Memoirs* of which the 1731 edition had formed the last volume, and representing Prévost's own meticulous revision and correction of the earlier text (*Histoire Du Chevalier Des Grieux Et de Manon Lescaut, A Amsterdam, Aux dépens de la Compagnie MDCCLIII*, but in fact published in Paris by François Didot). The present translation follows most recent French editions in preferring the 1753 version. The text used is therefore that of the current Classiques Garnier edition, edited by Frédéric Deloffre and Raymond Picard (Paris, 1995), as well as of the GF-Flammarion edition, edited by Jean Sgard (Paris, 1995). Prévost's paragraphing and, as far as is consistent with modern English usage, his punctuation have also been followed, to the extent of omitting quotation marks, whose absence permits a free movement between direct and indirect speech, important in this novel.

In his revised version of 1753 Prévost included a whole new episode—that of the Italian prince—whose purpose, he tells us, is to portray more fully the character of Manon; he altered the emphasis of the end of the novel, substituting for the religious conversion that is claimed for Des Grieux in 1731 a more secular return to family and class values; and he corrected a number of instances of hyperbolic or colourful language that must by then have seemed to him inappropriate.[1] Some of the savour and freshness of the original is inevitably lost in the process. However, the greater coherence of style and characterization that is gained enhances the persuasiveness of the novel, and is wholly in line with Prévost's original conception; while from the innumerable small adjustments to the rhythm, word order, and phrasing of the novel that Prévost made in 1753, and above all from the excision of any word that can

---

[1] For some of the more significant of these changes see the Explanatory Notes.

be dispensed with, there emerges a narrative of such energy, suspense, and compelling eloquence as amply to justify this choice of text.

NOTE ON THE ILLUSTRATIONS

The revised edition of *Manon Lescaut*, which Prévost prepared for publication in 1753, included eight illustrations of the text, two of them by Hubert-François Gravelot (1699–1773), the remaining six by Jean-Jacques Pasquier (1718–78), who may also have been responsible for the vignette that appears on the first page. Although Prévost clearly laid great store by the illustrations, the extent to which he was personally involved in their preparation is not known. However, they are a clear indication of the care with which the new edition of *Manon* was prepared and of the publisher's confidence in its commercial success. The engravings are notable, too, for their contribution to the history of book illustration. Gravelot—an important intermediary between French and English book illustration in the mid-century—had worked in England, collaborated with Hogarth, produced the engravings for Richardson's *Pamela* (1742) and for Fielding's *Tom Jones* (1750), and would later do so for Rousseau's *La Nouvelle Héloïse*. Pasquier had worked with Gravelot on the engravings for *Tom Jones*, and was responsible for the series of illustrations to Prévost's highly successful translation of Richardson's *Clarissa*, which appeared the year before the revised *Manon Lescaut*. Illustrated editions of novels were not new in France, but the particular style achieved by Gravelot especially—not allegorical, after the fashion of sixteenth- and seventeenth-century engraving, but, at the same time, something more than merely faithful to the text—exercised a great influence on subsequent book illustration.

The engraving on the first page, which reuses, it has been conjectured, an earlier work by Pasquier himself, is an example of this allegorical style. It shows an older man of biblical appearance guiding a young man towards what is presumably a crucifix mounted on a rock. The inscription, borrowed from Horace (*Odes*, i. 27), reads 'what torments you endure in Charybdis, young man worthy of a nobler love'. The name of Charybdis, a dangerous whirlpool in Greek mythology, was often invoked in the eighteenth century to warn against the wiles of high-class prostitutes bent on the ruin of some young man of good family. The vignette, then, presents the story that follows as a victory for sacred over profane love, for Tiberge's influence on Des Grieux over that of Manon. It thus reinforces the moralizing interpretation advanced in the author's Foreword to the novel, and was no doubt intended to avoid a repetition of the scandal that had accompanied its first appearance in France in 1733. The attractions of love are none the less allegorized elsewhere in the engraving, where a band of winged cupids aim their darts at the young man, bind him with garlands, and try to turn him back towards the female figure who emerges from a flowery bower and stretches out her arms towards him.

If the vignette makes the moral case for the novel, the eight illustrations that follow appeal to the reader's sympathies and sensibilities. Each of them comments on a significant moment in the story. These moments are rendered faithfully and, at one level, realistically, thus compensating, through some precise observation of contemporary dress, décor, and manners, for the reticence of a narrative notoriously sparing of descriptive detail. The drama of such moments—whether comic or tragic—is not lost either; while the best of the engravings communicate, in addition, an air of tension and instability that is entirely faithful to the spirit of the book.

SELECT BIBLIOGRAPHY

Modern Editions of Manon Lescaut

Histoire du Chevalier des Grieux et de Manon Lescaut, ed. F. Deloffre and R. Picard: Nouvelle édition revue et augmentée par F. Deloffre; avec mise à jour bibliographique (Paris: Classiques Garnier, Dunod, 1995).
Histoire du chevalier Des Grieux et de Manon Lescaut, ed. J. Sgard (Paris: GF-Flammarion, 1995).
Manon Lescaut, ed. P. Byrne (London: Bristol Classical Press, 1999).

I should like to acknowledge here my debt to all three of these recent critical editions (referred to in the Explanatory Notes as, respectively, Deloffre–Picard, Sgard, and Byrne). English-speaking readers who wish to read *Manon Lescaut* in French will find the Byrne edition, which offers the text in French, and—in English—explanatory notes and a perceptive discussion of all aspects of the novel, particularly valuable.

Introductory Studies

Two excellent brief critical guides are also widely available:

Francis, R. A., *Prévost: Manon Lescaut* (London: Grant & Cutler, 1993).
Mylne, V., *Prévost: Manon Lescaut* (London: Edward Arnold, 1972).

Further Critical Works

There is an extensive critical literature on Manon Lescaut. The following list is limited to more recent studies, most of them in English.

Betts, C. J., 'The Cyclical Pattern of the Narrative in Manon Lescaut', *French Studies*, 41 (1987), 395–407.
Donohue, J. I., 'The Death of Manon: A Literary Inquest', *L'Esprit Créateur*, 12 (1972), 129–46.
Fort, B., 'Manon's Suppressed Voice: The Use of Reported Speech', *Romantic Review*, 76 (1985) 172–91.
Gasster, S., 'The Practical Side of Manon Lescaut', *Modern Language Studies*, 15 (1985), 102–9.
Gilroy, J. P., *The Romantic Manon and Des Grieux: Images of Prévost's Heroine and Hero in Nineteenth-century French Literature* (Sherbrooke, Quebec: Naaman, 1980).
Gossmann, L., 'Prévost's Manon: Love in the New World', *Yale French Studies*, 40 (1968), 91–102.

Gossmann, L., 'Male and Female in Two Short Novels by Prévost', *Modern Language Review*, 77 (1982), 29–37.

Mauron, C., 'Manon Lescaut et le mélange des genres', in *L'Abbé Prévost: actes du colloque d'Aix-en-Provence, 20 et 21 décembre 1963* (Gap: Ophrys, 1965), 113–18.

Segal, N., *The Unintended Reader: Feminism and 'Manon Lescaut'* (Cambridge, 1986).

Sgard, J., *Prévost romancier* (Paris: Corti, 1968).

—— *L'Abbé Prévost: labyrinthes de la mémoire* (Paris: PUF, 1986).

—— *Vingt études sur Prévost d'Exiles* (Grenoble: Ellug, 1995).

Singerman, A. J., 'A "fille de plaisir" and her "greluchon": Society and the Perspective of Manon Lescaut', *L'Esprit Créateur*, 12 (1972), 118–28.

Stewart, P., *Rereadings: Eight Early French Novels* (Birmingham, Ala.: Summa Press, 1984).

Further Reading in Oxford World's Classics

Voltaire, *Letters concerning the English Nation*, ed. Nicholas Cronk.

—— *Candide and Other Stories*, trans. and ed. Roger Pearson.

Jean-Jacques Rousseau, *Confessions*, trans. Angela Scholar, ed. Patrick Coleman.

1697	Birth of Antoine-François Prévost in Hesdin on the borders of Artois and Picardy (in what is now the department of Pas-de-Calais), the second of five sons (five daughters die during childhood) of Liévin Prévost, public prosecutor to the king, and of Marie Duclaie.
1711	Death of Prévost's mother. He is sent to the Jesuit college in Hesdin.
1712	Follows his older brother to Paris. Enlists as a volunteer to fight in the War of the Spanish Succession.
1713–15	Studies at the Collège d'Harcourt in Paris. Accepted as a novice by the Jesuits.
1717–18	Second noviciate, at La Flèche. Rejoins the army, as an officer this time, in the war against Spain (1718–19). According to some sources he deserts and flees to Holland.
1720	An unhappy love affair (according to Prévost's own account) leads him to seek refuge, not with the Jesuits, but at the Benedictine monastery of Saint-Wandrille in Normandy.
1721	Takes his vows in the strict Benedictine congregation of Saint-Maur at Jumièges.
1721–6	Studies, teaches, and preaches at various abbeys in Normandy. Contributes to a pamphlet, *Les Aventures de Pomponius*, in which various Jesuits as well as courtiers at the Regent's court are satirized; is finally ordained.
1727	Prévost is moved to Paris and then to the monastery of Saint-Germain-des-Prés. He works on the collective Benedictine publication, the *Gallia Christiana*; and wins second prize in a literary competition for his *Ode sur saint François Xavier*.
1728	Publication of volumes 1 and 2 of the fictional *Mémoires et aventures d'un homme de qualité* (1728–31, 7 volumes). His request to transfer to the—less austere—general Benedictine order is granted, but he departs without waiting for formal permission to arrive, leaving behind him a letter of protest to his superiors. A warrant for his arrest is issued. Prévost flees to England, and announces his conversion to Anglicanism.
1728–30	In London Prévost acts as tutor to Francis Eyles, the son of Sir John Eyles, former Lord Mayor of London, former governor

of the Bank of England, a Member of Parliament, and a director of the South Sea Company. He learns English, moves in literary circles, frequents the theatre, begins to translate English writers (Congreve, Farquhar, Vanbrugh, Dryden, Otway, Addison), and starts work on a new epic novel, his *Histoire de M. Cleveland, fils naturel de Cromwell, ou Le Philosophe anglais* (1731–9, 8 volumes), the story of the adventures of a melancholy and romantic hero, whose philosophy does not cure him of the ills of love. Prévost's secret engagement to the daughter of the house, Mary Eyles, is discovered. He is dismissed and flees to Holland.

1731   During the early months of the year Prévost interrupts work on the next volumes of *Cleveland* in order to write volumes 5–7 of the *Mémoires d'un homme de qualité* (published in Amsterdam in May), the last of which is devoted to the *Histoire du Chevalier Des Grieux et de Manon Lescaut*. Volumes 1 and 2 of *Cleveland* appear in July, volumes 3 and 4 in October. At some point in late spring or early summer of this year Prévost meets and subsequently forms a liaison with the fascinating and ruinously extravagant Lenki Eckhard.

1733   Bankrupt and deeply in debt to his publishers, Prévost flees to England, accompanied by Lenki. In London he starts a periodical he calls *Le Pour et contre* (1733–40), on the model of Addison's *Spectator*, and which—more comprehensively than Voltaire's *Lettres philosophiques* or *Lettres anglaises* (1733–4)— acquaints French readers with English life and letters. In December Prévost is imprisoned for attempting to borrow money against a promissory note forged in the name of his former pupil Francis Eyles, who has him released. Meanwhile, in Paris, *Manon Lescaut* receives its first French edition, followed, several months later, by the seizure and suppression of unsold copies.

1734   Prévost returns clandestinely to France, is granted papal absolution for his apostasy and permission to move to the general order of Benedictine monks. Enjoys literary success in the salons of Paris.

1735   He obtains a small benefice, is obliged to undergo a further noviciate, and publishes the first volume of a third long memoir-novel, *Le Doyen de Killerine*, which is set against the background of the court of the exiled James II in Saint-Germain. He is officially warned against attempting to publish further novels.

1736   Acquires a post as chaplain to the powerful Prince de Conti, by whom he is unpaid but housed and protected.

1739   Permission is at last given for the publication of the last two volumes of *Cleveland* and of volumes 2 and 3 of *Le Doyen de Killerine*.

1740   Faced with financial ruin, Prévost appeals to Voltaire, who declines to help him; he publishes a second short novel, the *Histoire d'une Grecque moderne*, which, based on a contemporary scandal, is assured of commercial success.

1741   Threatened with imprisonment for his association with a dissident journalist, Prévost seeks refuge, first in Brussels and later in Frankfurt, where he receives pardon and permission to return to his family in Artois. He seems to have parted company, on her marriage, with a certain Mme. Chester, presumed to be Lenki Eckhard, who, in spite of the marriage her name implies, had rejoined him in France some time after his return there from London.

1742–50 During these years of intense literary activity Prévost publishes the lives of William the Conqueror, and (translated from the English) of Cicero, as well as a translation of Cicero's letters; he embarks on a *Histoire générale des voyages* (1745–70, in 21 volumes, of which he provides the first seventeen, and of which the first seven are translated from the English), a highly influential survey of the history, geography, and peoples of newly discovered lands; he settles in Chaillot, the village just outside Paris where Des Grieux and Manon had taken refuge.

1750   Prévost's dictionary, the *Manuel lexique*, appears, a translation, in part, from the English.

1751   His translation of Richardson's *Clarissa, or the History of a Young Lady* (1747–8) appears, under the title *Lettres anglaises, ou Histoire de Miss Clarisse Harlowe*. Prévost's version, with its accompanying illustrations, of this story of the triumph of virtue and sentiment is to delight and influence Rousseau, among others.

1753   The revised edition of *Manon Lescaut*, with illustrations by Pasquier and Gravelot, appears in Amsterdam and Paris.

1755–63 Prévost continues to produce works of journalism and fiction as well as translations, including Dryden's *All for Love*, Richardson's *History of Sir Charles Grandison*, and Hume's *History of the Stuarts*. At some point he settles at Saint-Firmin, near Chantilly. Rousseau, who knew him during these later years, speaks of him in his _Confessions_ as 'a very likeable, very simple man, whose works, deserving of immortality, sprang straight from the heart, and in whose temperament and society there was none of that sombre colouring he gave to his writings'.

1763   Prévost, on his way to visit some neighbouring Benedictine monks, dies of a stroke.

THE STORY OF THE
CHEVALIER DES GRIEUX AND
MANON LESCAUT

FOREWORD BY THE AUTHOR

of the

Memoirs of a Man of Quality

Although I could have included the *Adventures of the Chevalier Des Grieux* among my *Memoirs*, I decided that, there being no necessary connection between the two works, the reader would derive more pleasure from seeing them presented separately.* An account of such length would have interrupted for too long the thread of my own history. Although I am far from claiming correctness as one of my virtues as an author, I know very well that a narrative ought to be pruned of details that would otherwise make it heavy and confused. Such indeed is Horace's precept:

> Ut jam nunc dicat jam nunc debentia dici
> Pleraque differat, ac praesens in tempus omittat.*

Nor is there any need to invoke so grave an authority to prove so simple a truth; for the prime source of this rule is common sense.

If the public have found anything to please or interest them in the story of my life, it will, I dare say, be no less satisfied with this addition. It will see, in M. Des Grieux's conduct, a terrible example of the power of the passions. The portrait I have to paint is of a young man who, in his blindness, rejects happiness in order to plunge voluntarily into the uttermost depths of misfortune; who, possessing all the qualities that mark him out for brilliance and distinction, prefers, from choice, a life of obscurity and vagrancy to all the advantages of fortune and nature; who foresees his own misfortunes without having the will to avoid them; who feels and is oppressed by them, without benefiting from the remedies that are continually offered him and which could at any moment end them; in short, an ambiguous character, a mixture of virtues and vices, a perpetual contrast between good impulses and bad actions. Such is the subject of the picture I will present. People of good sense will not look upon a work of this kind as a fruitless endeavour. For they will find, not only that it is a pleasure to read, but that it contains few events that cannot serve as an aid to moral instruction; and it does the public no small service, in my view, to instruct while entertaining them.*

One cannot reflect for long on moral precepts without being astonished at seeing them, at one and the same time, revered and neglected, and without wondering what could be the reason for this vagary of the human heart, whereby it clings to principles of goodness and perfection from which it deviates in practice. If people of a certain order of intelligence and refinement were to ask themselves what is the most usual subject of their conversations, or even of their solitary musings, they would easily conclude that these almost always turn on moral considerations. The sweetest moments of their lives are those they spend, either alone or with a friend, discoursing freely and openly upon the charms of virtue, the pleasures of friendship, the ways and means of reaching happiness, the weaknesses in our nature that prevent us from achieving it, and the remedies by which these might be cured. Horace and Boileau, describing a life of true contentment, identify such conversations as one of its most pleasing features.* How is it, then, that we so readily descend from these heights of lofty speculation, and find ourselves on a level once again with the ordinary run of humanity? There is, however, unless I am much mistaken, a satisfactory explanation for this contradiction between our ideas and our conduct: which is that, moral precepts being nothing more than vague and general principles, it is difficult to apply them to particular and detailed instances of behaviour and action. Let us take an example. Well-born souls sense that gentleness and humanity are lovable virtues, and are disposed, out of inclination, to practise them; but when the moment comes to exercise them, they are often seized by hesitation. Is this really the occasion to use them? Do we know what limits we should place on them? Might one not be deceived as to their object? A hundred difficulties intervene. One is afraid of being duped, while trying to be benevolent and liberal; of seeming weak, by appearing too soft-hearted and sensitive; in a word, of exceeding or not adequately fulfilling duties that are enshrined in too obscure a fashion within our general notions of humanity and gentleness. In such uncertainty, only experience or example can rationally determine which way the heart should incline. Now experience is not an advantage that it is open to everyone to acquire, since it depends on the various situations in which, by chance, we find ourselves. For many people, then, this leaves only example that can offer any guidance as to how they should exercise virtue. It is precisely for this sort of reader that works such as the present one are of exceptional utility, when, that is, they have been written by a person of honour and good sense. Every deed that is related adds a further degree of illumination, a lesson that is a substitute for experience; every adventure provides a model according to which one could fashion oneself; all that is needed is some adjustment to the reader's own circumstances. The whole work is a moral treatise, appealingly presented as a practical example.

A severe reader will perhaps be offended at seeing me, at my age, take up my pen again to relate tales of fortune and love; but if the reflections I have just offered are sound, they will be my justification; if they are false, that I am in error will be my excuse.

Note. *It is in order to yield to the entreaties of those who are fond of this little work that it has been decided to purge it of a great number of gross errors which have crept into successive editions. Some additions have also been made, which seemed necessary for the fuller portrayal of one of the principal characters.*

The vignette and the illustrations speak for themselves and require no further commendation or praise.

Quanta laboras in Charybdi | Digne Puer meliore flâmma

FIRST PART

I must begin by taking my reader back to the time in my life when I first met the Chevalier Des Grieux. It was about six months before my departure for Spain. Although I rarely left the retirement in which I was then living, my desire to help my daughter sometimes led me to undertake various short journeys, which I tried to keep as brief as possible.* I was returning one day from Rouen, where she had asked me to take up with the *parlement** of Normandy the matter of her entitlement to some estates, the claim to which I had inherited from my maternal grandfather and had bequeathed to her. Setting out again on the road through Évreux, where I spent the first night, I arrived next day in time for dinner at Pacy, some eleven or twelve miles further on. I was surprised, on entering this little market-town, to see all the inhabitants in a state of alarm. They came tumbling out of their houses and ran together in a great crowd towards the door of a mean-looking inn, in front of which stood two covered wagons. The horses were still harnessed and steaming, as though from heat and fatigue, showing that these two vehicles had only just arrived. I stopped for a moment to ask what the uproar was about, but received little clarification from a populace which, consumed with curiosity, paid no attention to my questions but pressed on towards the inn with much jostling and confusion. When at last a guard, wearing a bandolier and carrying his musket over his shoulder, appeared in the doorway, I beckoned him over. I asked him the reason for this commotion. It's nothing, Monsieur, he said, only a dozen prostitutes I'm taking, with my companions, to Le Havre-de-Grâce, where we're going to ship them off to America.* Some of them are pretty, and clearly this is exciting the curiosity of these worthy countryfolk. I would have left after this explanation, if I had not been stopped short by the exclamations of an old woman who was coming out of the inn, clasping her hands and crying out that here was a barbarous thing, a thing to make you weep with horror and pity. But what is it all about? I asked her. Ah, Monsieur! She replied, go inside and judge for yourself if this is not a sight to break the heart! Curiosity made me get down from my horse, which I left with my groom. Pushing my way with difficulty through the crowd, I went inside, where a touching enough scene did indeed meet my eyes. Among the dozen prostitutes who stood chained together about the waist in groups of six, there was one whose air and cast of feature were so little in keeping with her present condition that in any other situation I would have taken her for a person of the first rank. Her sad expression and the filthy state of her linen and dress detracted so little from her beauty that the sight of her filled me with respect and compassion. She nevertheless tried, as far as her chains would allow her, to turn away from the spectators and to hide her face from their gaze. The efforts she made to conceal herself were so natural that they seemed to arise from an inborn sense of modesty. Since the six constables who were escorting this unhappy band were also present, I took their leader to one side and asked him what light he could shed on the fate of this lovely girl. He could tell me very little. We took her from the Hôpital,* he said, on the orders of the Lieutenant-General of Police. I don't imagine she was shut up in there for good conduct. I questioned her several times on the way here; I couldn't get a word out of her. But even though no one's told me to treat her with more consideration than the others, I can't help feeling some respect for her, since it seems to me she's worth a bit more than her

Although he had seemed calm enough while telling this story, he let fall a few tears on reaching its end. It struck me as one of the most extraordinary and touching I had ever heard. I will not press you, I said to him, to reveal anything you wish to keep secret; but if I can be useful to you in any way, I will be glad to do you service. Alas! he replied, I cannot see the least ray of hope. I must submit to the full harshness of my destiny. I will go to America. At least there I will be free to be with the woman I love. I have written to one of my friends who will make sure there is help waiting for me at Le Havre-de-Grâce. My only difficulty is in getting there, and in procuring some relief on the way for this poor creature, he said looking sadly at his mistress. Very well, I said, I will resolve your difficulty. Here is some money which I beg you to accept. I am only sorry that there is nothing more I can do for you. I gave him four louis d'or without the guards noticing,* for I was sure that if they knew that he had this money they would sell their services to him at an even greater price. It even occurred to me to strike a bargain with them that would secure the young lover the freedom to converse with his mistress all the way to Le Havre. I beckoned their leader over and put this proposition to him. He seemed ashamed, for all his impudence. It's not that we refuse to let him talk to the girl, he replied in some embarrassment; but he wants to be with her the whole time; this puts us out, and it's only fair we should make him pay for this. And how much, I asked him, would it take for you not to feel put out? He had the audacity to ask for two louis. I gave them to him on the spot. But take care you don't try any cheating, I said, for I'm leaving my address with this young man, who will let me know if you do; and you may depend on it, it's well within my power to have you punished. This whole affair cost me six louis d'or. The good grace and lively gratitude with which the young stranger thanked me confirmed me in my view that he had not been born a nobody, and was worthy of the liberality I had shown him. I said a few words to his mistress before leaving. She replied with such sweet and enchanting modesty that, as I left, I could not help reflecting on the incomprehensible nature of women.

Shortly afterwards I returned to my place of retirement and so never learned the sequel to this adventure. Almost two years passed, during which I had forgotten about it completely, when a chance encounter gave me another opportunity to acquaint myself in depth

with its every detail. I was on my way back from London with my pupil, the Marquis de..., and had just arrived in Calais. We were staying, if I remember rightly, at the Lion d'Or, where, for one reason and another, we were obliged to remain for a whole day and the following night. Strolling about the streets that afternoon, I thought I caught sight of the same young man I had met in Pacy.* He was poorly dressed, and much paler than on our first meeting, and, having only just arrived, was carrying an old saddlebag over his arm. Nevertheless, he was too handsome not to be easily recognized, and I remembered him at once. We must go and meet that young man over there, I said to the Marquis. When he in his turn had recognized me, his joy was beyond words. Ah Monsieur! he cried, kissing my hand, how glad I am of the chance to assure you once more of my undying gratitude! I asked him where he had come from. He replied that he had just arrived by sea from Le Havre-de-Grâce, having not long since returned from America. You don't seem to be too well off, I said to him; go to the Lion d'Or, where I'm staying, and I'll join you there in a moment. In fact I returned almost at once, impatient to hear the details of his misfortunes and what had brought him back from America. I paid him every possible attention, and gave orders that he should lack for nothing. He did not wait to be pressed, but at once began to tell me the story of his life. You have treated me so honourably, Monsieur, he said, that I would consider myself guilty of base ingratitude if I were to keep anything from you. I want you to know not only my misfortunes and my sufferings, but also my transgressions and my most shameful weaknesses. I feel certain that, while condemning me, you will be unable to keep from pitying me.

I should here inform my readers that I wrote his story down almost immediately on hearing it, and that in consequence they can be sure that nothing is more accurate and more faithful than the narrative that follows. By faithful, I mean even in its relation of the thoughts and feelings which our young hero communicated with the best grace in the world. Here then is his story, to which I will add nothing, until its conclusion, that does not come from him.

I was seventeen years old, and was just completing my studies in philosophy at Amiens, where my parents, who belonged to one of the best families in P..., had sent me. I was leading a life so prudent and well ordered that my teachers held me up as an example to the entire

college. Not that I made strenuous efforts to deserve their praise; but I am by nature disposed to be mild and peaceable. I applied myself to my studies out of inclination, while signs I gave of a natural aversion to vice were attributed to me as virtues. My birth, my scholastic successes, and an agreeable appearance had won me the acquaintance and respect of everyone of any consequence in the town. I spoke so well—and to such general acclaim—in the public debates at the end of the year, that the Bishop, who was present, suggested that I go into the Church, where I could not fail to earn greater distinction than as a Knight of Malta, for which my parents had destined me. They already made me wear its cross, and with it the title of Chevalier Des Grieux.* The holidays were approaching, and I was getting ready to return home to my father, who had promised to send me to the Academy very soon. My one regret on leaving Amiens was that I would be parting from a friend to whom I had always been deeply attached. He was several years older than I. We had been brought up together, but since his family fortunes were modest in the extreme, he was obliged to enter holy orders and to stay on in Amiens after I had left, in order to continue with the studies appropriate to that profession. He had a thousand good qualities. You will come to know him, as my story unfolds, for his readiness to use the best of these on my behalf, and especially for a zealousness and generosity in friendship that surpass the most famous examples of Antiquity.* If I had followed the advice he gave me then, I would always have prospered and been wise. If, in the abyss into which my passions soon plunged me, I had at least heeded his reproaches, I might have salvaged something from the shipwreck of my fortune and reputation. But the only fruit he reaped from his efforts on my behalf was the bitterness of seeing them in vain, and sometimes harshly repaid by an ungrateful wretch who felt them as an affront, and dismissed them as an impertinence.

I had already decided the date of my departure from Amiens. If only, alas! I had decided to leave a day sooner, I would have returned to my father's house as innocent as when I left it. On the evening before the day when I was to leave the town, I was out walking with my friend, whose name was Tiberge, when we saw the coach from Arras arrive, and followed it to the inn where these vehicles stop. Our only motive was curiosity. Several women alighted and at once went inside. But there was one, a very young girl, who remained

companions. There's a young man over there, added the guard, who might be able to tell you more than I can about the cause of her misfortune; he's been following her ever since we left Paris, and has hardly stopped weeping for a moment. He must be her brother or her lover. I turned towards the corner where the young man was sitting. He seemed lost in a deep reverie. I have never seen a livelier image of grief. He was dressed very simply; but one can tell at a glance a man of birth and education. I went over to him. He rose; and I discerned in his eyes, his face, and all his movements so refined and noble an air that I instinctively felt disposed to wish him well. I would not for the world disturb you, I said, sitting down beside him, but would you be so good as to satisfy my curiosity concerning that lovely young woman over there, who, it seems to me, was never meant for the sad state I see her in? He replied, politely, that he could not tell me who she was without making himself known to me also; and that he had powerful reasons for wishing to remain anonymous. I can nevertheless tell you something those wretches know only too well, he continued, gesturing towards the constables, which is that I love her with so violent a passion that it has made me the most unhappy of men. I did everything I could in Paris to procure her freedom. Pleading, subtlety, force, all were in vain; I have made up my mind to follow her, to the ends of the earth if need be. I will embark with her. I will go to America. But what truly is inhuman, he added, again indicating the guards, is that these cowardly rascals won't let me go near her. I had planned to attack them openly, a few miles from Paris. I engaged four men who, in return for a considerable sum, promised to help me. The traitors left me to fight it out on my own, and ran off with my money. The impossibility of succeeding by force made me lay down my arms. I proposed to the guards that they at least allow me to follow them, and offered to pay them. Lured by the prospect of gain, they agreed. But they wanted to be paid every time they allowed me to speak to my mistress. My purse was soon empty; and now that I haven't a sou, they have the barbarity to push me back brutally every time I take a step towards her. Only a moment ago, when I dared to approach her in spite of their menaces, they had the insolence to threaten me with the butts of their rifles. To satisfy their greed and put myself in a position where I can continue the journey on foot, I have to sell a wretched horse that has served as my mount until now.

Des Grieux and Manon in the courtyard of the inn at Amiens
(J.-J. Pasquier)

behind, standing alone in the courtyard while an elderly man, who
appeared to be her escort, busied himself retrieving her luggage
from the coach. She seemed to me so enchanting that I, who had
never thought about the difference between the sexes nor looked at a
girl with any attention—I, I repeat, whose wisdom and restraint
were admired by all—found myself inflamed all of a sudden to the
point of rapture. I had always been timid to a fault, and easily put out
of countenance; but far from being deterred by these weaknesses
now, I at once approached the mistress of my heart. Although she
was younger even than I was, she received my polite overtures without the least sign of embarrassment. I asked what brought her to
Amiens, and if she was acquainted with anyone there. She replied
openly that she had been sent there by her parents, to become a nun.
Love, which had only a moment before entered my heart, had
already so opened my eyes that I at once saw this plan as a mortal
blow to my desires. She could see from the way in which I spoke to
her what my feelings were, for she was much more experienced than
I. It was against her will that she was being sent to the convent, in
order, no doubt, to check that predisposition to pleasure which had
already declared itself, and which has since been the cause of all her
misfortunes and of mine. I protested against so cruel a proposal on
the part of her parents, with every argument that dawning love and
my student eloquence could furnish. She affected neither severity
nor disdain. She told me, after a moment's silence, that she could see
only too well that she was meant to be unhappy, but that this was
apparently Heaven's will, since it left her no means of avoiding it.
The sweetness of her glance, an enchanting air of sadness as she
pronounced these words—or rather, my evil star already in its
ascendant and drawing me to my ruin—did not allow me to hesitate
for a moment over my reply.* I assured her that, if she would only
put her trust in my honour and the infinite tenderness she already
inspired in me, I would devote my life to delivering her from her
parents' tyranny, and to making her happy. I have marvelled a
thousand times, thinking it over, where, at the age I was then, I could
have acquired such boldness and ease of expression; but we would
not have made a divinity of Love, if it were not for the wonders it so
often works. I added a thousand other things, no less pressing. My
beautiful stranger knew very well that one is not, at my age, a
deceiver; she confessed that if I could see some way to procuring her

freedom, she would consider herself indebted to me for something dearer than life itself. I repeated that I was ready to undertake anything; but being too inexperienced to envisage there and then how I might be of service to her, I fell back on this general assurance, which was of no very great assistance either to her or to me. Since her aged Argus had now rejoined us,* my hopes would have foundered if her wits had not been sharp enough to compensate for the dullness of mine. As her escort drew near, I was astonished to hear her address me as 'cousin', and to say that, having had the good fortune to meet me by chance in Amiens, she had decided to postpone her entry into the convent until the following day, so as to procure herself the pleasure of having supper with me. Entering readily into the spirit of this ruse, I suggested she take rooms in an inn whose host, now settled in Amiens after many years as coachman to my father, was wholly devoted to carrying out my orders. I guided her there myself, while the aged escort seemed inclined to grumble and my friend Tiberge, who understood nothing of this whole scene, followed without a word. He had not heard our conversation, but had continued strolling about the courtyard while I talked of love to my fair mistress. Fearing some sensible objections on his part, I got rid of him by asking him to undertake an errand for me. I therefore had the pleasure, when we arrived at the inn, of talking alone with the sovereign of my heart. I soon realized that I was less of a child than I had thought. My heart opened up to a thousand pleasurable emotions, of which I had not had the least idea. A gentle warmth spread through my veins. I was in a kind of transport, which for a time deprived me of the power of speech and found expression only through my eyes. Mademoiselle Manon Lescaut—for so she told me she was called—seemed well pleased with the effect of her charms. I even noticed, or thought I did, that she was no less moved than I was. She admitted that she found me greatly to her liking, and said she would be entranced to owe her freedom to me. She wished to know who I was, and her attachment to me grew with my reply, for, of humble birth herself,* she was flattered to have made the conquest of such a lover. We discussed what we should do so that we could be together. After much reflection, we found no other course but to run away. But first we would have to deceive the vigilance of her escort, who, although only a servant, was a man to be reckoned with. We decided that during the night I would hire a chaise, and that I would return to the inn early next morning before he was awake; that we would steal away in secret, and go straight to Paris, where we would be married as soon as we arrived. I had about fifty écus, the fruits of some small savings; she had almost twice that amount. We imagined, like the inexperienced children we were, that this sum would last us for ever; and we were no less confident about the success of our other measures.

After the most delightful supper I had ever known, I took my leave of her in order to put our scheme into operation. My arrangements were the easier to make in that, since I had intended returning home next day, my small amount of baggage was already packed. I thus had no difficulty in getting my trunk removed and securing a coach for five o'clock the next morning, at which time the gates of the town should be open. But I encountered an obstacle I had not anticipated, and which almost ruined my whole enterprise.

Although only three years older than I, Tiberge was a young man of mature good sense and orderly conduct. He was extraordinarily fond of me. The sight of so pretty a girl as Mademoiselle Manon, the eagerness with which I had offered to accompany her, and the lengths to which I had gone to invent some errand that would rid me of him, were reasons enough for him to suspect that I might be in love. He had not dared go back to the inn where he had left me, for fear his return would offend me; but had gone instead to wait at my lodgings, where, on my arrival, I found him, even though it was by now ten o'clock in the evening. His presence was highly unwelcome to me. He could see very well the constraint it put me under. I feel sure, he said without prevarication, that you are hatching some scheme you want to keep secret from me. I can see it in your eyes. I replied, somewhat brusquely, that I was not obliged to keep him informed of all my plans. No, he rejoined, but you have always treated me as your friend, a title that assumes a degree of openness and trust. He pressed me so long and hard to reveal my secret to him that, never having kept anything from him before, I confided my passion in full. He listened with an air of displeasure that made me tremble. I regretted above all having been so indiscreet as to let him know I was planning to run away. He told me he was too much my friend not to oppose this with everything in his power; that it was therefore his intention to present me, in the first instance, with every argument he thought likely to deflect me from this wretched course, but that if I did not as a result abandon it, he would inform those who most certainly would put a stop to it. Whereupon he delivered a very solemn speech, which went on for more than quarter of an hour, and which ended with him again threatening to denounce me, if I did not give him my word I would behave more sensibly and reasonably in future. I was in despair at having given myself away so inopportunely. I nevertheless reflected—for had not love during the last two or three hours sharpened my wits to an extraordinary degree?— that I had not told him that my plan was to be put into operation the next day; and I decided to trick him by means of an equivocation. Tiberge, I said, I have always until now believed you to be my friend, and by confiding in you, have wanted to put this to the test. It's true I am in love; I haven't deceived you about that; but as to running away, that is an enterprise not to be embarked upon lightly. Come and meet me here tomorrow morning at nine o'clock. I'll take you to see my mistress, if this is possible,* so that you can judge for yourself whether she merits my taking this step for her. After a thousand protestations of friendship, he left me. I spent the night putting my affairs in order and, arriving towards daybreak at the inn where Manon was staying, found her waiting for me. She was at her window overlooking the street, and as soon as she caught sight of me came down and opened the door herself. We slipped out without a sound. She had no baggage apart from a change of clothing, which I took charge of myself. The chaise was ready to depart; and we had soon left the town far behind us. I will relate in due course how Tiberge behaved when he realized I had tricked him. In spite of this, the ardour of his friendship remained undiminished. You will see to what extraordinary lengths he carried it, and what tears I ought to shed when I consider what has always been its reward.

We made such rapid progress that we were in Saint-Denis before nightfall. I had travelled on horseback alongside the chaise, which allowed us to talk only when we changed horses; but when we saw how close we were to Paris, and therefore to safety, we stopped for a little refreshment, for we had eaten nothing since leaving Amiens. However great my passion for Manon, she managed to persuade me that she felt no less for me. We were so unrestrained in our caresses that we had not the patience to wait until we were alone. Our postilions and the people at the inn looked on in astonishment, surprised, as I observed, to see two such children apparently in love to the point of distraction. Our plans for marriage were forgotten in Saint-Denis; we defrauded the Church of its rights, and found ourselves man and wife without giving the matter a moment's thought. There is no question but that, given my affectionate and constant nature, I could have been happy with Manon my whole life long, if only she had been faithful to me. The more I came to know her, the more new and lovable qualities I discovered. Her mind and heart, her gentleness and beauty, these formed a chain so strong and so enchanting that I would have thought it perfect happiness to remain for ever within its bounds. How cruel a reversal! What has brought me to despair could have been my felicity. I have been made the most wretched of men by that very constancy that should have earned me the happiest of fates and love's sweetest rewards.

We took a furnished apartment in Paris. It was in the Rue V... and, as ill-luck would have it, near the house of M. de B..., the well-known tax-farmer.* Three weeks passed during which I was so taken up with my passion for Manon that I gave little thought to my family and to the grief my absence must be causing my father. However, since there was no trace of debauchery in my conduct, and since Manon too behaved with a good deal of reserve, the tranquillity of our life together helped reawaken in me, little by little, thoughts of my duty. I decided to become reconciled, if this was possible, with my father. My mistress was so truly lovable that I did not doubt that she would win him over, if only I could find a way of letting him discover her merit and worth for himself: in other words, I deceived myself into thinking I could procure his permission to marry her, having been disabused of my hopes of doing so without his consent.* I communicated this scheme to Manon, intimating that, along with motives of love and duty, that of necessity must enter into our considerations too, for our funds were sorely depleted and I was beginning to revise my opinion as to their inexhaustibility. Manon received my suggestion coldly. Since, however, the difficulties she raised all sprang from the tenderness of her feelings for me, and from her fear of losing me if my father, having discovered our hiding-place, refused to accede to our plans, I had not the least foreboding of the cruel blow that was about to be dealt me. To the argument that we were driven by necessity, she replied that we had enough to live on for some weeks yet, and that afterwards she would appeal to some of her relations in the provinces, who were fond of her and to whom she would write for help. She softened her rejection of my plan with such tender and passionate caresses that I, who lived only through and for her, and who did not for a moment doubt the sincerity of her heart, approved of all her arguments and all her decisions. I had entrusted to her the management of our purse and the task of settling our day-to-day expenses. I noticed, shortly afterwards, that our table was better supplied than before, and that she had allowed herself several new and expensive sets of clothes. Since I knew only too well that we could scarcely have more than twelve or fifteen pistoles left, I indicated my astonishment at this apparent increase in our means. She implored me, laughing, not to worry. Did I not promise you, she said, that I would find resources? I loved her with too much simplicity of heart to doubt her reassurances.

One day, when I had gone out in the afternoon, telling her I would be away for longer than usual, I was astonished on my return to be kept waiting for two or three minutes at the door. Our only servant was a young girl of about our own age. When at last she opened the door to me, I asked her what had kept her so long. She replied, in some confusion, that she had not heard me knock. But I only knocked once, I said; so if, as you say, you didn't hear me, why did you come and open the door? She was so put out by this question that, not having enough presence of mind to know how to reply, she began to cry, assuring me it was not her fault, and that Madame had forbidden her to open the door until M. de B... had left by the other staircase, which communicated with the dressing-room. This reply threw me into a state of such agitation that I could not bring myself to enter our apartment.* I decided to go out again, on the pretext of some matter or other, and instructed the young girl to tell her mistress that I would be returning shortly, but on no account to let her know that she had mentioned M. de B... to me.

So great was my consternation that I shed tears as I descended the stairs, without recognizing as yet what emotion it was that caused them to flow. I went into the first coffee-house I came to; and, sitting at a table, put my head in my hands so as to reflect on what was happening in my heart. I did not dare dwell on what I had just heard. I wanted to think of it as an illusion, indeed two or three times I was on the verge of returning home as though nothing had happened. It seemed to me so impossible that Manon should have betrayed me that I feared I was insulting her even by suspecting it. I adored her, there was no question of that; I had given her no proofs of love greater than those I had received from her; why then should I accuse her of being less sincere and less constant than I was? What reason could she have had to deceive me? It was only three hours ago that she had heaped the tenderest caresses upon me, and had received mine with rapture; I did not know my own heart better than I knew hers. No, no, I continued, it is impossible that Manon should betray me. She could never forget that I live only for her. She knows only too well that I adore her. Is that a reason for her to hate me?

M. de B...'s visit and his furtive departure remained, nevertheless, a source of perplexity. I also remembered Manon's little acquisitions, which had seemed to me to go beyond what our wealth would permit. They now seemed to hint at the liberality of some new lover. And then there was the confidence she had shown about finding sources of income unknown to me! It was very hard to give to so many enigmas as favourable a meaning as my heart would have wished for. On the other hand, she had scarcely been out of my sight since the day we arrived in Paris. Projects, outings, amusements—we had done everything together: for how, in God's name, could we have endured a minute's separation? We had to be always reassuring one another of our love; otherwise we would have died of grief. Indeed, I could scarcely think of a single moment when Manon could have been busy with someone other than me. At last I believed I had solved the mystery. M. de B..., I said to myself, is a man who is involved in great affairs and has many grand connections; Manon's relatives must have used this man to send money to her. She may already have received some by this route, and perhaps he came today to bring her more. No doubt she is amusing herself by hiding it from me, and intends to give me a pleasant surprise later on. Perhaps she would have told me about it if I had gone home as usual, instead of coming here to brood; at any rate, she will not try to hide it from me once I've brought the subject up.

I argued this view so persuasively that it did a great deal to dispel my unhappiness. I went straight home. I embraced Manon with my usual tenderness. She responded with affection. I was tempted at first to tell her my conjectures, which now more than ever I thought were correct; but I held back in the hope she might perhaps forestall me by telling me everything that had happened. Supper was served. I sat down at table with an air of great cheerfulness; but in the light of the candle that stood between us I thought I saw signs of sorrow on the face and in the eyes of my beloved mistress. This thought filled me in turn with sadness. I noticed that her gaze was fixed on me, but not in a way it had ever been before. I could not tell if it was a look of love or of pity, although it seemed to spring from some gentle and languishing emotion. I returned her gaze; and perhaps she found it no easier to judge the state of my heart from my eyes. We neither of us thought of speaking or eating. At last I saw tears fall from her lovely eyes—perfidious tears! Heavens, dearest Manon! I cried, you are weeping; you are so distressed it makes you weep, and yet you tell me nothing of the cause of your grief. A few sighs were her only reply, which redoubled my anxiety. I rose trembling to my feet; I implored her, with all the fervour of passionate love, to tell me the reason for her tears; I shed tears myself while drying hers; I was more dead than alive. A barbarian would have been moved by these signs of my anguish and fear. While I was thus wholly preoccupied with her, I heard the noise of several people coming up the stairs. There was a gentle tap at the door. Manon gave me a kiss and, escaping from my arms, slipped quickly into the dressing-room and shut herself in. I supposed that, conscious of some disorder in her dress, she wanted to avoid the gaze of the unknown visitors who had knocked. I went to open the door myself. No sooner had I done so than I found myself seized by three men I recognized as my father's footmen. They did me no violence; but while two of them held me by the arms, the third went through my pockets, removing a little knife, which was the only weapon I had on my person. They asked forgiveness for the lack of respect they were obliged to show me; they told me quite openly that they were acting on my father's orders, and that my older brother was waiting downstairs in a carriage. I was so confused that I allowed myself to be led away without attempting to resist or reply. My brother was indeed waiting for me. They put me into the carriage beside him, and the coachman, evidently acting under orders, drove at full speed to Saint-Denis. My brother embraced me tenderly but did not speak, so that I had all the leisure I needed to muse on my ill-fortune.

At first I found the whole thing so obscure that I could see nothing on which to base the least conjecture. I had been cruelly betrayed; but by whom? Tiberge was the first to come to mind. Traitor! I said, if what I suspect turns out to be true, it will cost you your life.

However, I reflected that, since he did not know my address, he could not have disclosed it to anyone else. As for accusing Manon, that was a treachery my heart did not dare contemplate. The extraordinary sadness I had seen her all but overwhelmed by, her tears, the tender kiss she had given me as she left the room—these, it is true, remained a mystery; but I was inclined to dismiss them as some sort of presentiment on her part of our common misfortune; and, while filled with despair at the misadventure that had wrested me from her, I was credulous enough to imagine she was still more to be pitied than I was. On further reflection, I persuaded myself that I must have been seen in the streets of Paris by some people who knew me, and who had informed my father. I drew some comfort from this idea. I supposed I would be let off with nothing worse than reprimands and a degree of harsh usage I would have to endure in the name of paternal authority. I resolved to suffer it all with patience, and to promise everything that was demanded of me, in order to secure an opportunity to return to Paris as early as possible, and to restore life and joy to my beloved Manon.

We soon reached Saint-Denis. My brother, surprised at my silence and imagining it to be the result of apprehension, took it upon himself to comfort me, assuring me that I had nothing to fear from my father's severity, provided I was prepared to resume my duties as a son with proper meekness, and to merit the affection he felt for me. We spent the night in Saint-Denis, where he took the precaution of making the three footmen sleep in my room. The thing that caused me real distress, however, was finding myself in the same inn I had stopped at with Manon on our way from Amiens to Paris. The landlord and servants recognized me, and immediately guessed my true story. I heard the landlord say: Well I never, it's the fine young gentleman who came this way not six weeks ago with a little lady he was so fond of. What a charmer she was too! Poor little things, how they doted on one another! And what a pity, by heavens, to separate them! I pretended to hear nothing of this, and appeared in public as little as possible. My brother had arranged for a chaise to be waiting for us at Saint-Denis; we set off next morning, and arrived home on the evening of the following day. He spoke to my father before I did, hoping to dispose him in my favour by telling him how meekly I had submitted to being brought there; with the result that I was received less harshly than I had expected. My father contented himself with some general reproaches concerning my misconduct in staying away from home without permission. As for my mistress, he said that, having delivered myself into the hands of a woman we did not know, I amply deserved what had happened to me; that he had had a better opinion of my good sense; but that he hoped I would be wiser in future for this little adventure. I chose to take from this speech only what was consistent with my own ideas. I thanked my father for the goodness he had shown in forgiving me, and promised to behave in a more submissive and orderly fashion in future. In my heart of hearts I was exultant, since, the way things were turning out, I did not doubt I would find an opportunity to steal away from the house very soon, even, perhaps, before the night was ended.

We sat down to supper; I was teased about the conquest I had made at Amiens and about my elopement with so faithful a mistress. I accepted these jests with a good grace. I was charmed, even, at being allowed to talk about what was constantly occupying my mind. However, something I heard my father say caught my ear and made me listen with the utmost attention. He spoke of treachery and of some self-interested service Monsieur B... had rendered him. I was taken aback at hearing him pronounce this name, and humbly begged him to explain at greater length what he meant. He turned to my brother and asked him if he had not told me the whole story. My brother replied that I had seemed so calm on the way home he had not thought I needed this remedy in order to cure me of my folly. I noticed my father hesitating as to whether or not to tell me everything he knew. I pressed him so urgently to do so that he obliged me, or delivered me a mortal blow rather, by recounting the most horrible of stories.

He asked me first of all if I had always been so ingenuous as to believe my mistress loved me. I replied, boldly, that I was so certain of this that nothing could make me suspect otherwise. Ha! ha! he cried, laughing heartily, that is excellent! A fine fool you are to be sure, but I like these sentiments in you. It's a pity, my poor Chevalier, indeed it is, to make you enter the Order of Malta, when you show such aptitude for the role of the patient and complaisant husband. He made a thousand more jokes in the same vein, aimed at what he called my foolishness and credulity. At last, as I remained silent, he went on to tell me that, according to such calculations as he had been able to make about my time since leaving Amiens, Manon had been in love with me for about twelve days: for, he added, I know you left Amiens on the twenty-eighth day of last month; today is the twenty-ninth of this; it is eleven days since Monsieur B... wrote to me; and I suppose he would have needed seven or eight to become perfectly acquainted with your mistress; so, if you take eleven plus eight from the thirty-one days that fall between the twenty-eighth of one month and the twenty-ninth of the next, that leaves twelve, give or take a day or two. Whereupon the laughter started up once again. I listened to all this with a seizure of the heart I feared I might succumb to before we reached the end of this sad comedy. You had better know, my father went on, since at present you do not, that Monsieur B... has won the heart of your princess; for he is mistaken if he thinks he can fool me into believing that he decided to steal her away from you out of disinterested zeal to be of service to me. Such nobility of sentiment is scarcely to be expected from a man like him, whom, moreover, we do not know. He discovered from her that you are my son; and, so as to be relieved of your importunate presence, wrote to tell me where you were and what a dissolute life you were leading, giving me to understand at the same time that force would be needed to secure you. He offered to facilitate the means whereby I might seize you, and it is thanks to information supplied by him and your mistress that your brother was able to find a moment when he could catch you unawares. Congratulate yourself now, if you can, on the length of your triumph. You know well enough how to take by storm, Chevalier, but you do not know how to consolidate your conquests.*

I no longer had strength enough to endure a speech whose every word pierced my heart. I rose from the table, but had not taken four steps towards the door before falling to the ground, bereft of all consciousness and feeling. Prompt assistance soon restored me. I opened my eyes only to pour forth a torrent of tears, and my mouth to utter the saddest and most touching lamentations. My father, who has always loved me tenderly, now employed all this affection in trying to comfort me. I listened, but did not hear him. I flung myself at his knees; I begged him, hands clasped together in supplication, to let me return to Paris, so that I might find B... and plunge a dagger into him. No, no, I protested, he has not won Manon's heart; he has used violence; he has resorted to some spell or potion to seduce her; perhaps he has taken her by brutal force. Manon loves me. Do I not know this to be true? He must have threatened her, dagger in hand, and compelled her to abandon me. What would he not have done in order to rob me of so enchanting a mistress! Oh gods above! Could it be possible that Manon has betrayed me, and that she no longer loves me?

Since I talked only of returning to Paris straight away, and indeed kept rising to my feet in order to leave, my father saw that, possessed as I was, nothing would be able to stop me. He took me to a room at the top of the house, where he left me with two servants he ordered to keep watch on me. I was beside myself. I would have given my life a thousand times over for a single quarter of an hour in Paris. I realized that, having declared myself so openly, I would not easily get permission to leave my room. I measured the height of the windows by eye; seeing no means of escape by that route, I approached my two servants and, in a friendly tone, promised, with a thousand protestations as to my good faith, that I would one day make their fortunes if they would only consent to letting me go free. I pressed, I cajoled, I threatened; but these efforts, too, were in vain.

At this point I abandoned all hope. I resolved to die, and threw myself on to my bed, intending not to leave it again until life itself had gone. I remained in this state for the whole of the night and the following day. I refused the food they brought me next morning. My father came to see me in the afternoon. Hoping to comfort me in my distress, he spoke words of the greatest kindness and consolation. He ordered me so absolutely to eat something that, out of respect for his orders, I did so. Several days passed, during which I ate nothing except in his presence, and in order to obey him. He continued the whole time to present me with arguments calculated to restore me to my senses, and inspire contempt in me for the unfaithful Manon. It was true that I no longer respected her: how could I have respected the most fickle, the most perfidious creature in the world? But her image, those enchanting features I carried deep in my heart, persisted there still. I knew myself only too well. I may die, I said; indeed I ought to do so, after so much shame and grief; but never, were I to suffer a thousand deaths, would I be able to forget the faithless Manon.

My father was surprised to see me still so powerfully affected. He knew me to have principles of honour; and since he could not doubt that her treachery had made me despise her, imagined my constancy to be the effect, not so much of this passion in particular, as of a fondness for women in general. He became so attached to this idea that, moved solely by tender affection, he raised the matter with me one day. Up until now, Chevalier, he said, I have always intended you to wear the Cross of Malta; but I see that your tastes do not incline you in that direction. You like pretty women. I have a mind to find one you would like. Tell me frankly what you think of this idea. I replied that I no longer distinguished between women, and that after the misfortune that had befallen me I detested them all equally. But I will find you one, continued my father smiling, who will resemble Manon, and be more faithful. Ah, if you care for me at all, I said, it is her and her alone you must return to me. I promise you, dearest Father, she has not betrayed me. It is B..., perfidious wretch that he is, who is deceiving us all, you, her, and me. If you knew how tender and sincere she is, if only you could see her, you would love her too. What a child you are! retorted my father. How can you be so blind, after everything I have told you about her? She alone it was, who handed you over to your brother. You ought to forget her very name and, if you have any sense, take advantage of the indulgence I am showing you. I saw all too clearly that he was right; and that some involuntary impulse was making me take the side of my faithless mistress in this way. Alas! I continued after a moment's silence, it is only too true that I am the wretched object of the basest betrayal that ever was. Yes indeed, I continued, shedding tears of vexation, I see very well that I am a mere child. It cost them little enough to deceive me, credulous fool that I am. I know well enough, however, how to take my revenge. My father asked me what I had in mind. I will go to Paris, I told him, I will set fire to B...'s house, and burn him alive along with the perfidious Manon. This outburst made my father laugh, and only served to have me held the more securely in my prison.

I spent six whole months there, the first of which saw little change in my state of mind. My feelings were nothing but a continual alternation of hate and love, of hope and despair, according to the image of Manon that was uppermost in my mind. At times I thought of her as the most adorable girl that ever was, and I yearned to see her again; at others I saw in her nothing but a false and perfidious mistress, and swore a thousand times over to seek her out only to punish her. They brought me books, which helped to restore some calm to my soul; I reread all my favourite authors; I became acquainted with new ones. I rediscovered an infinite taste for study. You will see what benefit this was to me in what follows. The insights I had acquired through love enabled me to elucidate a large number of places in Horace and Virgil that had hitherto seemed to me obscure. I wrote a lover's commentary on the fourth book of the *Aeneid*; I intend to publish it some day; and I flatter myself it will please the public. Alas! I said to myself as I wrote it, it was a heart such as mine that faithful Dido deserved.*

Tiberge came to see me one day in my prison. I was surprised by the fervour with which he embraced me. It was the first time he had given me cause to regard his affection for me as anything other than a simple college friendship, such as often springs up between young men of like age. I found him so changed and matured, in the five or six months that had passed since I last saw him, that his appearance and manner of speaking inspired me with respect. He talked to me as a wise mentor, not as a schoolfriend. He regretted the aberration I had fallen into. Believing me to be on the road to recovery, he congratulated me on my cure; finally he exhorted me to profit from this youthful error, and open my eyes to the vanity of earthly joys. I looked at him in astonishment. He observed this. My dear Chevalier, he said, I am saying nothing that is not profoundly true, and of which I have not become convinced through serious examination. I used to have as great a fondness for pleasure as you; but Heaven had given me, at the same time, a love of virtue. Bringing reason to bear on the matter, I compared the fruits of the one with those of the other, and it was not long before I discovered their differences. Heaven aided me in these reflections. I have conceived for the world a contempt that has no equal.* Can you guess what it is that keeps me here, he added, and prevents me from seeking the solitude of the convent? Only the tender friendship I feel for you. I know your excellent qualities of heart and mind; there is no good of which you would not be capable, if you chose. But the poison of pleasure has led you astray. What a loss for virtue! Your flight from Amiens caused me so much grief that I have not known a moment's true contentment since. You can judge this for yourself by the measures it led me to take. He went on to tell me that, realizing I had deceived him and had run away with my mistress, he had followed me on horseback; but that, since I had a start of four or five hours, he had been unable to catch me up, even though I had left Saint-Denis only half an hour before he arrived; that, feeling certain I must still be in Paris, he had spent six weeks there vainly searching for me; that he had been to all the places where he hoped he might find me, and one day, at last, had recognized my mistress at the theatre, but so dazzlingly attired he imagined she must owe this fortune to some new lover; that he had followed her carriage all the way to her house; and had learned from a servant that she was maintained at the expense of Monsieur B... But I did not leave it at that, he continued. I went back the next day, to find out from her in person what had become of you; but she turned her back on me the moment I mentioned your name, and I was obliged to return to the country without any further explanation. There I learned of your fate and of the extreme des-pondency into which it had plunged you; but I did not want to see you until I could be sure of finding you in a calmer frame of mind.

So you have seen Manon, I replied with a sigh. Alas! You are more fortunate than I, condemned never to see her again. He reproached me for this sigh, which showed some weakness for her still on my part. He spoke so flatteringly and so artfully of my good character and worthy impulses that, from this first visit, he inspired in me a strong desire to renounce all worldly pleasures, as he had done, and enter holy orders.

I was so taken with this idea that, when I was alone once more, I thought of nothing else. I remembered the Bishop of Amiens, who had given me the same advice, and the favourable predictions he had made as to my future success if I should decide to embrace this way of life. Piety, too, played its part in my deliberations. I will lead a good and Christian life, I said; I will devote myself to study and religion, which will so occupy my mind that I will be prevented from dwelling on the dangerous pleasures of love. I will despise what the common run of men admire, and since I dare to hope that my heart will desire only what it can respect, I will have as few anxieties as desires. I at once devised a peaceful and solitary way of life for the future. I imagined a secluded house, with a little wood and a stream of clear water at the end of the garden, a library of choice books, a small number of friends possessed of virtue and good sense, a table which, though frugal and modest, was tastefully furnished. I added a correspondence by letter with a friend living in Paris, who would keep me informed of the news of the day, less to satisfy my curiosity than to afford me a diverting spectacle of human folly and turmoil. How could I fail to be happy? I added; will not all my aspirations be fulfilled? And it is true that this plan was wholly consistent with my natural inclinations. But when all these wise arrangements were in place, I felt that my heart still yearned for something more, and that, to have nothing left to wish for in the most delightful solitude, I would have to share it with Manon.*

Nevertheless, as Tiberge continued to pay me frequent visits in order to further the project he had inspired in me, I found an opportunity to raise it with my father. He declared that it had always been his intention to leave his children free to choose their course in life, and that, whatever I might wish to do, the only right he reserved for himself was that of offering advice. The advice he gave was very wise, aimed less at discouraging me in my enterprise than at enabling me to embrace it in the full knowledge of what I was undertaking. The start of the school year was approaching. I agreed with Tiberge that we would enrol together at the seminary of Saint-Sulpice, he to complete his theological studies, and I to begin mine. His merits were already so well known to the diocesan bishop that, before our departure, this prelate conferred on him a considerable benefice.*

My father, who believed me completely cured of my passion, made no difficulty about letting me go. We arrived in Paris. I exchanged my Cross of Malta for clerical dress, and the title of Chevalier for that of Abbé Des Grieux. I applied myself so diligently to my studies that, within a very few months, I had made extraordinary progress. I devoted part of the night to them, and did not waste a moment during the day. I soon acquired such a reputation for brilliance that people were already congratulating me on the high honours I could not fail to win; and, without my having solicited it, my name was included on the list of those eligible for a vacant living. Nor was I devoid of piety; I performed all my devotional exercises with fervour. Tiberge was delighted by what he regarded as his own work; and I several times caught him in tears as he congratulated himself on what he called my conversion. That human resolutions should be subject to change is not something that has ever surprised me: being born of a particular passion, they may be destroyed by another; but when I think of the sanctity of the resolutions that had brought me to Saint-Sulpice, and of the inner joy Heaven granted me so long as I continued to carry them out, I tremble at the ease with which I was able to break them. If it is true that divine aid is at any moment as powerful a force as passion, let someone explain to me by what evil star we find ourselves suddenly swept away, along a course that deflects us from our duty, unable to offer the least resistance or feel the least remorse. I believed myself cured once and for all of the frailties of love. I felt that I would rather have read a page of Saint Augustine or spent quarter of an hour in Christian meditation than enjoy all the pleasures of the senses, not excepting those that Manon could have offered me. In spite of which, an unlucky moment sent me falling from the precipice once more; and my fall was the more irremediable in that, suddenly finding myself again in the very depths from which I had escaped, the new levels of dissipation into which I now sank took me further still towards the bottom of the abyss.

I had been in Paris for almost a year without making any enquiries about Manon. At first, practising such restraint had cost me dear; but Tiberge's wise and ever-present counsel, together with my own reflections, helped me to emerge victorious. The last few months had passed so peacefully that I believed myself on the point of forgetting that bewitching and perfidious creature for ever. The moment came for me to take part in my first public exercise in disputation at the School of Theology. I invited several people of consequence to honour me with their presence. My name was thus made public in every part of Paris; it reached the ears of my inconstant mistress. She could not be certain that, under my new title of abbé, she had identified me correctly; but a vestige of curiosity, or perhaps some feeling of remorse at having betrayed me (I have never been able to decide which of these feelings it was) excited her interest in a name so similar to mine; she came to the Sorbonne with several other ladies. She was present at my disputation; and had little difficulty, no doubt, in remembering me.

I had not the least idea that this visit had taken place. As everyone knows, private compartments for ladies are provided in such places, where they are hidden behind a screen. I returned to Saint-Sulpice, covered in glory and laden with compliments. It was six o'clock in the evening. A minute later someone came to tell me that there was a lady asking to see me. I at once went to the parlour. Gods above! What an astounding apparition! I found Manon there. It was she, but lovelier and more dazzling than I had ever seen her. She was in her eighteenth year. Her charms were beyond description. There was an air about her, so delicate, so sweet, so appealing—the air of Love itself. Her whole person seemed to me an enchantment.

I stood speechless at this sight; and, unable to guess the cause of her visit, waited, fearful and trembling, and with lowered eyes, for her to offer some explanation. For a while her confusion was equal to my own; but, seeing that I remained silent, she put her hand to her eyes to hide a few tears. She confessed, timidly, that her infidelity had given me every reason to hate her; but added that, if it was true that I had ever felt any tenderness for her, then it had been very hard of me to let two years go by without taking the trouble to enquire as to her fate; and it was still harder of me to see the state to which she was reduced in my presence, without saying a word to her. The turmoil in my soul, as I listened, cannot be expressed.

She sat down. I remained standing, my body half turned away from her, not daring to look her in the face. Several times I attempted a reply, but had not the strength to finish it. At last, making an effort, I cried out in anguish: Faithless Manon! Ah, faithless, faithless Manon! Weeping bitterly, she repeated that it was not her intention to try and justify her treachery. What do you intend then? I cried again. I intend to die, she replied, if you will not give me back your heart, for I cannot live without it. Demand my life, then, traitor! I continued, myself shedding tears I tried in vain to hold back. Demand my life, which is the only thing I have left to sacrifice for you; for my heart has never ceased to be yours. I had scarcely uttered these last words when she rose, transported, and rushed to embrace me. She showered me with a thousand passionate caresses. She called me by all the names love has invented to express its tenderest and most ardent feelings. I was slow to respond as yet. What a change, indeed, from the tranquil state I had been in, to the tumultuous emotions I now felt reawaken! I was filled with terror; I trembled, as at night, when you find yourself in an isolated stretch of country: it is as if you have been transported to a whole new order of being; you are seized with a secret dread, from which you recover only after examining your surroundings at length.

We sat down side by side. I took her hands in mine. Ah Manon! I said, looking at her sadly. I did not expect the black betrayal with which you have repaid my love. It was all too easy for you to deceive a heart whose absolute sovereign you were, a heart which found its whole felicity in pleasing and obeying you. Tell me, have you found

The scene in the parlour (Gravelot)

others that are as tender and submissive? Surely not, for Nature makes few that are tempered like mine. Tell me at least, have you sometimes regretted losing such a heart? What trust can I put in the kindness that brings you back today to offer my heart such sweet consolation? I see only too clearly that you are more bewitching than ever, but, in the name of all the torments I have suffered for you, tell me, fairest Manon, will you be more faithful?

She spoke so touchingly of her remorse, she promised with so many vows and protestations to be faithful, that she moved me beyond anything words can say. Dear Manon! I said, with a profane mingling of amorous and theological expressions, you are too adorable for a mere created being. I feel my heart succumb to a delectation whose victory it cannot deny. Everything they say at Saint-Sulpice about free will is an idle fancy. I already see that I will lose my fortune and my reputation for your sake. I can read my destiny in your lovely eyes. But for what losses will your love not console me! Fortune's favours mean nothing to me; fame seems mere smoke; all my plans for a life in the Church were foolish delusions; in short, I despise every blessing except those I hope to share with you, for they could not withstand for a moment, in my heart, a single one of your glances.*

While promising I would forget all her faults, I nevertheless wanted to know how it was that she had allowed herself to be seduced by B... She told me that, seeing her at her window, he had fallen passionately in love with her; he had made his declaration like a true tax-farmer, which is to say, by informing her in writing that payment would be in proportion to the favours received; she had immediately capitulated, but without any intention beyond that of extracting from him a sum considerable enough to allow us to live comfortably; he had dazzled her with promises of such magnificence that she had, by degrees, allowed herself to be swayed; but that I could nevertheless judge of her remorse by the signs of grief she had displayed on the evening of our separation; and that, in spite of the opulence in which he had maintained her, she had never tasted true happiness with him, not only because she did not find in him, so she said, that delicacy of feeling and refinement of manner she had grown accustomed to in me; but also because, in spite of the pleasures he ceaselessly provided for her, she preserved deep in her heart the memory of my love, as well as a sense of remorse at her own infidelity. She spoke of Tiberge and the extreme confusion into which his visit had plunged her. A sword thrust deep into my heart, she added, would have caused less tumult in my blood. I turned my back on him, unable to endure his presence for a moment. She went on to tell me how she had come to hear of my being in Paris, of the change in my situation, and of my disputation at the Sorbonne. She insisted that she had been so agitated during the debate that she had had great difficulty, not only in restraining her tears but even her groans and cries, which had more than once been on the point of breaking out. Finally, she told me that she had been the last to leave the place, so as to conceal her agitation, and that, following only the impulses of her heart and the impetuosity of her desires, she had come straight to the seminary, resolved to die there if she did not find me disposed to forgive her.

Could there anywhere be so barbarous a heart as not to be touched by so fervent and so tender a repentance? I, for my part, felt at this moment that I would have sacrificed all the bishoprics in Christendom for Manon. I asked her how best she thought we should arrange our affairs in future. She said we must leave the seminary immediately and postpone any further discussion until we were in a safer place. I made no objection, but agreed to everything she wanted. She returned to her carriage, saying she would wait for me at the corner of the street. I slipped out myself a moment later, without the porter noticing me. I got in beside her. We went to a tailor's. I put on officer's braid again, as well as my sword. Manon supplied the means, for I was without a sou; and fearful lest I encounter some obstacle to leaving Saint-Sulpice, she had opposed my returning to my room for even a moment to collect some money. Moreover, my funds were modest; while she, thanks to B...'s liberality, was rich enough to despise what she was making me abandon. We discussed, while still at the tailor's, what course of action we should take. In order to impress upon me the sacrifice she was making in giving up B..., she decided not to show him the least consideration. I will leave him his furniture, she said, it belongs to him; but as is only fair, I will keep the jewels and the almost sixty thousand francs I have had from him over the past two years. I have never given him any hold over me, she added; which means that we can remain in Paris without fear, and find a comfortable house where we can live happily together. I pointed out to her that while there might be no danger in this for her, there was a great deal for me, who could not fail, sooner or later, to be recognized, and who would continually be exposed to the misfortune I had already suffered. She gave me to understand that she would be reluctant to leave Paris. I was so afraid of vexing her that there was no danger I would not have risked in order to please her; nevertheless, we arrived at a reasonable compromise, which was to rent a house in some village close to Paris, from where it would be easy for us to get into town, whenever pleasure or necessity called us there. We chose Chaillot, which is not far away. Manon immediately returned home. I went to wait for her at the little gate of the Jardin des Tuileries. She returned an hour later in a hired carriage, accompanied by her maidservant and some trunks containing her clothes and everything else she possessed that was of any value.

We did not delay, but went straight to Chaillot. We stayed at the inn the first night, so as to give ourselves time to look for a house or at least a comfortable apartment; and by the end of the next day had found one that was to our liking.

For a while my happiness seemed so securely based as to be unshakeable. Manon was all sweetness and eagerness to please. So delicate were the attentions she showed me that I believed myself only too perfectly recompensed for all my past sufferings. Since both of us had by now acquired a little experience, we gave serious consideration to the solidity of our fortune. Sixty thousand francs, which was the full extent of our wealth, was not a sufficient sum to cover an entire lifetime. Nor, moreover, were we disposed to restrict our expenditure. Economy was not Manon's chief virtue, any more than it was mine. The plan I proposed was as follows: sixty thousand francs, I said to her, could last us for ten years. Two thousand écus is an adequate annual income, provided we continue to live here in Chaillot. We will lead a life that is decent but simple. Our only expenses will be the upkeep of a carriage and visits to the theatre. We will exercise moderation. You are fond of the opera: we will go twice a week. As for gaming, we will limit our play in such a way that our losses will never exceed two pistoles. It is impossible that there should be no changes in my family during the next ten years: my father is old and may die. I will inherit something, and all our worries will be at an end.

This arrangement would not have been the greatest folly of my life, if we had had the sense to submit to it with any consistency. But our good resolutions lasted scarcely a month. Manon was passionately fond of pleasure, I of her. New opportunities to purchase arose at every moment; and, far from lamenting the amounts she spent, sometimes in profusion, I was the first to procure her anything I believed likely to give her pleasure. She even began to find living in Chaillot burdensome. Winter was coming on; everyone was returning to town; and the country was becoming deserted. She suggested we again take a house in Paris. I could not agree, but hoping to please her by yielding to her in something, said we might rent a furnished apartment, so as to be able to spend the night there whenever we found ourselves late in leaving the assembly, where we went several times each week; for the disadvantage of having to return home at so inconvenient an hour was the excuse she gave for wanting to leave Chaillot.* We thus permitted ourselves two apartments, one in town and the other in the country, a change that soon threw our affairs into total disarray by giving rise to two misadventures, which between them brought about our downfall.

Manon had a brother, who was a guardsman.* He happened, most unfortunately, to be living in the same street as us in Paris. Seeing his sister one morning at her window, he recognized her and hurried round at once. He was a brutal man, devoid of every honourable principle. He came into the room swearing horribly; and, since he had heard part of his sister's adventures, assailed her with insults and reproaches. I had gone out only the previous moment, which was no doubt fortunate both for him and for me, who was anything but disposed to tolerate an affront. By the time I returned he had gone. I could see from Manon's air of sadness that something unusual had happened. She told me about the vexing scene she had just been subjected to, and of her brother's brutal threats. So great was my indignation that I would have rushed to exact vengeance then and there, if she had not restrained me with her tears. While I was discussing this mishap with her, the guardsman came back into the room unannounced. I would not have received him as courteously as I did, if I had known who he was; but, greeting us cheerfully, he took the opportunity to say to Manon that he had come to apologize for his outburst; that he had understood her to have fallen into dissolute ways, and that this had inflamed his anger; but that having enquired of one of our servants who I was, he had heard such favourable things about me as to make him eager to be on good terms with us.

Although there was something bizarre and shocking about his obtaining this information from one of my footmen, I accepted his compliments politely, thinking that this would please Manon. She appeared charmed to see him so ready to be reconciled with us. We invited him to dinner. In no time at all he was on terms of such intimacy with us that, hearing us speak of returning to Chaillot, he insisted on accompanying us. We were obliged to give him a seat in our carriage. It was, in short, an appropriation: for he soon became so used to the great pleasure he always found in our company, that he made our house his own and himself, as it were, master of everything that belonged to us. He spoke of me as his brother; and on the pretext that this relationship permits certain liberties, took it upon himself to invite all his friends to our house in Chaillot and entertain them there at our expense. He provided himself with magnificent new clothes and had the bill sent to us. He even got us to pay all his debts. I closed my eyes to this tyranny so as not to displease Manon, to the point of pretending not to notice the considerable sums of money he extracted from her from time to time. It is true that, being a great gambler, he was faithful in repaying her part of what he owed her whenever fortune favoured him; our own fortune, however, was too modest to support such unrestrained expenditure for long. I was about to express myself forcibly to him on the matter, so as to prevent any further such impositions, when a fateful accident spared me this trouble, only to plunge us into another, which ruined us irrevocably.

We had stayed on in Paris one day, intending to spent the night there, as we often did. The maidservant, who on these occasions remained in Chaillot, arrived next morning to tell me that my house had caught fire during the night, and that they had had great difficulty in putting it out. I asked her if our furniture had been damaged; she replied that the crowds of strangers who came to help had created such confusion that she could not be sure of anything. I trembled for our money, which I kept locked in a little chest. I at once went to Chaillot. My journey was in vain: the chest had disappeared. I discovered then that one can love money without being a miser. So violent was the grief that filled me at this loss that I thought I would go out of my mind. I suddenly realized to what new misfortunes I was about to be exposed; poverty was the least of them. I knew Manon; I had already learned too well, through bitter experience, that however faithful and however fond of me she was in times of prosperity, there was no counting on her when times were bad. She was too fond of pleasure and luxury to sacrifice them for me. I will lose her, I cried; and in that case, unhappy Chevalier, you will lose everything you love. This thought threw me into a state of such fearful distress that for some moments I considered putting an end to all my troubles through death. However, I still had enough presence of mind to resolve to consider first if any other course of action was open to me. Heaven inspired me with an idea that saved me from despair. I thought it would not be impossible for me to conceal the loss from Manon and, through some ingenious scheme or favourable turn of events, to provide for her honourably enough myself to keep her from suffering want. I have already worked out, I said, trying to comfort myself, that twenty thousand écus would last us for ten years; let us suppose, however, that these ten years have passed without any of the changes I hoped for in my family having taken place. What would I do? I do not know exactly, but does anything prevent me from doing now what I would have done then? Think how many people live in Paris who have neither my wit nor my natural qualities, and who nevertheless depend for their livelihood on their talents, such as they are! Has not Providence, I added, reflecting on the different conditions in life, arranged things very wisely? The great and the wealthy are, for the most part, fools: this is obvious to anyone who knows anything of the world. And is there not an admirable justice in this? If, as well as wealth, they also had wit, they would be too fortunate and the rest of mankind too wretched. Qualities of mind and body have rather been given to these latter, so that they may use them as a means of extricating themselves from wretchedness and poverty. Some of them acquire a share of the wealth enjoyed by the great by procuring them their pleasures, and so make dupes of them. Others devote themselves to their education, and so try to make honest men of them. It is rare, in fact, that they succeed in this; indeed, it is not part of Divine Wisdom's purpose that they should; but at least they reap one benefit from their labours, which is that they live at the expense of those they educate; and, whichever way you look at it, the foolishness of the great and the wealthy is an excellent source of revenue for the humble.

These reflections calmed my anxious head and heart a little. I decided first of all to go and consult M. Lescaut, Manon's brother. He knew Paris intimately; and I had all too often had occasion to note that neither property nor his soldier's pay were his most obvious sources of revenue. I had a mere twenty pistoles left, which fortunately I had been carrying in my pocket. I showed him the state of my purse, told him of my misfortune and my fears, and asked if there was any course of action open to me other than either dying of hunger or blowing my brains out in despair. He replied that blowing one's brains out was the last resort of the fool; and as for dying of hunger, plenty of clever people had seen themselves reduced to this, when all they lacked was the will to make use of their talents; it was up to me to decide what I was capable of; and I could rely on his help and advice in all my undertakings.

That is all very vague, M. Lescaut, I said. My situation requires a more immediate remedy; for what am I to say to Manon? As to Manon, he replied, haven't you always got, with her, a way to end your difficulties if you wanted to? A girl like her ought to support us all, you, herself, and me. He cut short the reply this impertinence merited, by going on to say that he could guarantee, before the day was out, a thousand écus to be shared between us, if only I would follow his advice; that he knew a nobleman so liberal in his purchase of pleasure that he felt sure a thousand écus would be as nothing to him if he could obtain the favours of a girl like Manon.* It was my turn to stop him. I had thought better of you, I replied; I had imagined that your motive in seeking my friendship sprang from a sentiment quite opposite to the one you are now expressing. He confessed, shamelessly, that he had always thought the same way, and that once his sister had violated the laws governing her sex, even though in favour of a man dearer to him than any other, he had sought a reconciliation with her only in the hope of profiting as much as he could from her misconduct. I saw well enough what dupes he had been making of us. Whatever the emotions aroused in me by this speech, however, my need of him was such that I was obliged to reply, lightly, that his advice was a last resort, to be used only in extremes. I asked him to propose some other way. He suggested taking advantage of my youth and the prepossessing appearance nature had given me in order to introduce me to some ageing and liberal lady. I did not like this course, which would have made me unfaithful to Manon, any more than the other; I mentioned gaming as the easiest means, and the one best suited to my situation. He said that gaming was indeed a useful expedient; but that some prior instruction would be necessary; that to begin by simply playing and, like everyone else, hoping for the best, was the surest way to total ruin; and that to imagine I could deploy on my own, without support, those little devices that an artful man uses in order to remedy the vagaries of fortune was too dangerous a game; there was a third way, that of working with others, but he feared that, given my youth, the confederates might not judge me to possess the skills required of a member of the League.* Nevertheless, he promised to use his good offices with them on my behalf; and—something I would not have expected of him—he offered me money, in case I should find myself hard pressed. The only favour I asked of him, under the circumstances, was not to say anything to Manon about the loss I had suffered, or about the subject of our conversation.

I left his house still less happy than when I had entered it. I even repented having confided my secret in him. He had done nothing for me that I could not have achieved just as easily without this disclosure, and I was in mortal terror lest he break his promise not to divulge anything to Manon. I also had reason to fear, from the sentiments he had expressed, that he was planning to profit from her, as he put it, by stealing her away from me; or at least by urging her to leave me and attach herself to some richer and more fortunate lover. Endless musings on the matter only increased my torment, and plunged me even deeper into the despair I had felt that morning. Several times it occurred to me to write to my father, and feign another conversion in order to obtain some financial assistance; but I at once recalled that, in spite of all his kindness, he had kept me under lock and key for six months following my earlier misdemeanour. I was quite sure that, after the commotion my escape from Saint-Sulpice must have caused, he would deal with me even more severely. At last, from this crowd of confused thoughts an idea emerged that immediately restored my peace of mind, and which I was astonished not to have considered sooner. This was to appeal to my friend Tiberge, in whom I was sure of always finding the same store of friendship and zeal. Nothing is more wonderful, or honours virtue more, than the confidence with which we turn to people whose probity we have long been acquainted with. With them, we feel, we run no risk. Even if they cannot always help us, at least we are certain of receiving from them only kindness and compassion. The heart that remains closed to the rest of mankind opens up naturally in their presence, like a flower that unfolds in the light of the sun, from which it expects only the mildest influence to flow.

To have remembered Tiberge so opportunely was, I thought, a sign of Heaven's protection, and I determined to find a way of seeing him before the day was over. I went home at once and wrote him a brief note, indicating a suitable place to meet. I urged silence and discretion as the most important services he could render me in my present circumstances. My joy at the prospect of seeing him erased the marks of anxiety Manon would otherwise not have failed to notice on my face. I spoke of our misfortune at Chaillot as of a trifle, which need not alarm her; and since there was nowhere in the world she was happier to find herself than in Paris, she was not vexed at my suggesting it would be as well for us to remain there until some of the slight damage caused by the fire at Chaillot had been repaired. An hour later I received a reply from Tiberge, promising to meet me at the appointed place. Full of impatience, I set out at once. Although I felt some shame at appearing before a friend whose very presence ought to have been a reproach to me for my dissolute way of life, my faith in his kind-heartedness and my concern for Manon sustained and emboldened me.

I had asked him to come to the gardens of the Palais-Royal. He was there before me. The moment he caught sight of me, he hurried forward and embraced me. He held me clasped in his arms for quite a long time, while I felt my cheek grow wet with his tears. I told him I could not appear before him without shame, and that I bore in my heart a deep sense of my ingratitude towards him; that the first thing I must beg of him was to tell me whether I might still be permitted to call him my friend, after so richly deserving to lose his esteem and affection. He replied, in the tenderest of tones, that nothing would ever make him renounce that name; that my misfortunes and even— if I would allow him to say so—my errors and aberrations had redoubled his tenderness for me; but that this tenderness was mingled with the keenest grief, such as we feel for someone dear to us whom, without being able to help, we see on the brink of perdition.

We sat down on a bench. Alas, I said with a sigh that came from the bottom of my heart, your compassion, dear Tiberge, must indeed be boundless if, as you claim, it is equal to my sorrows. I am ashamed, however, to let you see this misery, since its cause, I freely confess, is inglorious, although its effect is so lamentable that even someone who loved me less than you do would be moved by it. He asked me, as a mark of friendship, to describe fully and frankly everything that had happened since my departure from Saint-Sulpice. I did as he asked; and far from deviating from the truth in any way, or diminishing my faults so as to make them more pardonable, I spoke of my passion with all the ardour it inspired in me. I presented it as one of those special blows that fate delivers when it is bent upon the ruin of some poor wretch, and against which it is as impossible for virtue to defend itself as it was for wisdom to foresee. I painted a vivid picture of my agitation, of my fears, of the despair with which I had been filled only two hours previously, and into which I would again be plunged if I found myself as mercilessly abandoned by my friends as by fortune; in short, I so affected the excellent Tiberge that I could see he was as much moved by compassion for me as was I by the sense of my own sufferings. He embraced me again and again, exhorting me to take courage and be comforted, but since he was clearly taking it for granted that Manon and I must separate, I gave him plainly to understand that I regarded this separation itself as the greatest of my misfortunes; and that I was ready, not only to endure the uttermost depths of wretchedness, but to suffer the cruellest of deaths rather than accept a remedy more intolerable than all my woes put together.

Tell me then, he said, what kind of help I can give you, since you reject every course of action I suggest. I did not dare admit that what I needed was his money. Finally, however he took my meaning and, indicating that he believed he now understood me, hesitated for a while, like a man in suspense. Do not imagine, he presently went on, that my abstracted air means that the ardour of my zeal and friendship has cooled. But to what alternatives do I find myself reduced, if I must either deny you the only help you will accept or, if I offer it to you, offend against my duty; for, in helping you persevere in your dissolute ways, do I not become a party to them? But then again, he went on after a moment's reflection, it may well be that the extremities into which you have been driven by poverty leave you no freedom to choose the better way; only a quiet mind can savour truth and wisdom. I will find the means of getting you some money. But, my dear Chevalier, he went on, embracing me, allow me to add just one condition, which is that you tell me where you are living, and allow me to try at least to return you to the path of virtue, which I know you love, and from which only the violence of your passions has led you to stray. I readily granted him everything he asked, and implored him to lament my malign fate, which made me profit so ill from the advice of so virtuous a friend. He took me straight to a banker he knew, who advanced me a hundred pistoles in exchange for his promissory note, for there was nothing Tiberge had less of than ready cash. As I have already said, he was not rich. His benefice was worth a thousand écus, but since this was the first year he had held it, he had not as yet received any income from it; it was against its future returns that he was making me this advance.

I felt the full worth of his generosity. It moved me to the point where I truly deplored the blind and fatal passion that had made me abandon every duty. Virtue reawakened in my heart, and for a few moments was powerful enough to rise up in protest against my passion, and in this instant of enlightenment I did at least recognize the shame and indignity of my chains. But the struggle was feeble and short-lived. The sight of Manon would have brought me headlong from heaven itself, and I marvelled, on finding myself with her once again, that I could have considered as shameful for even a moment so justified a tenderness for so enchanting an object.

Manon was a creature of an extraordinary character. No girl was ever less attached to money than she was, but neither could she endure for a moment the fear of having to do without it. What she needed was pleasure and diversion. She would never have wanted a single sou, if only amusement could be had free of charge. The general state of our finances was of no interest to her, so long as she could spend the day in some agreeable fashion; so that, since she was neither excessively prone to gambling, nor likely to be dazzled by extravagant displays of wealth, nothing was easier than to make her happy, by continually devising entertainments that were to her taste. But such was her need for constant pleasure that, if it was not forthcoming, there was no relying on her temper or mood. Tenderly though she loved me, and although, as she readily admitted, I was the only one with whom she could truly taste the joys of love, I was fairly sure that this tenderness would not withstand some of her fears. She would have preferred me, with even a moderate fortune, to any man on earth; but I was in no doubt that, when all I had left to offer were fidelity and constancy, she would abandon me for some new B... I therefore resolved to regulate my own expenditure in such a way that I would always be in a position to provide for hers, and to deny myself a thousand necessities of life rather than deprive her of even its luxuries. The carriage worried me more than all the rest, for there was no prospect of my being able to maintain horses and a coachman. I confided my difficulty to M. Lescaut. I had not hidden from him the fact that I had received a hundred pistoles from a friend. He repeated that if I wanted to try my luck at cards, he was not without hopes that, were I to be so gracious as to devote some hundred francs to the entertainment of his associates, I might, on his recommendation, be admitted to the ranks of the League of Industry. In spite of the repugnance I felt for cheating, I allowed myself to be drawn into it out of cruel necessity.

M. Lescaut introduced me to them as one of his relatives that very evening. He added that I was the more likely to succeed because of my need of the greatest of fortune's favours. Nevertheless, to make it clear that I was not, in spite of my penury, a nobody, he told them I had it in mind to offer them supper. My offer was accepted. I entertained them magnificently. They discussed at length my pleasing person and agreeable attributes. They claimed that a great deal was to be hoped for from me, since, with something in my physiognomy that proclaimed a man of honour, no one would suspect me of guile. Finally they thanked M. Lescaut for having procured a novice of such merit for the Order, and they assigned one of the chevaliers to give me the necessary instruction during the next few days. The principal theatre of my exploits was to be the Hôtel de Transylvanie,* where there was a faro table in one room and various card-games as well as dice-boards in the gallery. This gaming academy was organized for the benefit of the Prince de R..., who was living in Clagny at the time, and most of whose officers were members of our League. Must I confess it to my shame? I soon profited from my master's lessons. I acquired, above all, great facility in handling the cards, in flipping, foisting, and palming them, and, with the assistance of a long pair of cuffs, in making them disappear and reappear so dexterously as to deceive the keenest eye and to ruin, without ceremony, any number of honest players. This extraordinary skill brought about so rapid an improvement in my fortune that, within the space of a few weeks, I had accumulated considerable sums of money, apart from those I shared in good faith with my associates. I was no longer afraid to reveal to Manon how much we had lost at Chaillot; and to console her for this vexatious news, I rented a furnished house, in which, with every appearance of stability and affluence, we were soon installed.

During this time Tiberge had continued to pay me frequent visits. He lectured me endlessly. He never tired of pointing out the damage I was doing to my conscience, my honour, and my fortune. I listened amicably to his advice; and although I was not in the least disposed to follow it, was grateful for his zeal, for I knew the source from which it sprang. Sometimes, even in Manon's presence, I would exercise my wit at his expense, exhorting him not to be more scrupulous than a great number of bishops and other priests, who know very well how to reconcile a benefice with a mistress. Only look, I said to him, indicating Manon's eyes, and tell me if there are frailties that may not be justified by so persuasive a cause. He bore all this with patience. He even tolerated it for quite some time; but when he saw that my wealth was increasing, and that not only had I not repaid him his hundred pistoles but, having rented a new house and doubled my expenditure, was about to immerse myself more deeply in pleasure than ever before, his tone and manner changed completely. He complained that my heart had grown hard; he threatened me with the wrath of Heaven, and predicted some of the misfortunes that were soon to befall me. It is impossible, he said, that the wealth that maintains you in your dissolute way of life should have come to you lawfully. You have acquired it dishonestly; it will be taken from you in the same way. The most terrible punishment that God could inflict on you would be to leave you to enjoy it in peace. All the advice I have given you, he added, has been useless; I see only too well that you will soon find it tiresome. Farewell, weak and ungrateful friend. May your criminal pleasures dissolve like shadows! May your prosperity and fortune perish without recall, while you remain alone and naked, knowing at last the vanity of those worldly things with which, in your madness, you are intoxicated. Only then will you find me ready to love and serve you, but today I break off all connection with you, and I abhor the life you are leading. He delivered this apostolic harangue in my room, with Manon watching. He stood up and made as if to leave. I tried to detain him, but was stopped by Manon, who said he was a madman and it was best to let him go.

His speech had made an impression on me nevertheless. I like to note in this way the various occasions when I have felt my heart turn back towards virtue, because it is to memories such as these that I have since owed part of the strength that has sustained me through the unhappiest moments of my life. Manon's caresses soon dispelled the distress this scene had caused me. We continued to lead a life devoted wholly to pleasure and love. The increase in our wealth redoubled our affection for one another: never were slaves of Venus and Fortune happier nor more fond! Why, in Heaven's name, do we call this world a vale of tears, when we can taste such rapturous joys there? But they have, alas, one defect—that they pass away too soon. If it was in their nature to last for ever, what other felicity would we seek? Ours suffered the common fate, which is to say that they were brief in duration and were followed by bitter regrets. The gains I had made at the gaming table were so considerable that I began to think of investing part of my money. Our servants were well aware of my success, especially my valet and Manon's maid, in front of whom we often discussed our affairs quite openly. The girl was pretty, my valet was in love with her. They were dealing with masters who were young and easygoing, and whom they thought it would not be difficult to deceive. They devised a plan to do so, and carried it out with such unfortunate consequences that they left us in a position from which we have never been able to recover.

One evening we went to have supper with M. Lescaut, and did not return home until almost midnight. I called for my valet, Manon for her maid; neither of them appeared. We were told they had not been seen in the house since eight o'clock, when they had gone out, having first supervised the removal of several chests, which they said was done on my orders. I felt some premonition of the truth, but nothing I suspected prepared me for what I saw on entering my room. The lock to my closet had been forced and my money removed, along with all my clothes. While I stood there alone, reflecting on this mishap, Manon appeared, greatly frightened, and told me her apartment had been similarly ransacked. This blow seemed so cruel that only by an extraordinary effort of will did I prevent myself from giving way to tears and lamentations. Instead, fearful of communicating my despair to Manon, I assumed an expression of calm. I promised her, jokingly, that I would soon have my revenge on some poor dupe at the Hôtel de Transylvanie. However, she seemed so struck by our misfortune that I was far more cast down by her despondency than she was persuaded, by my feigned gaiety, not to give in to it too easily. We are lost, she said, with tears in her eyes. I tried in vain to console her with caresses; my own tears betrayed my despair and anxiety. Indeed, we were so utterly ruined that we were left without so much as a shirt between us.

I decided to send for M. Lescaut immediately. He urged me to go that very moment and see the Lieutenant of Police and the Grand Provost of Paris. I did as he suggested; but this plunged me even deeper into misfortune; for not only did this step, and those I persuaded these two officers of justice to take on my behalf, yield nothing, but they gave Lescaut time to talk to his sister and to prevail upon her, in my absence, to take a horrible decision. He told her about M. de G... M..., an ageing voluptuary who was ready to pay lavishly for his pleasures, and he made her see so many advantages to being in his pay that, dismayed as she was by our ill-fortune, she agreed to everything he asked. This honourable bargain was concluded before my return, and its execution postponed until the following day, so that Lescaut would have time to inform M. de G... M... I found him waiting for me when I returned home; Manon, however, had retired to her apartment, leaving orders with her footman that she needed rest and must request me to leave her undisturbed that night. Lescaut left, having offered me some pistoles, which I accepted. It was close on four o'clock by the time I went to bed, where, still preoccupied in considering the means whereby I might restore my fortunes, I fell asleep so late that I woke again only towards eleven or twelve o'clock next morning. I got up at once and went to enquire after Manon's health; they told me she had gone out an hour before with her brother, who had come to fetch her in a hired carriage. Although it was a mystery to me why she should go on such an outing with Lescaut, I forced myself not to give way to my suspicions. I let several hours go by, which I spent reading. At last, no longer able to contain my anxiety, I began pacing to and fro in our apartments. Entering Manon's room, I caught sight of a sealed letter lying on her table. It was addressed to me, and written in her hand. I opened it with a shudder of mortal terror. It read as follows:

I swear, my dear Chevalier, that you alone are the idol of my heart, and that there is no one in the world I could love as I love you; but can you not see, my poor dear soul, that in the state we are reduced to, fidelity is a foolish virtue? Do you really think one can be truly loving when one is short of bread? Hunger would cause me to make some fatal error; I would one day breathe my last breath, believing it to be a sigh of love. I adore you, of that you may be sure. But leave the management of our fortune to me for a while. And woe betide anyone who gets caught in my net! It is my Chevalier I'm working for, to make him rich and happy. My brother will give you news of your Manon, and will tell you what tears she shed at having to leave you.

After reading this letter I was in a state of mind it is not easy to describe, for I do not know, even today, what the feelings were that caused me such agitation. It was one of those unique situations, the like of which one has never before experienced. You cannot explain them to others, because they can have no idea of them; and you can hardly fathom them yourself because, being the only ones of their kind, they correspond to nothing in your memory, and cannot even be compared with any other feeling you have known. And yet, whatever the precise nature of mine, it is certain that grief, resentment, jealousy, and shame all played their part. If only the greatest part of all had not been played by love! She loves me, I cried, I will and must believe it; but would she not need to be a monster to hate me? What rights has anyone ever had over another's heart that I do not have over hers? After everything I have sacrificed for her already, what more can I do? Nevertheless, she is abandoning me! And the ungrateful creature supposes that all she need do to be spared my reproaches is say she has never stopped loving me! She is afraid of going hungry. God of love! What vulgarity of feeling! And what a way of responding to the delicacy of mine! Was I afraid of hunger, I who, renouncing my fortune and the comforts of my father's house, exposed myself so readily to it for her sake? I, who restrict myself to the bare necessities so as to satisfy her every little humour and caprice? She adores me, so she says! If you adored me, ungrateful girl, I know where you would have turned for advice; at least you would not have left me without saying farewell. I'm the one who should be asked what cruel torments one feels at being parted from everything one adores. Only someone who had lost his mind would expose himself to all this of his own free will.

My lamentations were cut short by a visit I had not expected. It was Lescaut. You brute, I said to him, reaching for my sword,

where is Manon? What have you done with her? He was frightened
by this outburst; he replied that if this was how I received him, when
he came to inform me of the greatest service he could possibly have
done me, he would depart forthwith and never set foot inside my
house again. I sprang to the door and closed it carefully. Do not
imagine, said I, turning towards him again, that you can make a fool
of me a second time and trick me with your stories. Either prepare to
defend your life, or help me get Manon back! Heavens, how hasty
you are, he said; that's the very thing that brings me here. I've come
to tell you a piece of good fortune you know nothing about as yet, but
which you'll perhaps recognize that you owe to me. I pressed him to
explain at once what he meant.

He told me that Manon, unable to endure the thought of poverty,
and above all the idea of having so suddenly to give up all our
possessions and pastimes, had begged him to procure the acquaintance of M. de G... M..., who was said to be a generous man. He was
careful not to say that this plan had come from him, nor that it was
he who had prepared the way, before leading her along it. I took her
there myself this morning, he continued, and the gentleman was so
enchanted with her qualities that he at once invited her to accompany him to his country house, where he has gone to spend a few
days. As for me, added Lescaut, I suddenly saw how greatly this
could benefit you, and I artfully intimated that Manon had suffered
considerable losses, playing on his generosity with such success that
he began by making her a present of two hundred pistoles. I said that
this was a very fair sum for the time being, but that my sister would
be exposed in the future to even greater need; that she had, moreover, taken on the care of a younger brother, who had been left on
our hands after the death of our father and mother, and that, if he
thought her worthy of respect, he would not let her suffer on
account of this poor child, whom she looked upon as the other half
of herself. As you can imagine, this story touched him greatly. He
has agreed to rent a comfortable house for you and Manon; for the
poor little orphaned brother is none other than yourself. He has
promised to furnish it nicely for you, and to allow you every month
the goodly sum of four hundred livres which, if I calculate correctly,
will amount to four thousand eight hundred by the end of each year.
Before setting out for his country estate he left orders with his
steward to find a house, and have it ready for his return. At which

point you will see your Manon again, who asks me to embrace you for her a thousand times, and to assure you she loves you more than ever.

I sat down, musing on so bizarre a revolution in my destiny. I found myself so divided in my feelings and, in consequence, in a state of uncertainty so difficult to resolve, that I remained there for a long time without offering any reply to the endless questions Lescaut asked me, one after the other. It was at this moment that honour and virtue conspired to make me feel the prickings of remorse once more, and that, sighing, I cast my mind back to Amiens, my parents' house, Saint-Sulpice, and all the places where I had lived in innocence. What vast expanses separated me from that happy state! I saw it still, but how far off and faint it seemed, like a distant shadow that could even now summon up my regrets and desires, but too feebly to move me to endeavour. By what decree of fate, I asked myself, have I become so wicked? Love is an innocent passion; how has it been transformed for me into a source of wretchedness and error? Who has prevented me from living tranquilly and virtuously with Manon? Why did I not marry her before taking advantage of her love? Surely my father, who loved me so dearly, would have given his consent, if only I had had legitimacy on my side? Ah! My father would have learned to cherish her as an enchanting girl, only too worthy to be a wife to his son. How happy I would have been, with Manon's love, my father's affection, the respect of men of honour, the blessings of fortune, and the peace of mind that is born of virtue! Why, then, this cruel reversal? What infamous role is this I am asked to play? What! Am I to share...? But, dare I hesitate, if it is Manon herself who has ordained this, and if I will lose her if I do not consent? M. Lescaut, I cried, closing my eyes as though to dismiss such vexing thoughts, if it was your intention to do me a service, I thank you for it. It is true that you could have chosen a more honourable route; but what's done is done, I suppose. So let us concentrate on making the most of your efforts and on carrying out your plan. Lescaut, who had been discomfited by my anger and the long silence that followed it, was delighted to see me adopt a course of action quite different from the one he had doubtless feared I would take; he was anything but brave, and I later on had better proof of this. Yes indeed, he replied hastily, it's a very great service I've done you and, as you'll see, we will do even better out of it than you expect. We discussed how to allay any suspicions that G... M..., finding me taller and perhaps rather older than he had expected, might have as to our really being brothers. We could think of no better way than that I should assume a naive and provincial air in his presence, and make him believe I was intending to enter holy orders, and that it was for this reason I went every day to college. We decided too that, the first time I was allowed the honour of addressing him, I should be very poorly dressed. He came back to town two or three days later; he escorted Manon himself to the house his steward had prepared for her. She at once let Lescaut know of her return; and, the latter having informed me of it, we went together to her house. The aged suitor had already left.

Although I had submitted to her wishes with resignation, I could not, on seeing her again, suppress the murmurings of my heart. I seemed sad and despondent to her. My pleasure in being reunited with her could not quite dispel the pain of her infidelity. She, by contrast, appeared transported with joy at seeing me again. She reproached me for my coldness. I could not prevent the words 'perfidious' and 'faithless' from escaping my lips, each accompanied by a sigh. At first she made fun of my ingenuousness; but when she saw how sadly I kept my eyes fixed on her, and how difficult I found it to accept a change so contrary to my disposition and desires, she turned on her heel and went into her dressing-room. Following her a moment later, I found her bathed in tears. I asked what had caused them. I should have thought it was obvious, she replied; for how do you expect me to bear it, if all that the sight of me produces in you are vexed and sombre looks? You have been here an hour already without giving me a single caress, and you have received mine with all the majesty of the Grand Turk himself in his harem.

Listen Manon, I replied, embracing her, I cannot hide from you the mortal anguish that afflicts my heart. I will not speak for the moment of the alarm your unexpected flight occasioned me, nor of your cruelty in abandoning me without a single word of consolation, after spending the night in a different bed from mine. The spell your presence casts would make me forget much more than this. But do you suppose I can contemplate without sighing, and even without tears, I continued—shedding a few—the sad and wretched life you want me to lead in this house? Let us leave to one side the matter of my birth and my honour: between such feeble considerations and a love like mine there can be no contest; but this love itself, can you not imagine how grieved it is at finding itself so poorly recompensed, or so cruelly treated, rather, by a harsh and ungrateful mistress? She interrupted me: Stop, Chevalier, she said, there is no need to torment me further with reproaches that, coming from you, can only pierce me to the heart. I can see what is offending you. I had hoped you would consent to my plan for restoring our fortunes a little, and it was only to spare the delicacy of your feelings that I had begun to carry it out without your agreement; but since you do not approve of it, I shall give it up. She added that all she asked of me was a little indulgence for the rest of the day; that her aged suitor had already given her two hundred pistoles, and that he had promised to bring her that very evening a beautiful necklace of pearls and other jewels, as well as half the annual allowance he had promised. Just give me time to receive these presents, she said; I swear he won't be able to boast of any advantages I've let him take, for I've managed so far to put him off until we return to town. It is true he has kissed my hands a million times and more; and it is only fair he should pay for this pleasure, for which, taking into account his wealth and his age, five or six thousand francs is not too high a price.

Manon's decision pleased me much more than the prospect of five thousand francs; while my relief at having avoided the infamous role she had proposed for me was further reassurance that my heart had not yet lost all sense of honour. But I was born to know brief joys and lasting sorrows. Fortune delivered me from the brink of one precipice only to plunge me over another. As soon as I had shown Manon, through a thousand fond caresses, how happy her change of mind had made me, I said we must inform Lescaut too, so that we could act in concert. He grumbled at first; but the four or five thousand francs in ready money soon persuaded him to enter cheerfully into our plans. We decided, therefore, that we should all three of us stay to supper that night with M. de G... M..., for two reasons: first, so as to enjoy the entertaining spectacle of me passing myself off as Manon's student brother; secondly, so as to prevent the old libertine from making too free with my mistress, on the strength of any rights he might think he had acquired by paying her so liberally in advance. Lescaut and I were to leave when he went up to the room where he was expecting to spend the night; while Manon promised us that, instead of following him, she would quit the house and come and spend it with me. Lescaut undertook to have a carriage waiting at the door precisely when it was needed.

Suppertime arrived. M. de G... M... did not keep us waiting. He arrived to find Lescaut already with his sister. The first compliment the old man offered his fair lady was to present her with a pearl necklace, bracelets, and earrings, worth at least a thousand écus. He then counted out, in fine gold louis, the sum of two thousand four hundred livres, which was half of the allowance he had promised her. He embellished these gifts with many pretty speeches in the old-fashioned style. Manon could not refuse him a few kisses, each of which won her new rights to the money he was placing in her hands. I stood with my ear pressed to the other side of the door, listening and waiting for Lescaut to summon me inside.

As soon as Manon had locked away the money and the jewels, he came, took me by the hand, and, leading me to M. de G... M..., ordered me to bow to him. I did so, very low indeed, two or three times. Do forgive him Monsieur, said Lescaut, I'm afraid the poor child doesn't know any better. As you see, he's far from having acquired Parisian manners, but we're hoping he will improve with a little experience. You will often have the honour of seeing Monsieur when he's here, he added, turning to me. Be sure you profit from so good a model. The aged suitor seemed genuinely pleased to see me. He tapped me two or three times on the cheek, and said I was a pretty young fellow, but that I must be on my guard in Paris, where young people can so easily sink into debauchery. Lescaut assured him that I was by nature such a good boy that I talked only of becoming a priest, and liked nothing better than making little shrines.* He has a look of Manon about him, the old man continued, placing his finger below my chin and tilting my face towards him. Ah Monsieur, I replied with a foolish laugh, that's because her flesh and mine are so close they're almost one; indeed, I love my sister Manon just like my other self. Did you hear that? he said to Lescaut. He's quite a wit. It's a pity the poor child hasn't seen a little more of society.* Oh, Monsieur, I replied, I've seen plenty of it at home in the churches, and I dare say I'll find plenty more in Paris, and stupider than me. Upon my word, he added, that's admirably said for a boy from the provinces. Our whole conversation over supper was more or less in this vein. Manon, always playful, was several times on the verge of spoiling everything by her peals of laughter. I found a way, while we were

Manon's 'brother' is introduced to old G... M... (Gravelot)

eating, of telling him his own story and of the misfortune that was about to befall him. Lescaut and Manon listened in fear and trembling, especially while I was painting his portrait, which I did to the life; vanity, however, prevented him from recognizing himself, and I carried the whole thing off so artfully that he was the first to find it highly diverting. It was a truly comic scene; and, as you will see, I have dwelt upon it at length for a reason. At last it was time for bed; he spoke of love and a lover's impatience. Lescaut and I took our leave, he was conducted to his own bedroom, and Manon, who had left the room on some pretext, joined us at the street door. The carriage, which was waiting three or four doors down the street, moved forward to pick us up. In a moment we had left the district.

Although I could see that this act was a piece of real villainy, it was not the greatest injustice with which I felt I had to reproach myself. The money I had won at cards weighed more heavily on my conscience. Be that as it may, we profited as little from the one as from the other, and Heaven allowed the lesser of these two injustices to be the more severely punished.

M. de G... M... was not slow in realizing he had been duped. I do not know if he took steps that very evening to have us pursued, but he was wealthy enough for his enquiries not to be fruitless for long, while we were imprudent enough to rely for our safety on the size of Paris, and the distance that separated our neighbourhood from his. Not only did he discover our address and our present circumstances, but he was soon fully informed as to who I was, the life I had been leading in Paris, Manon's earlier liaison with B..., the deceit she had practised on him, and, in a word, all the more scandalous parts of our story. At this, he determined to have us arrested, and treated not so much as criminals as downright libertines.* We were still in bed when a sub-lieutenant of police, accompanied by half-a-dozen guards, entered our room. They at once seized our money, or rather G... M...'s, and, ordering us out of bed, marched us to the street door where we found two carriages waiting, in one of which poor Manon was carried off without a word of explanation, while I was pushed into the other and taken to Saint-Lazare. Only one who has suffered such reverses can know what despair they cause. Our guards were so heartless they would not let me embrace Manon, or say a single word to her. It was only much later that I discovered what had become of her. No doubt it was a blessing I did not find out earlier, for so terrible a catastrophe would have cost me my reason, and perhaps my life.

So it was that my unhappy mistress was carried off before my very eyes, and taken to a place of retreat it appals me even to name.* What a fate for so utterly enchanting a creature, who would have occupied the first throne in the world, if all men had my eyes and my heart! It was not that she was treated barbarously; but she was kept in close confinement, alone, and condemned to complete each day a particular task, the necessary condition for her securing a portion of disgusting food. I learned these melancholy details only much later, when I myself had endured several months of harsh and grievous punishment. Since my guards had not informed me of where they had been ordered to take me either, I learned of my fate only at the gates of Saint-Lazare. I would have preferred death itself at that moment to the state I believed I was about to be reduced to. I had terrifying notions of this place. My fright increased when, on my way in, the guards went through my pockets a second time to make sure I no longer had any arms or other means of defending myself. The Father Superior appeared at once; he had been forewarned of my arrival. He greeted me with great gentleness. No indignities, Reverend Father, I said to him.* I would rather lose my life a thousand times over than suffer a single one. There is no question of that, Monsieur, he replied; you will conduct yourself wisely, and we will be quite content with one another. He asked me to accompany him to a room at the top of the house. I followed him without demur. The guards came with us as far as the door, whereupon the Father Superior, taking me inside, signalled to them to withdraw.

So I am your prisoner! I said. Well then, Reverend Father, what do you intend to do with me? He told me he was delighted to see me adopt a reasonable tone; that he meant to make it his duty to inspire in me a taste for religion and virtue, just as it would be mine to profit from his exhortations and his advice; and that provided I chose to respond to the interest he took in me, I would find nothing but pleasure in my solitude. Ah, pleasure, I replied; you do not know, Father, the one thing that can give me that! I do know, he continued; but I hope that your inclinations will change. His reply suggested that he knew about my adventures, and perhaps even my name. I asked him if this was so. He told me frankly that he was fully informed about me.

This revelation was the harshest punishment of all. I dissolved into a flood of tears, accompanied by all the signs of dreadful despair. Faced with a humiliation that would make me the talk of everyone I knew and bring shame on my family, I was inconsolable. I spent a week in the deepest despondency, deaf and insensible to everything except my sense of my own disgrace. Even the thought of Manon added nothing to my grief; or rather, it entered into it, but only as a past sorrow that had been overtaken by this new pain, and the ruling passion of my soul was one of confusion and shame. Few people know how powerfully these particular impulses can act upon the heart. The ordinary run of men are susceptible to only five or six passions, within whose compass they live their whole lives, and to which all their emotions are reduced. Remove love and hate, pleasure and pain, hope and fear, and there is nothing left for them to feel. But people whose characters are more noble can be stirred in a thousand different ways; it is as if they had more than five senses, and could receive ideas and sensations that transcend the ordinary limits of human nature. And since they are conscious of possessing this superiority that raises them above the common herd, there is nothing of which they are more jealous. This is why they suffer contempt and ridicule with such impatience, and why shame is one of their most violent passions.

I had this miserable advantage at Saint-Lazare. So excessive did my melancholy seem to the Father Superior that, fearful of its consequences, he thought it best to treat me with great gentleness and indulgence. He visited me two or three times a day. He often invited me to take a walk in the garden with him, during which he expended all his zeal in offering me salutary exhortations and advice. I accepted them meekly. I even showed gratitude. This gave him reason to hope I might be converted. You are by nature so gentle and lovable, he said to me one day, that I cannot understand the irregularities of conduct of which you are accused. Two things astonish me: first, how, with so many good qualities, you should have abandoned yourself to such extreme licentiousness; and second—which I find more amazing still—how it is that, having persisted for several years now in so dissolute a way of life, you should accept my admonitions and my advice. If this is repentance, it is a remarkable example of Heaven's great mercies; if natural goodness, it is at least proof of a fundamental excellence of character that gives me grounds to hope we will not need to detain you for long, but will soon see you restored to an honourable and orderly way of life. I was delighted with his good opinion of me. I decided to enhance it still further by adopting a mode of conduct that would completely satisfy him, persuaded that this was the best means at my disposal of shortening my time in prison. I asked him for some books. He was surprised when, having left me to choose what I wanted to read, I decided on various serious authors. I pretended to apply myself to my studies with the utmost dedication, thus offering him proof, on every possible occasion, of the change he so wished to see in me.

This was purely external, however. I must confess, to my shame, that I played the hypocrite at Saint-Lazare. Whenever I was alone, instead of studying I did nothing but bewail my wretched lot. I cursed my prison and the tyranny that held me there. Besides, I no sooner felt some respite from the mood of deep despondency into which shame and humiliation had plunged me than I found myself a prey once again to all the torments of love. Manon's absence, my uncertainty as to her fate, the fear of never seeing her again, these were now the sole objects of my sorrowful musings. I pictured her in G... M...'s arms, for that had been my first thought; and far from imagining he had subjected her to the same treatment as me, I was convinced he had only had me taken away so that he might possess her in peace. I spent, in this way, days and nights which seemed to last for ever. My only hope was in the success of my hypocrisy. I watched the Father Superior carefully, noting his every expression and word, in the hope of ascertaining what he thought of me; and I made every effort to please him, for was he not the arbiter of my destiny? It was easy enough to see I was wholly in his good graces. I no longer doubted his willingness to help me. I plucked up courage one day, and asked if my release depended upon him. He told me it was not absolutely in his gift, but that, if he were to testify on my behalf, he hoped that M. de G... M..., at whose request the Lieutenant-General of Police had had me locked up, would consent to my being set free. Might I flatter myself, I continued meekly, that the two months in prison I have already endured will seem to him sufficient expiation? He promised he would raise the matter with him, if this was what I wanted. I at once asked him to do me this good office. Two days later he told me that G... M... had been so touched by the good report he had had of me that, not only did he seem disposed to let me see the light of day again, but he had even expressed a great desire to know me better, and was proposing to come and visit me in prison. Although his presence could never be anything but disagreeable to me, I regarded this visit as another step towards regaining my freedom.

He duly came to Saint-Lazare. I found his demeanour more grave and less foolish than it had been at Manon's. He made several speeches full of good sense about my bad behaviour. He added, apparently in order to justify his own irregularities of conduct, that while it was permissible for human weakness to procure for itself certain pleasures that nature demands, villainy and shameful tricks deserved to be punished. I listened with a submissive air that seemed to please him. I showed no offence, even when he ventured various jokes about my fraternal resemblance to Manon and Lescaut, and about the little shrines of which he supposed, so he said, I must have made a good number in Saint-Lazare, since I took such pleasure in this pious occupation. But, unfortunately for him and for me, he let slip the observation that Manon too would no doubt have made some very pretty ones at the Hôpital. In spite of the trembling that seized me at the very word Hôpital, I still found strength enough to ask him, mildly, to explain. Oh yes! he went on, she has been in the Hôpital, learning to be good, for two months now, and I trust she has benefited as much from her time there as you have at Saint-Lazare.

Had I been threatened with eternal imprisonment, or even death itself, I could not have suppressed the transport that seized me at this terrible news. I threw myself upon him, in such a fury of rage that it deprived me of half my strength. I nevertheless had enough left to knock him to the ground and to grab him by the throat. I was on the point of strangling him, when the noise of his fall, and some piercing cries I scarcely left him breath enough to utter, brought the Father Superior and several of the monks to my room. They delivered him from my grasp. I myself was almost entirely bereft of strength and breath. O God! I cried, exhaling a thousand sighs; O divine justice! After such infamy, how can I bear to live a moment longer? I again tried to throw myself on the barbarian who had just dealt me this mortal blow. They stopped me. My despair, my cries and tears, were beyond imagining. So extravagant was my behaviour that those present, not knowing its cause, looked at one another with as much fear as surprise. M. de G... M..., meanwhile, was readjusting his wig and his cravat, and in his resentment at having been so maltreated, ordered the Father Superior to keep me more closely confined than ever, and to inflict on me all the punishments that everyone knew were employed at Saint-Lazare. You are mistaken Monsieur, replied the Father Superior, that is not how persons of birth, such as the Chevalier, are dealt with here; he is, besides so mild and so well bred that I find it hard to believe he would be driven to such extremes without powerful reasons. This reply succeeded in disconcerting M. de G... M... He went away, declaring that he knew ways of making the Superior, and me, and anyone else who dared to defy him, bend to his will.

The Father Superior, having asked the monks to accompany him to the door, remained alone with me. He implored me to tell him straight away what had caused all this commotion. Oh Father! I replied, continuing to weep like a child, think of the most horrible cruelty you can, imagine the most barbarous of abominations: such is the deed that G... M..., unworthy wretch that he is, has been base enough to commit. Oh, he has pierced me to the heart! I will never recover. I will tell you everything, I added, sobbing. You are good, you will pity me. I gave him an abridged account of my long and unconquerable passion for Manon, of the flourishing state of our fortune before we were stripped of it by our own servants, of the offer G... M... had made to my mistress, of the arrangement they had come to between them, and the way in which it had been broken. I presented all of this, it is true, in a light as favourable to us as was possible. Such is the source, I continued, from which G... M...'s zeal for my conversion springs. His good work in having me shut up here was inspired by motives of pure vengeance. I forgive him; but, Reverend Father, that is not all. He has taken away from me, most cruelly, the other and dearer half of myself; he has had her shamefully imprisoned in the Hôpital; and today he has had the impudence to tell me all this with his own lips. In the Hôpital, Father, in heaven's name! My enchanting mistress, my heart's own queen, imprisoned in the Hôpital, like the most infamous of creatures! Where will I find the strength not to die of anguish and shame? The good Father, seeing me so grievously afflicted, tried to comfort me; he told me he had never quite understood my story in the way I had just told it; that he had known, it is true, that I was leading a dissolute life, but had imagined it was some family connection based on respect or friendship that had led M. de G... M... to take an interest in me; that he had only been able to explain it to himself in these terms; but that what I had just told him put my affairs in a completely different light, and he was in no doubt that the faithful account he meant to make of it to the Lieutenant-General of Police would contribute to my release. He then enquired why I had not yet thought of informing my family, since they had played no part in my imprisonment. I satisfied him on this score, pointing out the grief I had feared it would cause my father, and the shame I myself would have suffered. He promised me, lastly, that he would go straight away and see the Lieutenant of Police, if only, he added, to forestall some worse action on the part of M. de G... M..., who has left this house in no good humour, and who is a man of sufficient standing to make himself feared.

I waited for the Father Superior's return with as much agitation as if I were some poor prisoner about to be sentenced. It was indescrib-able torture to me to imagine Manon in the Hôpital. Apart from the infamy of the place, I did not know how she was being treated there; while the memory of certain details I had heard about this house of horrors kept me in constant torment. So determined was I to rescue her, at whatever cost and by whatever means, that had I been unable to leave Saint-Lazare in any other way, I would have set fire to it. I began, therefore, to examine the various measures I might take if the Lieutenant-General of Police continued to detain me against my will. I tested my ingenuity to the utmost; I reviewed all the possi-bilities. I found no certain means of escape, and feared that, follow-ing an unsuccessful attempt, I would be held more securely than ever. I recalled the names of several friends I hoped might help me; but how was I to let them know of my situation? At last I thought I had devised a plan so artful it might succeed; and I delayed putting the final touches to it until after the Father Superior's return, in case the failure of his mission should make its use necessary. He returned soon enough. I could not see on his face any of the signs of joy that accompany good news. I have spoken to the Lieutenant-General of Police, he said, but I arrived too late. M. de G... M... went to see him the moment he left here, and has so prejudiced him against you that he was on the point of issuing me with new orders to keep you still more closely confined.

However, he went on, after I had let him know the full facts of the affair he softened a good deal and, laughing a little at old G... M...'s lasciviousness, said that you must remain here for six months, in order to satisfy him; which was all to the good, since you could only benefit from such a stay. He urged me to treat you with respect; and you can rest assured you will have no grounds for complaint on that score.

The worthy Father's account was lengthy enough to give me time for some prudent reflection. I could see that if I showed too much eagerness for regaining my freedom I would risk upsetting my whole project. I therefore, on the contrary, intimated that, since I must of necessity remain there, it was a source of true consolation to know he held me in some esteem. Then, in all sincerity, I begged him to grant me a favour, which was of no importance to anyone else, but which would contribute greatly to my own peace of mind; this was to inform one of my friends, a saintly cleric living in Saint-Sulpice, that I was in Saint-Lazare, and to allow me to receive occasional visits from him. My request was promptly granted. The friend in question was Tiberge; not that I imagined he himself could help me regain my freedom; but I wanted to make use of him indirectly, without him being aware of his involvement. My plan, in short, was as follows: I would write to Lescaut, entrusting him and our mutual friends with the task of securing my release. But how could I get a letter to him? This was to be Tiberge's contribution. However, since he knew Lescaut was my mistress's brother, I feared he would be reluctant to undertake this commission. I would therefore enclose my letter to Lescaut inside another one, which I would send to an acquaintance, asking him to deliver the first letter promptly to its address; and since it was essential that I meet Lescaut, so that we could decide on a concerted course of action, I intended telling him to come to Saint-Lazare and to ask to see me under the name of my older brother, come to Paris expressly to find out about my affairs. We would then agree upon whatever means of escape promised to be quickest and most reliable. The Father Superior told Tiberge of my desire to see him. Faithful friend that he was, he had not lost sight of me completely, but knew about my latest misadventure. He had heard I was in Saint-Lazare, and perhaps was not sorry to learn of my disgrace, hoping it might recall me to my duty. He hurried to my room.

We greeted one another with great affection. He enquired as to my state of mind. I opened my heart to him unreservedly, except on the matter of my proposed escape. I do not want to appear in your eyes, dear friend, I said to him, as anything but what I am. If you had hoped to find here a friend as wise in his conduct as he is moderate in his desires, a libertine chastened by Heaven and reawakened to virtue, a heart, in short, set free from love and cured of Manon's charms, you have judged me too favourably. You find me just as you left me four months ago: still passionately in love, and still made wretched by that same fatal passion in which I never weary of seeking my happiness.

He replied that the confession I had just made was inexcusable; that it was common enough to see sinners so intoxicated with the illusory happiness that is born of vice as openly to prefer it to that of virtue; but such people were at least attached to images of happiness, and were duped by appearances; whereas to recognize, as I did, that the object of my attachment could bring me only guilt and misery, and yet to continue voluntarily to immerse myself in misfortune and crime, involved a contradiction between ideas and conduct that did little honour to my reason.

How easy it is to defeat you, Tiberge, I replied, when one abandons any attempt to oppose you with your own arms! Allow me to put forward an argument in my turn. Can you claim that what you call the happiness that is born of virtue is exempt from suffering, adversity, and anxious fear? How do you account for prison, crucifixion, and the tortures inflicted by tyrants? Will you maintain, as the mystics do, that what torments the body rejoices the soul? You would not dare to say such a thing: it is an unsustainable paradox. Your much-vaunted happiness, in other words, is mingled with a thousand woes; or, to be more precise, it is nothing but a tissue of sufferings through which one reaches towards felicity. Now if, by some force of the imagination we are able to take pleasure in these pains themselves, since they may lead us in the end to the happiness we long for, why, in my case, do you dismiss as contradictory and senseless a wholly similar aspiration? I love Manon; I am trying, through the thousand ills that beset me, to reach a place where I can live with her in happiness and peace. The path I tread is a painful one; but my hopes of arriving at the end I yearn for fill it with sweetness, and I will feel myself only too well rewarded by a single moment spent with her for all the griefs I have suffered in order to win it. Things seem to me equal, then, on your side and on mine; or if there is a difference, it is even to my advantage, for the happiness I hope for is close at hand, while the other is far off; mine partakes of the nature of pain, that is, it is felt by the body, while the nature of the other is unknown, accessible only through faith.

Tiberge seemed alarmed by this argument. He took two steps backwards, saying, with an air of the utmost seriousness, that what I had just said not only offended against good sense, but was a wretched sophism, born of impiety and irreligion: for, he added, the comparison you make, between the end of your own sufferings and that which religion proposes, smacks of the most profane and monstrous libertinism.*

I agree my comparison is not exact, I went on, but be careful, my argument does not turn on it. My purpose has been to explain something you regard as a contradiction, which is that one should persevere in a love that is unhappy; and I think I have proved successfully that, if there is a contradiction here, it is one that you cannot escape from any more than I can. It is in this respect only that I have treated these things as equal, and I insist that they are so. You will no doubt reply that the end of virtue is infinitely superior to that of love. Who would deny it? But is that the question here? Is it not rather as to which of them better enables us to endure suffering? And to judge this, we need only look at each according to its effects. How many deserters there are from the rigours of virtue, how few from the cause of love! You will again reply that, if the exercise of virtue involves suffering, this is not infallibly or necessarily so; that tyrannies and torture are a thing of the past, and that we are surrounded by any number of virtuous people who lead pleasant and tranquil lives. To which I will likewise reply that love also can be peaceful and blessed with good fortune; I will further add—and here is another difference, and one that is extremely favourable to me— that love, while it often deceives, at least promises only satisfaction and joy, whereas what religion leads us to expect are doleful mortifications and gloomy observances. Do not be alarmed, I added, seeing him ready to take offence at this affront to his zeal. All I am trying to establish here is that nothing is less calculated to cure the infatuated heart than to disparage the joys of love, and to promise greater happiness in the exercise of virtue. Made as we are, nothing is more certain than that all our felicity consists in pleasure. I defy anyone to argue otherwise. Now the human heart has no need for long reflection to feel that, of all pleasures, the sweetest are those of love. It soon discovers that when other, more enticing joys are promised elsewhere, this is mere deceit, and one that inclines it thereafter to view with suspicion even the most solid of promises. To those preachers who want to recall me to the path of virtue, I say: Tell me that it is necessary and indispensable; but do not disguise its rigours and pains. Persuade me that the delights of love are fleeting, that they are forbidden, that they will be followed by eternal torment, and—something that will make even more impression on me—that the sweeter and more enchanting they are, the more magnificently Heaven will reward our sacrifice of them; but confess, too, that with hearts made as ours are, we can expect no greater felicity here below.

These last remarks restored Tiberge's good humour. He agreed that my way of thinking was not wholly unreasonable. The only further objection he made was to ask why I did not at least embrace my own principles, and sacrifice love to my hopes of this reward, of which I had formed so high an idea. Ah, dearest friend, I answered, it is because I recognize only too well my wretchedness and weakness. Alas, yes! It is indeed my duty to act in accordance with my convictions, but is this action within my power? What aid would I not need, in order to forget Manon and her charms! God forgive me, exclaimed Tiberge, but I think we have here another of our Jansenists.* I do not know what I am, I replied, and it is not at all clear to me what one ought to be; but I feel only too keenly the truth of what they say.

This conversation at least served to reawaken my friend's compassion for me. He saw that there was more weakness than wickedness in my dissolute ways. Faithful friend that he was, after this he was the more ready to give me the help without which I would infallibly have perished in wretchedness. Nevertheless, I did not give him the least intimation of my plan to escape from Saint-Lazare. I asked him only to take charge of my letter. I had it ready when he arrived; nor was I short of pretexts to explain why I had felt it necessary to write. He was faithful enough to deliver it exactly as I requested; and Lescaut received, before the end of the day, the one that was meant for him.

He came to see me the following day, having succeeded in gaining admission under my brother's name. I was overjoyed when he appeared in my room. I closed the door carefully. Let us not lose a moment, I said to him: first give me the news of Manon, and then some good advice as to how I can break free of my chains. He assured me he had not seen his sister since the day preceding that of my arrest, that only through assiduous enquiries had he discovered what had happened to her and to me; and that he had presented himself two or three times at the Hôpital, only to be refused permission to speak to her. G... M..., you wretch, I cried, I'll make you pay for this!

As to setting you free, Lescaut went on, this is a less easy enterprise than you might suppose. We spent yesterday evening, two of my friends and I, studying the outside of this building, and we concluded that, since your windows look over an interior courtyard surrounded by high walls, as you've pointed out yourself, it would be very difficult to get you out by that route. Besides, you're on the third floor, and we can't hope to get ladders and ropes all the way up here. So, the outside of the building offers no means of escape. It's to the inside we must look if we are to devise some ruse. That won't do either, I replied; I have examined everything, especially since my confinement has been a little less strictly enforced, thanks to the Father Superior's indulgence. My door is no longer locked; I am free to walk in the galleries which the monks use; but all the staircases are blocked off by heavy doors, which they are careful to keep fastened night and day, so that it is going to take more than ingenuity if I am to slip away unnoticed. Wait though, I went on, after considering for a moment what struck me as an excellent idea, could you bring me a pistol? Very easily, said Lescaut; but are you proposing to kill someone? I assured him that killing was so far from my intentions that the pistol need not even be loaded. Bring it to me tomorrow, I added, and then be sure you are waiting at eleven o'clock in the evening, with two or three of our friends, opposite the door to this building. I hope to be able to join you there. He pressed me in vain to tell him more. I said that an enterprise such as I had in mind would seem practicable only after it had succeeded. I asked him to cut short his visit, so that he would have no difficulty in coming again the following day. He gained admittance as easily as before. He wore an air of great gravity—no one would not have taken him for a man of honour.

As soon as I found myself in possession of the instrument of my freedom, my doubts as to the success of my venture all but disappeared. It was bizarre, it was bold; but, given the motives that impelled me, of what was I not capable? I had noticed, since being allowed to leave my room and walk about the galleries, that the porter came every evening at the same time, and delivered the keys to all the doors in the house to the Father Superior, after which a deep silence reigned, indicating that everyone had retired for the night. At this point I could make my way unhindered, by a communicating gallery, from my own room to that of the Father Superior. My plan was to gain possession of his keys, frightening him with my pistol if he was at all reluctant to hand them over, and to use them to reach the street. I waited impatiently for the moment to arrive. The porter came at his usual time, that is, a little after nine o'clock. I let a further hour go by, so as to make sure that all the monks and servants were asleep. I set out at last, carrying my weapon and a lighted candle. I tapped, gently at first, at the Father's door, hoping to wake him without making any noise. He heard me at the second knock and, imagining no doubt that one of the monks was ill and needed his help, got up and came to open it. He nevertheless took the precaution of asking, through the door, who was there and what was wanted of him. I was obliged to give my name; but I affected a plaintive tone, so as to make him think I was feeling unwell. Ah, my son, it's you! he said, opening the door. What brings you here so late? I entered his room and, drawing him to the end furthest away from the door, declared that it was impossible I should remain in Saint-Lazare a minute longer; that night-time offered the best moment to leave without being seen, and that I trusted, given the friendship he had shown me, that he would agree either to opening the doors for me, or to lending me his keys so that I could open them myself.

These courtesies must have taken him completely by surprise. He said nothing, but stood gazing at me for quite some time. Since I myself had none to lose, I went on with my speech, assuring him I was very touched by all the kindness he had shown me, but that, freedom being the most precious possession of all, especially to someone who had been deprived of his unjustly, I was determined to secure my own that very night, at whatever cost; and, in case he should take it into his head to raise his voice and call for help, I showed him the perfectly respectable reason for remaining silent I was carrying beneath my frock-coat. A pistol! he said. What! After all the consideration I've shown you, you would take my life, would you, my son? God forbid that I should need to, I replied. You have far too much sound wit and common sense to oblige me to do any such thing; but I want my freedom, and am so determined to have it that, if my plan should fail through any fault of yours, you are done for. But my dearest child, he went on, pale and frightened, what harm have I done you? What reason could you have for wanting me dead? None at all, I retorted impatiently. I have no intention of killing you, if you want to live. Open the door for me, and we will remain the best of friends. I caught sight of the keys lying on the table. I picked them up and asked him to follow me, and to make as little noise as possible. He had no choice but to obey. As we progressed from one door to the next, he repeated, with a sigh, as he opened each one, Ah my son, who would have believed it? Not a sound, Father, I repeated in turn. At last we arrived at a sort of barrier just inside the main door to the street. Believing myself already free, I was following hard on the heels of the Father Superior, my candle in one hand and my pistol in the other. While he hurried to open it, a servant who slept in a little room nearby, hearing the sound of bolts being drawn, gets up and puts his head round his door. The worthy Father apparently thought that this man could stop me. Most unwisely, he ordered him to come to his assistance. He was a powerfully built rascal, who immediately threw himself upon me. I did not spare him; I let him have it, right in the chest. Now see what you've done, Father, said I to my guide, not without a touch of pride. But don't let that stop you finishing your work, I added, pushing him towards the final door. He dared not refuse to open it. I went through without hindrance and, not four paces further on, found Lescaut and two of his friends waiting for me, just as he had promised.

We set off at once. Lescaut asked me if he hadn't heard a pistol being fired. That's your fault, I told him; why did you bring it to me loaded? I thanked him, nevertheless, for having taken this precaution, without which I would certainly have been in Saint-Lazare for a very long time. We spent the night at a victualler's, where I began to make up for the bad diet I had endured for almost three months. I could not give myself over wholeheartedly to pleasure, however. I suffered mortally, not on my own account, but for Manon. We must rescue her, I said to my three friends. This was my sole aim in seeking my own freedom; and it is an undertaking to which I beg you to bring all your ingenuity; as for me, I will give it my life itself. Lescaut, who lacked neither good sense nor caution, argued that we should rein ourselves in for a while; that my escape from Saint-Lazare, and the unfortunate incident as I left, would inevitably create a stir; that the Lieutenant-General of Police would mount a search for me, and that he had a long arm; finally, that if I did not want to expose myself to something even worse than Saint-Lazare, I would be well advised to lie low for a few days, in order to give the first zeal of my enemies time to cool down. This was wise advice, and had I been equally wise I might have followed it. But so much delay and circumspection were not at all compatible with the vehemence of my passion. My only concession, in the end, was to promise I would spend the following day asleep in bed. He locked me in his room, and I remained there until evening.

I spent part of this time devising schemes and stratagems to help Manon. I felt sure that her prison was even more impenetrable than mine. Force and violence would be of no use; what was needed was guile; but the goddess of invention herself would not have known where to begin. Seeing no way of proceeding, I postponed further consideration of the matter until after I had acquired some information about the internal disposition of the Hôpital.

As soon as darkness had restored my freedom, I asked Lescaut if he would accompany me on this mission. We engaged one of the porters in conversation. He seemed a sensible man. I pretended to be a stranger to the city, who had been impressed by what he had heard about the Hôpital and the system observed there. I questioned him about it in the most minute detail, and, moving from one particular to the next, at length arrived at the administrators, whose names and circumstances I enquired into. The answers he gave on this last subject suggested what seemed to me an admirable idea, which I put into effect immediately. I asked him—for this was essential to my plan—whether any of the administrators had children. He said he could not answer with total certainty, but that he knew that one of the principals, M. de T..., had a son of marriageable age, who had come to the Hôpital several times with his father. This assurance was all I needed. I broke off our conversation as soon as I could and, as we made our way home, confided to Lescaut the plan I had devised. It is quite likely, I said, that M. de T...'s son, who is rich and of good family, will have a certain taste for pleasure, like most young men of his age. In other words, he cannot be averse to women, nor wish to be thought so gauche as to refuse his assistance in an affair of the heart. My plan is to involve him in Manon's release. If he is a man of honour and breeding, he will offer to help us out of generosity of spirit. If he lacks this impulse, he will at least do something for so enchanting a young woman, if only in the hope of sharing her favours. I must see him no later than tomorrow, I added. This plan has given me new courage, which seems to me to augur well for it. Lescaut himself agreed that my scheme had some plausibility, and that we might reasonably hope that something would come of it. I spent the night in a less gloomy frame of mind.

Next morning I dressed as respectably as I could in my impoverished state, and took a hackney-carriage to the house of the younger M. de T... He was surprised to receive a visit from a complete stranger. His open expression and courteous manner seemed to me to augur well. I told him frankly why I had come, and, so as to arouse his natural feelings, spoke of my passion and my mistress's merit as two things whose only equal was each other. He said that although he had never seen Manon, he had heard about her—if, that is, I meant the girl who had been old G... M...'s mistress. I was in no doubt that he already knew of the part I had played in this adventure, and in order to win him over still more by seeming to confide in him, I related in detail everything that had happened to Manon and me. So you see, Monsieur, I continued, the chief concern of my life and my heart is in your hands. The one is not dearer to me than the other. I feel I need have no reserve with you, for I know you have a generous spirit; besides, the similarity in our ages leads me to hope we will find ourselves alike in disposition too. He seemed touched by these marks of openness and candour. His reply was that of a man of the world and a man of honour—things that experience of the world does not always give, and often takes away. He told me he would always rank my visit among the favours that fortune had bestowed on him, that he would look upon my friendship as one of his happiest acquisitions, and that he would strive to merit it by his zeal in doing me service. He could not promise to restore Manon to me, since, he said, such influence as he possessed was modest and not to be relied on, but he offered to procure me the pleasure of seeing her, and to do everything in his power to return her to my arms. I was happier with this uncertain influence of his than I would have been with a confident assurance that all my desires were about to be fulfilled. The very modesty of the promises he made me indicated, in my eyes, a sincerity with which I was charmed. In short, I saw in his good offices the fulfilment of my hopes. His promise to take me to see

Manon would alone have made me ready to do anything I could for him in return. I expressed something of these feelings to him, in a way that persuaded him that my nature, too, was far from ignoble. We embraced tenderly, and, from that moment on, became friends, out of the simple goodness of our hearts, and prompted solely by that instinct that draws men of warmth and generosity of spirit together. He went still further in the marks of esteem he showed me; for, having reflected on the whole course of my adventures, and concluded that I was unlikely, having just left Saint-Lazare, to find myself in easy circumstances, he offered me his purse, and pressed me to accept it. I could not do so, but said: You are too good, Monsieur. If such kindness and friendship were to be employed in helping me see my beloved Manon again, I would be your servant for life. And if you could restore this dearest of creatures to me completely, I could never discharge the debt, were I to shed for you my last drop of blood.

We parted only after agreeing the time and place of our next meeting. He was too considerate to postpone it beyond that very afternoon. I waited for him in a coffee-house where, towards four o'clock, he joined me, and together we made our way to the Hôpital. My knees trembled as I crossed its courtyards. Power of love! I said, so I am again to see the idol of my heart, the object of so many tears and anxieties! O Heaven! Preserve me long enough to reach her, and then you may dispose as you will of my life and fate. I have no other favour to ask of you.

M. de T... spoke to several of the gaolers, who were only too anxious to please him in any way they could. He had us shown to the place where Manon had her room; we were accompanied by a key of terrifying proportions, which served to open her door. I asked the valet who was guiding us, and whose responsibility it was to look after Manon, what she did to pass the time in such a place. He told us he had never seen such angelic sweetness; that she had not once spoken a harsh word to him; that she had wept continuously during the first six weeks of her stay there, but that for some time now she seemed to bear her misfortune with greater patience; and that she busied herself with her sewing from dawn till dusk, except for a few hours which she spent reading. I asked him again if she had been properly looked after. He assured me that she had never lacked the necessities of life, at least.

The reunion in La Salpêtrière (Pasquier)

We arrived at her door. My heart was beating violently. Go in without me, I urged M. de T..., and prepare her for my visit. I am afraid that if I appear without warning, the shock might be too much for her. The door opened. He went inside. I remained in the gallery. I could nevertheless hear everything that was said. He told her he had come to bring her comfort; that he was a friend of mine, and that he took a great interest in our happiness. She at once enquired of him eagerly if he knew what had become of me. He not only knew, he said, but could bring me to her, so that I might throw myself at her feet, as fond and as faithful as ever. When? she asked. Perhaps this very day, he replied; the happy moment need not be delayed; he will appear this very minute, if you wish. She realized I was just outside the door. She rushed headlong towards it and, at this moment, I entered. We embraced with an outpouring of that tenderness which an absence of three months makes so enchanting to perfect lovers. Our sighs, our faltering endearments, the thousand murmured words of love we exchanged again and again, provided M. de T..., for quarter of an hour, with a scene that greatly affected him. I envy you, he said to me, as he persuaded us to sit down; there is no destiny, however glorious, I would not forgo for so lovely and so passionate a mistress. And as for me, I rejoined, I would reject every empire on earth in exchange for the happiness of being loved by her.

The rest of this conversation—so long awaited—could not fail to be infinitely touching. Poor Manon related her adventures to me, and I told her mine. Reflecting on her present situation, and the one I had just escaped from, we shed bitter tears. M. de T... comforted us with renewed promises of how ardently he would work to end all our woes. He advised us, so as to make it easier for him to procure future interviews, not to prolong this first one unduly. We were reluctant to accept advice so little to our taste. Manon, especially, could not bring herself to let me go. A hundred times she made me sit down again, catching hold of my clothes and my hands. Alas! What a place to leave me in! she said. Can I be certain of ever seeing you again? M. de T... promised he would often return with me to see her. As to this place, he added gallantly, we should no longer call it the Hôpital, but rather Versailles, since a lady worthy to reign over every heart is imprisoned here.

On my way out I rewarded the valet liberally, to encourage his zeal in looking after her. This young fellow was not as base of soul or as hard of heart as the rest of his kind. He had witnessed our interview and been touched by the tender spectacle it offered. The louis d'or I gave him was enough to win him over completely. As we went down again into the courtyard, he drew me to one side. Monsieur, he said, if you were to think of taking me into your service, or of offering me some decent compensation for the loss of the position I occupy here, I think I could secure Mademoiselle Manon's freedom without too much difficulty. I pricked up my ears at this suggestion, and although I possessed nothing, promised him rewards beyond his wildest dreams. I reckoned it would always be easy enough to recompense a man of his sort. You can be sure that there is nothing I would not do to repay you, my friend, I said, and that your fortune is as certain as my own. I asked him what his plan was. None other, he replied, than to open the door to her room one evening, and accompany her as far as the one that gives on to the street, where you must be ready to receive her. I asked him if he was not afraid she would be recognized, as they made their way through the galleries and the courtyards. He admitted there was a danger of this, but said that such a plan was bound to involve some risk. Although I was delighted to see him so resolute, I called to M. de T... to join us, so that I could explain this plan to him, along with my only reason for doubting its success. He saw more problems than I did. He agreed that Manon could perfectly easily escape in this way; but, he continued, if she is recognized, if she is apprehended while trying to flee, it might well be the end of her. Besides, you would have to leave Paris immediately, for however carefully you hid yourself, they would be certain to find you. They would redouble their efforts to do so, on your account as much as on hers. A man on his own can evade arrest, but it is almost impossible for him to escape notice in the company of a beautiful woman. However sound I recognized this argument to be, it counted for nothing with me against so immediate a hope of setting Manon free. I said as much to M. de T..., and begged him to excuse, in the name of love, a little imprudence and temerity. I added that it had already been my intention to leave Paris and, as before, to settle in some neighbouring village. We therefore agreed with the valet not to put off the plan any later than the following day; and, determined to do everything we could to assure its success, we decided to provide Manon with men's clothing, so as to make it easier for her to leave unnoticed. It was not easy to get this into the prison, but I soon thought up a way of managing it. I simply asked M. de T... to wear two light jackets the following day, one on top of the other, and I took charge of all the rest.

We returned to the Hôpital next morning. I had with me stockings, linen, and so on, for Manon; while, over my frock-coat, I wore a top-coat which concealed anything too bulky I might be carrying in my pockets. We remained in her room for no more than a moment. M de T... left her one of his two jackets; I gave her my frock-coat, since my top-coat would disguise its absence well enough to allow me to leave the building. Her dress was thus complete, apart from a pair of breeches which, unfortunately, I had forgotten. The omission of this necessary item would doubtless have caused us much mirth, if the difficulty into which it plunged us had not been so serious. I was in despair lest a bagatelle of this sort should spoil our entire plan. I saw at once what I must do, however, which was to give my breeches to Manon and to leave the building myself without them. My top-coat was long, and I managed, with the aid of a few pins, to make myself respectable enough to get past the porter on the door. The rest of the day seemed to me endless. Darkness fell at last, we arrived in our carriage, and positioned it just below the door to the Hôpital. We had not been there long when we saw Manon appear with her guide. The carriage door was open. They climbed in. I took my beloved mistress in my arms. She was trembling like a leaf. The coachman asked me where he should take us. To the ends of the earth, I cried, or at least to a place where I need never again be parted from Manon.

This outburst, which I had been unable to contain, narrowly missed having the most vexatious consequences. The coachman pondered my words; and when, a moment later, I gave him the name of the street we wanted, replied that he feared I was involving him in some suspect affair, that he could clearly see that the handsome young fellow called Manon was a girl I was abducting from the Hôpital, and that he was in no mood to ruin himself for love of me. This fastidiousness on the part of such a scoundrel was only a ruse to make me pay more dearly for his coach. But we were still too close to the Hôpital not to go along with it. Hold your tongue, I told him, and you'll earn yourself a louis d'or; after which he would have helped me burn down the Hôpital itself. We arrived at Lescaut's lodgings. It was late, and M. de T..., having promised to see us again the next day, had already left. Only the valet remained.

I was holding Manon so tightly in my arms that we occupied only a single place in the carriage. She was weeping with joy, and I felt my cheeks grow wet with her tears. But when we arrived at Lescaut's door and had to get out, I had a second quarrel with the coachman, this time with dreadful consequences. I regretted having promised him a louis, not only because the amount was excessive, but for another and much more powerful reason, which was that I could not pay it. I summoned Lescaut. He came down from his room to open the door to us. I whispered in his ear the difficulty I found myself in. Inclined to ill-temper, and not at all accustomed to humouring coachmen, he replied that I must be mad. A louis d'or! he added, I'll give the scoundrel twenty good strokes of my cane! I tried pointing out quietly to him that this would ruin us, but to no avail. He snatched my cane from me, and seemed bent on setting about the coachman with it. Perhaps this was not the first time the man had fallen foul of a guardsman or a musketeer; at any rate he fled in terror, along with his carriage, and shouting that I had cheated him but that I hadn't heard the last of it. I called to him repeatedly to stop, but in vain. His flight left me greatly agitated. I had no doubt he would inform the Superintendent of Police. You have done for me, Lescaut, I said. I can't stay here now: it isn't safe; we must get away this very minute. I gave Manon my arm, and we at once left that dangerous street. Lescaut accompanied us. There is something wonderful in the way that Providence orders events. We had been walking for no more than five or six minutes when a man whose face I could not make out recognized Lescaut. No doubt he had been searching for him in the streets close to where he lived, intent on the fateful resolve he now carried out. It's Lescaut! he cried, firing a shot at him; he'll sup with the angels tonight! He ran off straight away. Lescaut fell to the ground without the least sign of life. I urged Manon to flee, for there was nothing we could do to help a corpse, and I was afraid of being apprehended by the night-watch,* which might appear at any moment. I turned into the first little side-street we came to, along with Manon and the valet. She was so distraught I could hardly support her. At last, at the end of the street, I caught sight of a hackney-carriage. We got in, but when the coachman asked where he should take us, I was puzzled to know what to reply. I had no secure refuge to go to, no trusted friend I dared turn to for help. I was without money, having scarcely more than half a pistole in my purse. Manon was so overwhelmed with terror and fatigue that she sat half-swooning at my side. Lescaut's murder, moreover, haunted my imagination; nor could I as yet be easy in my mind about the night-watch. What was I to do? Fortunately I remembered the inn at Chaillot, where Manon and I had spent a few days when we first went there to live. I hoped not only to be safe in this village, but to be able to live there for some time without being pressed for payment. Take us to Chaillot, I said to the coachman. He refused to go there so late for anything less than a pistole. Here was a new and unexpected setback. At last we agreed on six francs, which was all that remained in my purse.

I did what I could on the way to comfort Manon; but deep down in my heart I was in despair. I would have welcomed death a thousand times over, if I had not been holding in my arms the only thing that made life dear. This thought alone was enough to restore me. At least she is here in my embrace, I said to myself; she loves me, she is mine. Tiberge can say what he likes, this is no mere phantom of happiness. I could watch the whole universe perish and not be moved. And why? Because all my affection is hers: I no longer have any to spare. I meant this quite sincerely; nevertheless, while setting such little store by earthly goods, I felt that some small share in them at least would be necessary, if I were to be in a position to regard all the rest with even more sovereign contempt. Love is mightier than wealth, mightier than riches and plenty; but it needs their support; and nothing causes the fastidious lover deeper despair than to see himself reduced, through their lack, to the vulgar concerns of baser souls.

It was eleven o'clock by the time we arrived in Chaillot. We were warmly welcomed by the people at the inn, who remembered us. They were not surprised to see Manon wearing men's clothes, since in Paris and its surroundings everyone is used to women appearing in all manner of guises. I made sure she was waited upon with every attention a man of fortune could command. She did not know how short of money I was; and I was careful not to reveal anything of this to her, being resolved to return alone to Paris the next day and seek to remedy this vexatious malady.

During supper she seemed to me thin and pale. I had not noticed this at the Hôpital, since the room in which we had met there was anything but brightly lit. I asked if this was not the result of the fright she had received on seeing her brother murdered. She assured me that, affected though she had been by this event, her pallor came only from her having endured three months' separation from me. Do you love me, then, so excessively? I asked. A thousand times more than I can say, she replied. Then will you never again leave me? I added. No, never, she replied; and this reassurance was accompanied by so many caresses, and so many vows, that it truly did seem impossible to me that she should ever forget them. I have always felt certain she was sincere; why would she have pretended to that extent? But she was even more inconstant, or rather, she was no longer anything—did not even recognize herself—when, seeing all about her women who lived in ease and plenty, she found herself in poverty and want. I was about to receive a final proof of this, one that surpassed all the others, and which brought about the strangest adventure that has ever befallen a man of my birth and destiny.*

Knowing this to be her temperament, I went straight back to Paris the next day. Her brother's death and our own lack of linen and clothes provided such good reasons for my visit that I required no other pretext. I left the inn, telling Manon and our host that I intended to take a hired carriage; but this was mere talk. Obliged by necessity to travel on foot, I walked very fast until I reached the Cours-la-Reine, where, as I had planned, I stopped. I needed a moment of solitude and calm in which to collect myself and decide what I was going to do in Paris.

I sat down on the grass. I embarked upon a sea of arguments and reflections, which in the end I narrowed down to three principal items. I must seek immediate help, so as to procure an infinite number of immediate necessities; I must look for some opening that would at least offer me hope for the future; and, no less importantly, I must take advice and put in place measures that would assure Manon's safety as well as my own. Having racked my brains trying to work out a plan of campaign that comprised all three, I concluded that at that moment it would be as well to eliminate the last two. A room in Chaillot was not a bad hiding-place; and, as to our future needs, I decided it would be time enough to think of them when I had satisfied our present ones.

My first task, in other words, was to replenish my purse. M. de T... had generously offered me his; but I was extremely reluctant to remind him of this. A fine figure I would cut, revealing my poverty to a stranger, and begging him for a share of his wealth! Only a mean and cowardly spirit, impervious to the ignominy of such a thing, would be capable of it; or else a humble Christian, so elevated of soul as to be above shame. I was neither a coward nor a good Christian, and I would have given half my blood to avoid this humiliation. But will Tiberge, I said to myself, will my good friend Tiberge refuse me anything he has the power to give? Assuredly not. He will be moved by my poverty; but he will slay me with his moralizing. I will have to suffer his reproaches, his exhortations, his threats; he will make me pay so dearly for his help, that I would rather give the other half of my blood than expose myself to so vexatious a scene, which can only leave me troubled and full of remorse. But in that case, I continued, I must abandon all hope, since no other course is open to me than these two, even though I would rather shed half my blood than take either one of them, which is to say, shed all my blood rather than take both. Yes, all my blood, I added after a moment's reflection; I would rather, without a doubt, give it all, than be reduced to abject supplication. But what is at stake here is indeed my blood! For what is at stake is Manon's life and well-being, her love and her fidelity. What else do I possess to weigh in the balance against her? Until now, nothing at all. She has taken the place of fame, happiness, and fortune. There are no doubt many things I would give my life to either obtain or avoid; but valuing something more than my life is not a reason for valuing it more than Manon. This argument was conclusive. I was soon on my way, resolved to go first and see Tiberge, and after him, M. de T...

As soon as I reached the city I took a hackney-carriage, even though I had no means of paying for it, but was relying for this on the help I had come to solicit. I asked to be taken to the Jardin du Luxembourg, from where I sent word to Tiberge, telling him I was waiting for him. He spared my impatience by appearing promptly. I did not attempt to prevaricate, but revealed to him the full urgency of my need. He asked me if the hundred pistoles I had returned to him would be enough and, without making any difficulties, went there and then to fetch them for me, with that air of openness and of pleasure in giving that only love and true friendship can inspire. Although I had never been in doubt as to the success of my request, I was surprised to have achieved it at so little cost, that is, without him scolding me for my lack of repentance. But if I thought I was to be spared his reproaches, I was mistaken; for when he had finished counting out his money, and I was about to leave, he asked me to take a turn about the gardens. I had not mentioned Manon. He had no idea that she was free and living with me again; so that the lecture he delivered concerned only my daring escape from Saint-Lazare and his fears that, instead of profiting from the lessons in wisdom I had received there, I would return to my dissolute way of life. He told me that, coming to visit me in Saint-Lazare the day after my disappearance, he had been shocked beyond words to learn of the manner of my flight; he had talked the matter over with the Superior; the worthy Father had still not recovered from his fright; he had nevertheless been magnanimous enough to conceal the details of my departure from the Lieutenant-General of Police, and had prevented the death of the porter from being known outside; I had therefore no cause for alarm on that score; but if I still retained the least feeling for virtue, I would profit from the fortunate turn that Heaven had given my affairs; I should start by writing to my father and seeking a reconciliation with him; and if I would, for once, follow his advice, he was of the opinion I should leave Paris and return to the bosom of my family.

I heard this speech through to the end. It contained much that was a source of satisfaction to me. I was delighted, first of all, to have nothing to fear as far as Saint-Lazare was concerned. I was free to roam the streets of Paris again. I congratulated myself, too, on Tiberge's not having the least idea that Manon had been rescued and was living with me once more. I noticed, indeed, that he had avoided any mention of her, in the apparent belief that, since I seemed so calm on her account, she must mean less to me than before. I made up my mind, if not to go back to my family, then at least to write to my father as he advised, and to indicate that I was ready to return to a proper respect for the duty I owed him and the wishes he entertained for me. My hope was to persuade him to send me some money, under the pretext that I was preparing for my examinations at the Académie;* for I would have had great difficulty in convincing him that I had any intention of returning to holy orders. Nor, when it came down to it, did I feel any aversion towards fulfilling the promise I intended making to him. I was, on the contrary, only too ready to apply myself to some worthwhile and honourable project, so long as this could be reconciled with my love for Manon. My cherished aim was to live with my mistress and at the same time complete my studies. The two were perfectly compatible. I was so pleased with all these ideas that I promised Tiberge I would send a letter to my father that very day; and accordingly, on leaving him, went into a public writing-room, where I composed such a tender and submissive letter that, on rereading it, I flattered myself that it would so move his father's heart as to procure me something.

Although, thanks to Tiberge, I was now in a position to hire a carriage and to pay for it too, I took pleasure and pride in going to M. de T...'s house on foot. I delighted in exercising a freedom my friend had told me need hold no further fears. It suddenly occurred to me, nevertheless, that his reassurances applied only to Saint-Lazare, and that I might be held answerable for the affair at the Hôpital as well, not to mention the death of Lescaut, in which I was involved as a witness at least. This reflection so terrified me that I took refuge in the first alleyway I came to, from where I summoned a carriage. I went straight to M. de T...'s house. He laughed at my fears. They struck even me as laughable, once he had assured me that on neither account did I have cause for alarm. He told me that, thinking he might be suspected of having played some part in Manon's abduction, he had gone to the Hôpital the following day and asked to see her, pretending not to know what had happened; that far from holding either him or me responsible, they were eager to share with him the strange news of her escape, and to marvel that so pretty a girl as Manon should have decided to run away with a valet; but that he had contented himself with coolly observing that this was no surprise to him, since people will do anything to gain their freedom. He went on to tell me that he had gone next to Lescaut's house, hoping to find me there with my enchanting mistress; the landlord, a coach-builder, had denied seeing either of us, but had said that this was hardly surprising since, if it was Lescaut we wanted, we would doubtless have been told that he had just been killed, at more or less that very time. Whereupon he had related, readily enough, everything he knew about the cause and circumstances of this death. About two hours previously one of Lescaut's friends, a guardsman, had come to see him and had proposed a game of cards. In no time at all Lescaut was winning, so that in the space of an hour the other man had found himself the poorer by a hundred écus, which was all the money he possessed. Seeing himself without a sou, the unfortunate man had begged Lescaut to lend him half the sum he had just lost; and, this request giving rise to various disagreements, they had quarrelled with the utmost bitterness. Lescaut had refused to go outside and draw his sword, and the other man had sworn, on leaving him, to blow his brains out; which is what he had done that very evening. M. de T... had the courtesy to add that he had been very anxious on our account, and that his services were still at my disposal. For my part, I had no hesitation in telling him where we had taken refuge. He asked if he might be permitted to come that evening and have supper with us.

Since all that remained for me to do was select some undergarments and clothes for Manon, I replied that we could set out at once, if he would be kind enough to stop with me for a moment at various shops along the way. I do not know if he thought I had made this suggestion with a view to exciting his generosity, or if he was simply prompted by some noble impulse; but, having agreed to set off with me then and there, he took me to a number of shops that supplied his own house; he persuaded me to choose several fabrics that were considerably more expensive than I had intended; and when I came to pay for them, absolutely forbade the shopkeepers to accept a sou from me. This gallantry was performed with such good grace, that I felt I might profit from it without dishonour. Together we took the road to Chaillot, where I arrived in a less anxious frame of mind than when I had left.

At this point I intervened, and invited the Chevalier Des Grieux, who had devoted more than an hour to telling us this story, to rest for a while, and keep us company at supper. He could tell from our attentiveness with what pleasure we had listened to him. He promised us that we would find something of even greater interest in the sequel to his story; and when we had finished supper, he continued in the following manner.

END OF THE FIRST PART

SECOND PART

My presence and M. de T...'s assiduities soon dispelled any distress Manon might still have been feeling. Let us forget the past and all its terrors, dearest love, I said to her as we arrived, and start again. We will be happier than ever. Love, after all, is a good teacher; Fortune cannot inflict on us as much pain as it affords us pleasure. The scene at supper was a truly joyous one. With Manon at my side and my hundred pistoles, I was prouder and happier than the richest tax-collector in Paris, for all his heaped-up treasures. We should measure our wealth according to the means we have of satisfying our desires. As for me, not a single one remained to be fulfilled. The future itself caused me little concern. I thought it unlikely that my father would refuse to give me enough to live decently on in Paris, since, being now in my twentieth year, I was approaching the moment when I could, by rights, claim my share of my mother's estate. I did not conceal from Manon the fact that my present wealth did not exceed a hundred pistoles. It was enough to enable us to wait with an easy mind for my fortunes to improve, as it seemed to me they could not fail to do, either through the laws of inheritance or the resources of the gaming-table.

Therefore, for the first few weeks,* I thought only of enjoying the situation I found myself in; and since a powerful sense of honour, as well as a lingering unease concerning the police, made me put off from day to day renewing my connection with the Associates of the Hôtel de T..., I contented myself with gambling in various less disreputable gatherings, where, since fortune favoured me, I was spared the humiliation of having to resort to cheating. I spent part of each afternoon in town, and returned home in time for supper, accompanied as often as not by M. de T..., whose friendship for us grew from day to day. Manon found ways of warding off boredom. She made friends with several young women, whom the fine weather had brought back to our neighbourhood. Walks and other little pastimes appropriate to their sex kept them occupied. A game of cards, whose limits they set in advance, would furnish the means to hire a carriage. They would go together to take the air in the Bois de Boulogne and, when I returned in the evening, I would find Manon waiting for me, happier, more beautiful, and more passionate than ever.

Some clouds, it is true, gathered on the horizon and seemed to threaten the whole edifice of my happiness. But they were briskly dispersed; and Manon, with her playful high spirits, gave such a humorous turn to the denouement of this little drama that I still find sweetness in a memory that evokes so vividly her affectionate heart and her accomplishments of mind and wit.

The valet, who alone comprised our household, took me aside one day and, greatly embarrassed, said he had a secret of particular importance to communicate to me. I urged him to speak freely. After prevaricating for a while, he gave me to understand that a certain foreign nobleman appeared to have taken a great fancy to Mademoiselle Manon. My agitation made itself felt through every vein in my body. And she to him? I interrupted, more brusquely than was wise if I was to receive the further clarification I sought. Frightened by my vehemence, he replied anxiously that his intelligence did not extend that far; but that, having noticed that the stranger came every day without fail to the Bois de Boulogne and, leaving his carriage and wandering alone among the byways, seemed to be looking for an opportunity to observe or encounter Mademoiselle, it had occurred to him to strike up an acquaintance with his servants, so as to discover their master's name; they believed him to be an Italian prince, and themselves suspected him of some amorous entanglement; to which he added, trembling, that he had been unable to gather any further information, because the Prince, emerging from the wood at that moment, had approached him in a friendly fashion and asked his name, after which, apparently guessing that he was in our service, had congratulated him on serving the most enchanting woman in the world.

I waited impatiently for the sequel to this story. He concluded it, however, with nothing more than a few timid apologies, designed solely, I thought, to dispel the agitation I had so unwisely betrayed. I pressed him in vain to continue, and to conceal nothing. He protested that he had told me all he knew and that, the events he had just related having occurred only the previous day, he had not seen the Prince's servants since. I tried to calm his fears, not only with words of praise but with a very respectable reward; and without revealing that I suspected Manon in the least, urged him, in more measured tones, to watch the stranger's every move.

Deep down, his alarm had afflicted me with cruel doubts. For might it not have led him to suppress part of the truth? After further thought, however, I recovered from my fit of agitation, and even regretted having allowed myself this sign of weakness. It was not Manon's fault if others fell in love with her. There was nothing to suggest she knew anything about her conquest; and what sort of life would I lead if I were to persist in so readily allowing jealousy to enter my heart? I went back to Paris the following day, still with no plan beyond that of increasing my fortune yet more rapidly by playing for higher stakes, so that I might be in a position to leave Chaillot the moment I had cause for anxiety. I heard nothing that evening that threatened my peace of mind. The stranger had reappeared in the Bois de Boulogne and, using what had happened on the previous day as a pretext for approaching my confidant again, had spoken to him of his love for Manon, although not in terms that implied any understanding with her. He had questioned him minutely on a thousand details. Finally he had tried to win him over by promising a handsome reward; and, taking out a letter he was carrying in his pocket, had vainly offered him several louis d'or if he would deliver it to his mistress.

Two days passed without further incident. The third was more stormy. I learned, returning quite late from town, that during her walk that day Manon had distanced herself for a moment from her companions; and that the stranger, who was following not far behind, had approached her in response to a signal she gave him, whereupon she had handed him a letter, which he received with transports of joy. The only expression of this he had time to give, however, was an impassioned kiss he bestowed upon the paper on which her words were written, for she had immediately slipped away again; but for the rest of the day she had seemed to be in a mood of extraordinary gaiety; nor had her high spirits abandoned her when she returned home. I trembled, needless to say, at every word. Are you quite sure your eyes have not deceived you? I asked my valet gravely. He called on Heaven itself to bear witness to his good faith. I do not know to what lengths my anguished heart might not have driven me, if Manon, hearing me arrive, had not come to find me, full of complaint and impatience at my long-delayed return. She did not wait for me to reply before showering me with caresses; and when she found herself alone with me, reproached me bitterly for the habit I had got into of coming home so late. Feeling free to continue because of my silence, she said that it was three weeks at least since I had spent an entire day with her; that she could not bear such long absences, but must ask me to devote at least a day to her from time to time; and that she wanted me to be with her the following day from morning till night. I will be there, never fear, I replied somewhat brusquely. She paid no attention to my ill-humour; but, borne along by her own gaiety, which struck me as unusually lively, painted a thousand amusing pictures of the way in which she had spent the day. What a strange girl she is! I said to myself. And after such a prelude, what must I expect? I was reminded of the circumstances of our first separation. And yet I thought I discerned in her, beneath all the gaiety and the extravagant caresses, a note of truth that was entirely in accord with these appearances.

During supper I had no difficulty in attributing the melancholy I could not quite suppress to a loss I complained of having made at cards. I regarded it as greatly to my advantage that the idea of my not leaving Chaillot next day should have come from her. It gave me time to consider what I should do. The fact that I would be with her the whole day relieved me of all sorts of fears I would otherwise have had; and although I had seen nothing so far that obliged me to divulge the discoveries I had made, I had already decided to transfer my household to town the day after that, and to settle in a neighbourhood where I would have no princes to contend with. This decision procured me a more peaceful night; but it did nothing to ease the dread and anguish I felt at the prospect of a new infidelity.

When I awoke next morning, Manon announced that, even though I was to spend the whole day in our apartment, she saw no reason why my appearance should be neglected, and that she would like to dress my hair with her own hands. I had a handsome head of hair. She had several times amused herself arranging it, but today devoted more care to it than she had ever done before. I was obliged, in order to please her, to sit down at her dressing-table, and to suffer all the little adjustments she invented for my adornment. She often, as she worked, made me turn my face towards her and, resting her hands on my shoulders, contemplated me with an avid curiosity. Then, expressing her satisfaction with a kiss or two, she would return me to my original position in order to continue her work. This little game kept us occupied until dinnertime. The pleasure she took in it seemed to me so natural, and her gaiety so unaffected, that, unable to reconcile such consistency in appearances with the black betrayal I believed she was contemplating, I was several times tempted to open my heart to her and relieve myself of a burden that was beginning to weigh heavily on me. But I persuaded myself, from one moment to the next, that she herself would broach the subject, and I savoured in advance the delicious triumph it would bring me.

We returned to her room. She again began arranging my hair and, anxious to please her, I was preparing to indulge her every whim, when the footman came to announce that the Prince de... was asking to see her. The name itself was enough to send me into transports of rage. What's this? I cried, pushing her away. Who? Which prince? She did not reply. Show him up, she said coldly to the footman; then, turning towards me, continued bewitchingly: Dearest love, whom I adore, I beg of you a moment of indulgence, a single moment, only one. Only do as I ask, and I will love you a thousand times more. I will be grateful to you my whole life long.

I was speechless with indignation and surprise. She resumed her earnest entreaties; I, meanwhile, tried to find expressions of contempt with which to reject them; at last, hearing the door of the anteroom open, she seized with one hand the hair that was floating free on my shoulders, and took hold of her toilet mirror with the other; summoning all her strength, she dragged me in this state to her door, then pushing it open with her knee, offered the stranger— whom the noise seemed to have arrested in the middle of the room— a spectacle that must have caused him no small astonishment. I saw a man who was very well dressed, but not very good looking. Although the situation into which he had been thrust was awkward, he nevertheless made a deep bow. Manon did not give him time to open his mouth. She held out her mirror to him: Look into this glass Monsieur, she said, examine yourself carefully, then do me justice. You ask me to love you. Here is the man I love, the man I have vowed to love my whole life long. Make the comparison yourself. If you think you can vie with him for my heart, pray tell me on what grounds? For I assure you that, in the eyes of your very humble

Manon confounds the Italian prince (Pasquier)

consider myself under an obligation to avert the effects of the evil I have caused.

I thanked M. de T... for his kindness in rendering me so important a service, and admitted, in a display of trust equal to his own, that Manon's character was indeed as G... M... imagined it to be; that is, that the very name of poverty was intolerable to her. However, I continued, so long as it is only a question of more or less, I do not think she will abandon me for someone else. I am already in a position to let her lack for nothing; and I am confident that my fortune will increase from day to day. Only one thing troubles me, I added, which is that G... M... might use his knowledge of our whereabouts to do us some disservice. M. de T... assured me I need have no fears on that score; that G... M... was capable of amorous folly, but not of baseness; and that if he should stoop to some perfidy, he who now stood before me would be the first to punish him, and thereby make amends for his misfortune in having occasioned it. I am much obliged to you for these sentiments, I replied, but the damage would already be done, and the remedy very uncertain. Prevention is our wisest course; we must leave Chaillot, and find somewhere else to live. You are quite right, M. de T... replied, but you will have difficulty in managing this as quickly as you would need, for G... M... could be here by midday; he told me so himself yesterday, which is what prompted me to come this morning and warn you of his intentions. He might arrive at any moment.

Alerted to the urgency of this matter, I began to view it in a more serious light. Clearly I could not avoid G... M...'s visit, any more than I could prevent him from declaring himself to Manon. Therefore I decided to warn her of my new rival's intentions myself. I imagined that, knowing me to be informed of the propositions he was putting to her, and receiving them before my very eyes, she would be resolute enough to reject them. I put this to M. de T..., who responded by saying that it was a very delicate matter. So it is, I said, but whatever reasons anyone could have for being certain of a mistress, I have for relying on the affection of mine. Only a truly magnificent offer could tempt her, for as I have already told you, she has no interest in money for its own sake. She loves ease and comfort, but she loves me too; and given the present state of my affairs, I hardly think she will choose the son of a man who had her shut up in the Hôpital in preference to me. In short, I persisted with my plan,

servant, all the princes in Italy are not worth a single one of these hairs I have in my hand.

During this crazy speech, which was clearly premeditated, I made repeated but unavailing attempts to disengage myself; and, taking pity on a person of some standing, felt inclined to make amends for the minor outrage he had suffered by my own politeness. But he recovered his composure easily enough, and his reply, which I found somewhat coarse, was enough to dispel any such impulse. Mademoiselle, Mademoiselle, he said with a forced smile, I have indeed had my eyes opened, and I find you much less of a novice than I had supposed. Whereupon he withdrew, without a glance in her direction, but adding quietly that French women were clearly no better than Italian. I was not tempted, under the circumstances, to persuade him to take a more favourable view of the fair sex.

Manon let go of my hair, threw herself into an armchair, and burst into long and loud peals of laughter. I did not try to hide the fact that I was touched to the depths of my heart by a sacrifice I could attribute only to love. Nevertheless, the joke seemed to me excessive. I reproached her for this. She told me that my rival, having importuned her on several occasions in the Bois de Boulogne, intimating by gestures and grimaces his feelings for her, had at length resorted to an open declaration, embellished with his name and his titles, in a letter he persuaded the coachman who drove her and her friends to deliver; he had promised her a dazzling fortune and eternal adoration beyond the mountains; she had returned to Chaillot determined to communicate this adventure to me but, imagining we could derive some amusement from it, had been unable to resist indulging this whim; she had written the Prince an encouraging reply, giving him permission to visit her at home, and had allowed herself the added pleasure of including me in her plan, without my having the least suspicion of this. I did not breathe a word about the intelligence that had come to me by a different route, but, intoxicated with love, approved of everything she had done.

I have observed, throughout my life, that Heaven has always chosen the moment when my fortunes seemed at their most secure to inflict its cruellest punishments on me. Assured of M. de T...'s friendship and Manon's love, I believed myself so fortunate that no one could have persuaded me I had any new misfortune to fear. Nevertheless, one so dreadful was being prepared that it reduced me

to the state you saw me in at Pacy and, by degrees, to such lamentable extremities you will hardly believe my account of them to be
true.

One day, when M. de T... had joined us for supper, we heard the
sound of a carriage stopping outside the door of the inn. Out of
curiosity, we enquired who it could be that was arriving at so late an
hour. It was, we were informed, the younger G... M..., the son, in other
words, of our bitterest enemy, of the old debauchee who had had me
put in Saint-Lazare and Manon in the Hôpital. The very mention of
this name brought the blood to my face. Heaven itself has surely sent
him here, I said to M. de T..., so that I might punish him for his
father's base cowardice. He will not escape me, not at least until we
have measured swords. M. de T..., who knew him, and was indeed one
of his closest friends, did his best to persuade me to view him in a
different light. He assured me that he was a truly amiable young
man, and so incapable of having had any part in his father's mis-
deeds, that I would not be in his company for more than a minute
before conceiving a sincere respect for him and a desire to obtain his
in return. After urging a thousand other things in his favour, he
asked if I would agree to his being invited to sit with us and share
what remained of our supper. Anticipating my objection, that to
reveal where Manon was living to the son of our enemy would be to
expose her to danger, he protested on his word of honour that, once
he knew us, we would have no more zealous defender. After such an
assurance, I made no further difficulties. Before bringing him to
meet us, M. de T... spent a little while informing him who we were.
His demeanour as he entered the room predisposed us in his favour.
He embraced me. We sat down. He admired Manon, me, everything that belonged to us, and ate with an appetite that did honour
to our supper. Once the table had been cleared, the conversation
grew more serious. He lowered his eyes when he spoke of the
excesses his father had perpetrated against us. He offered us his
most abject apologies. However, I would prefer not to prolong
these, he said, so as not to reawaken a memory that causes me so
much shame. Sincere though these apologies doubtless were to
begin with, they very soon became even more so, for he had not
been half an hour in our company before I noticed the effect
Manon's charms were beginning to have on him. His glance and
his manner grew gradually softer. He betrayed nothing of this in his

speech; but although it was not jealousy that had opened my eyes, I
had too much experience of love not to recognize for what it was
anything that came from that source. He stayed with us until after
nightfall, and took his leave only after congratulating himself on
having made our acquaintance, and asking permission to visit us
again from time to time with renewed offers of support. He left the
next morning with M. de T..., to whom he had offered a place in his
carriage.

I was not, as I have said, disposed to be jealous. I was readier than
ever to believe Manon's vows. This bewitching creature was so absolutely mistress of my soul, that I entertained not the slightest feeling
for her that was not one of love and esteem. Far from blaming her for
having taken young G... M...'s fancy, I was delighted with the effect of
her charms on him, and congratulated myself on being loved by a
girl with whom the whole world fell in love. Nor did I think it
appropriate to share my suspicions with her. Besides, we were busy
during the next few days with visits from her dressmaker, and with
debating whether we could go to the theatre without the fear of
being recognized. M. de T... came to see us again before the end of the
week. We consulted him on the matter. He saw that, in order to
please Manon, he had to approve. We decided to go with him that
very evening.

However, we could not carry out this plan, for reasons which he
explained after drawing me, as soon as he could, to one side. Since
we last met, he said, I have found myself in a most awkward situation, one consequence of which is my visit to you today. G... M... is in
love with your mistress, and has confided his secret in me. I am his
intimate friend, therefore ready to do him service in any way I can;
but I am no less yours. I thought his intentions unworthy, and said
so. I would have kept his secret, if he had been intending to try only
the usual methods of winning her over; but he is fully informed of
her character. He has found out, I do not know from where, that she
is fond of luxury and pleasure; and since he has considerable wealth
at his disposal, he assured me that he means to begin by tempting
her, not only with a substantial gift, but with the offer of an allowance of ten thousand livres. Other things being equal, I might have
found it much harder to betray him; but justice, as well as friendship,
pleads in your favour; the more so since I am myself the inadvertent
cause of his passion, having introduced him to you, and therefore

and, taking Manon to one side, told her frankly everything I had just learned.

She thanked me for my good opinion of her, and promised to respond to G... M...'s offers in such a way as to cure him of the desire ever to repeat them. No, I told her, it would be better not to offend him by being too brusque. He could harm us, if he chose. Then I laughed, adding, but no one knows better than you, wicked girl that you are, how to be rid of a disagreeable or inconvenient lover. After musing for a moment she cried out: I have just thought of an adorable scheme, and am immensely proud of inventing it. G... M... is the son of our bitterest enemy; we must take revenge on the father, and not through his son but through his purse. I will listen to him, accept his presents, and dupe him. It's an amusing idea, I said, but have you forgotten, my poor child, that the last time we took that route it led straight to the door of the Hôpital? However forcibly I pointed out the perils of this enterprise, her only reply was that we should be careful how we went about it. Show me a lover who does not enter blindly into all the caprices of an adored mistress, and I will concede that I was wrong to give in so easily to mine. The decision was taken to make a fool of G... M..., and by a bizarre twist of fate, it was he who made one of me.

At about eleven o'clock we saw his carriage arrive. He greeted us with elaborate apologies for the liberty he was permitting himself in coming to dine with us. He was not surprised to see M. de T..., who had promised the previous day to be there too, and had invented some business in order to avoid travelling in the same carriage with him. Although there was not a single one of us who did not have treachery in his heart, we sat down at table with a great air of friendship and trust. G... M... had no difficulty in finding an opportunity to declare himself to Manon. He cannot have found me a hindrance, for I deliberately absented myself for several minutes. Nor did it seem to me, on my return, that he had been driven to despair by any excessive severity. On the contrary, he was in the greatest good humour. I pretended to be so too: underneath it all, he was laughing at my naivety and I at his. For the rest of the afternoon each afforded the other a highly diverting spectacle. Before he left I procured him another moment of private conversation with Manon; so that he had as much reason to congratulate himself on my complaisance as on my hospitality.

As soon as he had climbed into the carriage beside M. de T...,
Manon ran to me with open arms and, bursting into peals of laughter, embraced me. She repeated, word for word, everything he had
said, everything he had promised her. It all came down to the same
thing in the end: that he adored her. He had offered to share with her
the forty thousand livres of annual income he already enjoyed, not to
mention what he might expect to receive on the death of his father.
She was to be mistress of his heart and fortune; and, as a token of his
good faith, he was ready to make her an immediate present of a
carriage, a furnished house in town, a maidservant, three footmen,
and a cook. Here is a son, I said to her, whose generosity is of quite a
different order from that of his father. But seriously, I added, doesn't
this offer tempt you? Me? she replied, adapting to the occasion some
lines from Racine:*

> Me? You suspect me of this base treachery?
> That I would willingly gaze on that odious face
> That ever recalls the Hôpital and my own disgrace?

No indeed, I replied, continuing the parody:

> I should hardly think, Madame, that the grim Hôpital
> Would help Love engrave that same face on your soul.

But a furnished house in town, complete with a carriage and three
footmen, is a powerful inducement; while Love offers few that are so
seductive. She protested that her heart would always be mine, and
that no features but my own would ever be engraved there. The
promises he has made me, she said, are a spur to vengeance rather
than a dart from Love's bow. I asked if she had any thought of
accepting the house and the carriage. She replied that she had
designs only on his money. The difficulty was in knowing how to
obtain the one without the other. We decided to wait until G... M... had
fully explained his plan to her in writing. The promised letter
arrived next day, delivered by a footman out of livery, who very
artfully procured himself a private interview with her. She asked him
to wait for her reply, and came at once with the letter to find me. We
opened it together. Along with the customary declarations of love, it
contained the details of what my rival was promising her. He set no
limits on what he was prepared to spend. He promised to give her
ten thousand francs, which would be hers the moment she took

possession of the furnished house, and to make good any subsequent diminution of this sum so that it would always be available to her in ready money. The inaugural day was not to be put off for long. He asked for only two days in which to get everything ready, and indicated the name of the street and house where he promised to be waiting for her on the afternoon of the second, if she thought she could slip away from me unnoticed. This was the only point on which he asked for reassurance; he seemed confident of all the rest; but he added that, if she foresaw any difficulty in escaping from me, he would find a way to facilitate her flight.

G... M... was wilier than his father; he wanted to be certain of his prey before parting with his money. We deliberated as to the course of action Manon should take. I again tried to persuade her to abandon the whole enterprise; I presented it to her in all its dangers. Nothing could shake her resolution.

She wrote a brief reply to G... M...'s letter, assuring him she would have no difficulty in coming to Paris on the appointed day, and that he might expect her with confidence. We then agreed that I would leave at once, and find new lodgings in some village on the other side of Paris, taking with me our small collection of belongings; on the following afternoon—on the day, that is, of her rendezvous—she would arrive in Paris in good time; as soon as she received the gifts he had promised her, she would suggest they go to the theatre; she would take with her as much of the money as she could carry, and entrust the rest to my valet, who she suggested should accompany her. This was the same man who had rescued her from the Hôpital, and he was extremely attached to us. I was to position myself at the entrance to the Rue Saint-André-des-Arcs in a hired coach, from where, at about seven o'clock, I would make my way, under cover of darkness, to the door of the theatre. Manon promised she would invent some excuse to leave her box for a moment, and would use it to come down and find me. The rest would be easy. In less than no time we would have rejoined our coach, left Paris by the Faubourg Saint-Antoine, and be well on our way to our new lodgings.

This plan, reckless though it was, seemed to us quite well conceived. But when it came down to it, it was nothing short of utter folly to imagine that, even if we had carried it out with complete success, we would have been able to escape its consequences. Nevertheless, we laid ourselves open, with the boldest self-confidence, to whatever might ensue. Manon left with Marcel, for this was our valet's name. It grieved me to see her go. Do not deceive me, Manon, I said as I embraced her; promise that you will be faithful. She reproached me tenderly for my lack of trust, and renewed every vow she had ever made me.

Her intention had been to arrive in Paris at about three o'clock. I left a little later, and spent the rest of the afternoon fretting in the Café de Féré on the Pont Saint-Michel. I remained there until nightfall, at which point I left, took a carriage, and asked it to wait, as we had agreed, at the entrance to the Rue Saint-André-des-Arcs, from where I continued on foot to the door of the theatre. I was surprised not to see Marcel, who was supposed to be meeting me there. I waited patiently for an hour, mingling with a crowd of footmen and keeping a watchful eye on all the passers-by. At last, seven o'clock having struck without my having seen anything that was consistent with our plan, I bought a ticket for the pit, from where I hoped to be able to see Manon and G... M... in one of the boxes. There was no sign of either of them. I returned to the door, where, beside myself with impatience and anxiety, I waited for another quarter of an hour. When no one appeared I returned to my carriage, even though I had not the least idea as to what I should do next. On seeing me approach, the coachman came forward to meet me, telling me, in tones of mystery, that a pretty young lady had been waiting for me in the carriage for the past hour; she had asked for me in terms that had enabled him to identify me easily, and having learned I was to return soon, had said she did not mind waiting. I at once imagined it must be Manon. I came nearer; but saw a pretty little face that was not hers. It was a perfect stranger, who first asked if she had the honour to address the Chevalier Des Grieux. I said that that was my name. I have a letter for you, she went on, which will explain the reason for my presence here, and to what I owe the advantage of knowing your name. I asked her to allow me a moment to read it in some nearby tavern. She preferred to come with me, and advised me to request a private room. Who is the letter from? I enquired as we went upstairs; she suggested I read it for myself.

I recognized Manon's hand at once. This, more or less, is the message she wanted to convey to me: G... M... had received her with an attentiveness and a magnificence beyond anything she could have imagined. He had showered her with gifts. He had promised her a future fit for a queen. Nevertheless, she assured me that, even in the midst of all this splendour, she had not forgotten me; but having been unable to persuade G... M... to take her to the theatre that evening, she was postponing the pleasure of seeing me until another day, and, in order to console me a little for the pain she realized this news might cause me, she had managed to procure me one of the prettiest girls in Paris, who was herself to be the bearer of this note. *Signed*, your faithful lover, MANON LESCAUT.

There was something so insulting and so cruel about this letter that, after remaining for a while torn between anger and grief, I resolved to try and forget my false and ungrateful mistress forever. I glanced at the girl beside me; she was extremely pretty. If only she could have been so irresistible as to make me false and faithless in my turn! But I did not find in her those fine eyes filled with languor, that divine form, that complexion blended from Love's fairest tints—in a word, that inexhaustible store of enchantments that nature had lavished on the perfidious Manon. No, no, I said, turning away from her, the faithless creature who asked you to come knew very well she was sending you on a fruitless errand. Go back to her; tell her from me to rejoice in her crime, and to rejoice in it, if she can, without remorse. Tell her I abandon her for ever, and that I renounce, at the same time, all other women too, who could never be as fair, but are doubtless as base and deceitful as she. I was on the point of descending the stairs, of departing and giving up forever any pretensions to Manon; indeed, since the mortal jealousy that had rent my heart had now disguised itself as a bleak and sombre calm, I believed myself close to being cured, and the more so since I found myself free of those violent transports that had tormented me on previous such occasions. But I was, alas, as much deceived by love as I believed myself to be by G... M... and Manon.

The girl who had brought me the letter, seeing me about to descend the stairs, asked what message she should take back to M. de G... M... and the lady who was with him. I had gone back into the room at this question; when suddenly, with a rapidity that would be inconceivable to anyone who has never known violent passion, I found myself transported from my supposed tranquillity into a terrible frenzy of rage. Go and tell that scoundrel G... M... and his perfidious mistress of the despair your accursed letter has plunged me into; but tell them too that they won't be laughing for long, and that I mean to stab both of them with my own hand. I threw myself into a chair. My hat fell one way, my stick the other. Two streams of bitter tears coursed down my cheeks. The fit of rage I had just suffered became at once one of profound grief. I groaned, I sighed, I wept as if I would never stop. Come closer, my child, I cried, turning to the girl, come closer; for have they not sent you to console me? Tell me then, have you consolations to offer one consumed by rage and despair, who intends to die by his own hand, after putting to death two traitors who do not deserve to live? That's right, come closer, I continued, seeing her venture a few timid and uncertain steps towards me. Come and dry my tears, come and restore peace to my heart, come and tell me you adore me, so that I may get used to being loved by someone other than my faithless mistress. You are pretty; perhaps in time I will learn to love you in return. The poor child, who could not have been more than sixteen or seventeen years old, and who seemed less brazen than the rest of her profession, was filled with amazement at so strange a scene. She came to me nevertheless, and even tried a few tentative caresses. I repulsed her immediately, pushing her away with both hands. What do you want of me? I cried. You are a woman, one of that sex I loathe and abhor. The very sweetness of your face threatens me with some new treachery. Be off with you at once, and leave me here alone. She curtsied and, without daring to reply, turned to leave. I cried out to her to stop. But at least tell me, I resumed, why, how, and for what purpose you were sent here? How did you discover my name and where to find me?

She told me she had known M. de G... M... for a long time, that he had sent for her at five o'clock that afternoon, and that she had followed his footman to a big house, where she found him playing piquet with a pretty lady; they asked her to take charge of the letter she had just delivered to me, and told her she would find me in a carriage at the end of the Rue Saint-André. I asked her if they had said anything else. She replied, blushing, that they led her to hope I might ask her to stay and keep me company. You were deceived, my poor child, I said to her, you were sadly deceived. You are a woman, you need a man; but you need one possessed of wealth and good fortune, and you will not find him here. You would do better to go back to M. de G... M... He has everything that is needed to be loved by beautiful women; he has fine furnished houses and carriages to give.

As for me, who can offer only love and constancy, women despise my poverty and make fun of my naivety.

I added a thousand other such complaints, now gloomy, now violent, according as to which of the passions that agitated me was dominant or in retreat. At length, however, exhausted with tormenting me, my transports abated sufficiently to leave room for some reflection. I compared this latest calamity with others of the same sort I had already suffered, and concluded that I had no more reason to despair now than on those previous occasions. I knew Manon; why distress myself so much over a misfortune I should have foreseen? Why not devote myself instead to seeking some remedy? There was still time. I ought at least to spare no effort, if, that is, I did not want to have cause later on to reproach myself that I had, through negligence, contributed to my own woes. I set to work immediately considering all the ways and means that seemed to offer some prospect of hope.

To attempt to wrest her from G... M...'s hands by force would be an act of desperation, very likely to ruin me, and without the least prospect of success. I felt certain, however, that the briefest conversation with her, if only I could procure it, would infallibly gain me some ground in her heart. I knew so well all its susceptibilities! I was so sure she loved me! Even the bizarre notion of sending a pretty girl to console me, I would have wagered came from her, born out of her pity for my sufferings. I decided to devote all my ingenuity to obtaining an interview with her; and, having considered the various ways of achieving this one after the other, finally settled on the following. M. de T... had begun to do me service in too affectionate a way to leave me in doubt as to his sincerity and zeal. I decided to go to him immediately and ask if he could arrange to have G... M... called away from home, on the pretext of important business he must attend to at once. Half an hour was all I would need to talk to Manon. My plan was to gain admittance to her room, which I thought I could easily do if G... M... were absent. Calmer for having reached this decision, I paid the young girl, who was still with me, liberally, and to forestall any inclination she might have felt towards returning to those who had sent her, took her address and allowed her to hope I might come there later and spend the night. I got back into my carriage and drove at full speed to M. de T...'s house. I was fortunate enough to find him at home. All the way there I had feared he might not be. A few words

were enough to acquaint him with my unhappy situation, and the
service I had come to ask of him. He was so astonished to hear that
G... M... had managed to entice Manon away that, not knowing the
part I had myself played in this misfortune, he generously offered to
gather his friends together and, sword in hand, to set my mistress
free. I managed to persuade him that the scandal this would cause
could well be fatal to Manon and me. Let us not shed blood, I said,
until extreme measures are called for. The plan I have in mind is
more moderate but will, I hope, be no less successful. He promised
he would do everything I asked of him without exception; and when
I again assured him that all I wanted him to do was to tell G... M... he
wished to speak to him, and to keep him occupied for an hour or so,
he declared his readiness to help and set out with me at once.

We discussed what pretext he could use that would keep G... M...
away from home for so long. I suggested he send him a short note,
supposedly written in some tavern, asking him to meet him there
immediately in connection with an affair of such importance it
would admit no delay. I will watch for his departure, I added, then
gain admittance to the house, which should not be too difficult since
I am known there only to Manon and to Marcel, my valet. As for
you, who will be with G... M... during this time, you can tell him that
the important affair you wanted to speak to him about concerns
money; that you lost yours playing cards, and went on to play for
much higher stakes, with only your word of honour as guarantee,
and with the same unfortunate result. It will take some time for
G... M... and you to go to wherever he keeps his safe-box, and this
will give me the chance I need to carry out my plan.

M. de T... followed this stratagem point by point. I left him in a
tavern finishing off his letter. I took up my position a few steps away
from Manon's house. I saw the courier arrive with M. de T...'s message, and G... M... leave on foot a moment later, followed by a servant.
I gave him time to get well away from the street, then approached
my faithless mistress's door. Angry though I was, I knocked with as
much respect as if I were entering a temple. Fortunately it was
Marcel who opened the door. I gestured to him to be silent.
Although I had no reason to fear the other servants, I quietly asked if
he could take me to Manon's room without my being seen. He said
this would be easy enough, provided we made no noise as we went up
the stairs. Quickly then, I said, and while I am there, try to prevent

anyone else from using the staircase. I reached her private apartment unhindered.

I found Manon reading. Now truly I had occasion to marvel at the character of this strange girl. Far from appearing frightened or apprehensive when, glancing up, she saw me, she showed only those signs of mild surprise one inevitably betrays on seeing someone one believes to be far away. Ah, it's you, my love! she said coming to embrace me with her usual tenderness. Good heavens! How bold you are! Who would have expected to see you here today? I disengaged myself from her embrace and, far from responding to her caresses, repulsed her with disdain, taking two or three steps backwards in order to distance myself from her. This response could only disconcert her. She did not move but, glancing at me, turned pale. I was, if the truth were told, so utterly enchanted at seeing her again that, in spite of having so much just cause to reproach her, I hardly had the strength to open my mouth to scold her. My heart was still bleeding, nevertheless, from the cruel injury she had done me. Hoping to rekindle my just resentment, I recalled its every detail; and I tried to disguise the love that shone from my eyes as some sterner emotion. As I remained silent for some time, and she saw the agitation I was in, I noticed she began to tremble, as if from fear.

This sight was more than I could bear. Ah Manon! I said to her tenderly, false and faithless Manon! With so much to complain of, where shall I begin? I see you pale and trembling, and am still so susceptible to your least distress, that I am afraid lest my reproaches cause you too much grief. But Manon, I must tell you that the pain of your betrayal has pierced me to the heart. You should not afflict a lover so, unless you mean to kill him. This is the third time, Manon—I have counted each one: there are things one cannot forget. You must decide this very moment what course you mean to take, for this cruelty is more than my sad heart can bear. I feel it almost failing me, and ready to break in grief. I cannot go on, I added, sinking into a chair; I scarcely have strength to speak or stand.

She did not reply, but as soon as I was seated fell to her knees and, laying her head in my lap, buried her face in my hands. The next moment I felt them grow wet with her tears. Gods above! What violent emotions raged in my breast! Ah Manon, Manon, I continued sighing, it is too late to weep for me now, when you have already caused my death. You are feigning a sorrow you cannot feel.

The greatest of your ills, without a doubt, is my very presence, which has always come between you and your pleasures. Open your eyes, see me for what I am; one does not weep such tender tears for a poor wretch already betrayed and now cruelly abandoned. Without changing her position she began kissing my hands. Inconstant Manon, I went on once more, ungrateful and false-hearted girl, where are they now, your promises and vows? Cruel and fickle lover, what have you done with that love that even today you swore was mine? And you, just Heavens, I added, will you suffer a perfidious mistress, false to the vows she called on you to witness, to mock you thus? Is perjury to be rewarded, while constancy and fidelity bring nothing but desertion and despair?

These words were accompanied by such bitter reflections that, in spite of myself, I let fall a few tears. Manon, hearing the change in my voice, perceived this. At last she broke her silence. I must indeed be guilty, she said sadly, since I am the cause of so much grief and anguish. But may Heaven punish me if I believed I was, or had any thought of being so! This speech seemed to me so destitute of sense and sincerity that I could not suppress a further fit of rage. What fearful hypocrisy! I cried. It is clearer than ever you are nothing but a deceiving slut. At last I know your wretched character for what it is. Farewell, worthless creature, I continued rising to my feet; I would rather die a thousand deaths than have anything more to do with you. May Heaven punish me in turn, if I ever show the least regard for you again! Stay with your new lover, love him, detest me, forsake honour, renounce reason; it is all one to me; I no longer care.

So terrified was she by this outburst that, still kneeling by the chair I had just left, she watched me, trembling and scarcely daring to breathe. I took a few more steps in the direction of the door, turning my head as I did so and keeping my eyes fixed on her. But I would have had to have lost every human feeling to harden my heart against so many charms. I was so little possessed of such cruel resolution that, finding myself carried all at once to the opposite extreme, I turned, or rather flung myself, without thinking what I was doing, towards her. I took her in my arms, I kissed her tenderly a thousand times. I begged forgiveness for my anger. I confessed I was a brute and did not deserve the happiness of being loved by a girl like her. I made her sit down and, kneeling in my turn, implored her not to move until she had heard me out. And there, in a few words, I included every respectful and tender protestation a submissive and impassioned lover can conceive in the apology I made her. I begged her to be merciful, and say she forgave me. Leaning forward, and putting her arms about my neck, she replied that it was she who was in need of indulgence, if she was to make me forget the grief she had caused me, and that she was beginning to fear, with reason, that I was not going to like what she had to say in her own defence. Me! I broke in at once; Ah! Far be it from me to ask you to defend yourself. I approve of everything you have done. It is not for me to require reasons for your conduct, being only too happy, only too blessed, so long as my beloved Manon does not deprive me of her heart's affection. But tell me, Manon, I continued, reflecting on the uncertainty of my fate, you who are all-powerful, who decide at your pleasure my sorrows and my joys, will you permit me, satisfied as you must now be by the signs I have given of humiliation and repentance, to speak of my suffering and distress? Am I to learn from you what is to become of me today, and whether you are irrevocably resolved on signing my death-warrant by spending the night with my rival?

She pondered her reply for some time. At last, resuming an air of tranquillity, she broke her silence: My dear Chevalier, she said, if only you had explained yourself at first as clearly as you have just done now, you would have spared yourself a great deal of upset, and me a most painful scene. Since your distress is the result of jealousy alone, I could have cured it straight away by offering to follow you to the ends of the earth. But I assumed it was the letter I wrote to you, with G... M... looking on, and the girl we sent you that were causing your vexation. I thought you might suppose that the letter was intended to make fun of you; and that the girl, who you no doubt imagined had come from me, was a declaration of my intention to abandon you. It was this thought that threw me into consternation just now; for, however innocent I knew myself to be, when I thought about it I could see that appearances were not in my favour. However, she continued, I prefer you to be my judge, after I have explained to you the truth of the matter.

She told me everything that had happened since she had found G... M... waiting for her in that very house. He had received her as though she truly were the first princess on earth. He had taken her round her new apartments, all of them furnished with admirable refinement and taste. He had counted out for her, in his study, the ten thousand livres he had promised, to which he added some jewellery, including the pearl necklace and bracelets she had already been given by his father. From there he led her into a drawing-room she had not seen before, where she found an exquisite little meal set out. She was served by new domestics he had just engaged for her, ordering them to regard her from now on as their mistress; finally, he had shown her the carriage, the horses, and all his other presents to her; after which he had suggested a game of cards, while they waited for supper. I freely admit, she continued, that all this magnificence impressed me greatly. I reflected, too, that it would be a pity to content myself with simply running off with the ten thousand francs, thus depriving us at a stroke of so many assets, that here was a ready-made fortune for both of us, and that we could live very agreeably at G... M...'s expense. Instead of suggesting we go to the theatre, I decided to sound out his opinion of you, so as to ascertain what opportunities we would have of seeing one another, always assuming that we carry out my plan. I found his character very amenable. He asked me what I thought of you, and whether I had any regrets at leaving you. I said you were so truly amiable, and had always dealt with me so honourably, that it was hardly natural I should hate you. He conceded that you had merit, and that he had always felt disposed to seek your friendship. He asked how I thought you would take the news of my departure, especially when you discovered I was now under his protection. I replied that our love had begun so long ago that there had been time for it to cool a little; that you were not, besides, in the easiest of circumstances, and perhaps would not regard my loss as so very great a misfortune, since it would relieve you of a heavy burden. I added that, being perfectly certain you would receive the news with composure, I had had no hesitation in telling you I was coming to Paris on a number of errands; that you had agreed to this and that, since you were coming yourself, had not seemed unduly anxious when I left you. If I thought, he said, that he was disposed to be on good terms with me, I would be the first to offer him my kind offices and attentions. I assured him that, knowing your character as I did, I did not doubt you would respond appropriately; especially, I told him, if he could be useful to you in your affairs, which had been in disarray ever since you had fallen out with your family. He interrupted me in order to protest again that he would render you every service in his power;

and that if you were ready to embark on a new love affair he would procure you a pretty mistress, whom he had left in order to attach himself to me. I applauded this idea, she added, the more completely to allay his suspicions; at the same time, more and more persuaded of the advantages of my project, I was eager to find some way of explaining it to you, for fear you would be excessively alarmed when I failed to keep our rendezvous. It was with this end in view that I suggested we send this new mistress to you that very evening; I was obliged to resort to some such ruse, as there was no prospect of him allowing me a moment to myself. He laughed at my proposal. He called his footman and, having asked if he thought it would take him long to track down his former mistress, sent him off this way and that to look for her. He assumed she would have to go to Chaillot to find you, but I told him that when I left you I had promised to meet you at the theatre; or, if for some reason I couldn't be there, that you had agreed to wait for me in a carriage at the end of the Rue Saint-André; consequently, it would be better to send your new lover there, so that you wouldn't be left alone fretting all night long. I also told him it was only fair I should send a few words informing you of this new arrangement, which otherwise you would find it difficult to understand. He agreed, but I was obliged to write while he looked on, so that I took the greatest care not to express myself too openly in my letter. That, added Manon, is exactly how things happened. I have hidden nothing from you as regards either my conduct or my intentions. The young girl arrived, I found her pretty; and since I did not doubt that my absence would cause you pain, I was sincere in hoping she might help to distract you for a while; for the fidelity I desire from you is that of the heart. I would have been delighted if I could have sent you Marcel; but I could not find a moment to explain to him what I wanted you to know. She concluded her story by describing the dilemma in which G... M... found himself on receiving M. de T...'s note. He hesitated as to whether he should leave me, she said, and he assured me he would not be gone for long. This is why your presence here fills me with anxiety, and why I seemed so surprised when you appeared.

I listened to this speech with a good deal of patience. It contained, to be sure, a number of things that were cruel and mortifying from my point of view, for so clearly did she intend an infidelity that she had not even tried to conceal it from me. She could not have been hoping that G... M... would leave her alone all night long, as though she were a vestal virgin. It was therefore with him that she was proposing to spend it. What a confession for a lover to have to hear! Nevertheless I regarded myself as partly responsible for this lapse, since not only had I acquainted her in the first place with G... M...'s feelings for her, but I had acquiesced, obligingly and blindly, in her plan for this whole rash venture. Besides which, thanks to some natural turn and bent of mind that is peculiar to me, I was touched by the artlessness of her account, and by the good-hearted and open way in which she had related even those circumstances that must offend me most. She sins, but without malice, I said to myself. She is frivolous and imprudent, but she is straightforward and sincere. Besides which, love alone was enough to make me close my eyes to all her faults. I was too filled with fond hopes of snatching her away from my rival that very evening. I said to her, nonetheless: And the night? With whom would you have spent it? This question, and the evident sorrow with which I asked it, embarrassed her. Her only reply was a few faltering *if*s and *but*s. I took pity on her discomfort and, interrupting her, said frankly that I expected her to follow me that very moment. Willingly, she said; but don't you, then, approve of my plan? Ah! Isn't it enough, I rejoined, that I approve of everything you have done up till now? What? She replied. Are we not even going to take the ten thousand francs with us. He gave them to me. They're mine. I urged her to abandon everything, and to think only of leaving at once; for, although I had been with her for scarcely quarter of an hour, I was afraid that G... M... would return. Nevertheless, she entreated me so earnestly not to leave empty-handed that, having obtained so much from her, I thought I should concede something in return.

While we were preparing to leave I heard a knock at the street door. I was in no doubt that it was G... M... and, agitated by this thought, declared to Manon that if he appeared he was a dead man. Indeed, I was not sufficiently recovered from my earlier transport to be able to contain myself at the sight of him. Marcel put me out of my misery by bringing me a note that had just been handed in at the door. It was from M. de T... He informed me that, since G... M... had gone back to his own house to fetch the money he had promised to lend him, he was taking advantage of his absence to communicate to me a highly diverting thought: which was, that it seemed to him I could not avenge myself more agreeably on my rival than by eating his supper and sleeping, that very night, in the bed he was hoping to occupy with my mistress; he thought it would be easy enough to achieve this, provided I could secure three or four men resolute enough to apprehend G... M... in the street, and trustworthy enough not to let him out of their sight until the following morning; he for his part would undertake to keep him occupied for at least another hour, on a pretext he was holding in readiness for his return. I showed this note to Manon, explaining to her the plan I had used to get myself admitted to her house. My ruse seemed admirable to her, as did M. de T...'s. We laughed heartily over them for a little while. But when I dismissed M. de T...'s as a jest, she surprised me by insisting on recommending it to me, in all seriousness, as something the very idea of which enchanted her. I asked her in vain where she imagined I would find, at such short notice, men willing to apprehend G... M... and trustworthy enough to hold him securely. She said we ought to try nevertheless, since M. de T... had promised us another hour, while her response to my other objections was to complain that I was acting the tyrant and not being at all nice to her. She could think of nothing more amusing than this plan. You will sit in his place at supper, she kept saying, you will sleep in his sheets, and early tomorrow morning you will carry off his mistress and his money. You will be avenged on both father and son.

I yielded to her entreaties, in spite of the secret murmurings of my heart, which seemed to presage an unhappy denouement to this affair. Leaving her house, I went in search of two or three guardsmen whose acquaintance I had made through Lescaut, and who I hoped would take on the task of apprehending G... M... Only one of them was at home; but he was a resourceful man, who no sooner understood the matter in hand than he assured me of its success; all he asked for were ten pistoles, which he would need to reward the three soldiers from the guards he was proposing to employ under his own command. I beseeched him to lose no time. He assembled them in less than a quarter of an hour. Meanwhile I waited at his house; and when he returned with his associates, led them myself to the corner of a street G... M... would have to take in order to reach the one where Manon lived. I urged the guardsman not to maltreat him, but to keep so close a watch on him until seven o'clock next morning that I could rely on his not escaping. He replied that his plan was to take him back to his own room, then make him undress or even get into bed,

while he and his three gallant comrades spent the night drinking and
playing cards. I stayed with them until G... M... appeared; at which
point I retreated into a dark corner a few steps further on, in order to
witness this most extraordinary of scenes. The guardsman accosted
him, pistol in hand, and explained, very civilly, that he had no
designs either on his life or his money; but that if he made the least
difficulty about following him, or uttered the least cry, he would
blow his brains out. G... M..., seeing the guardsman accompanied by
three soldiers, and no doubt frightened by even the wad of a pistol,*
offered no resistance. I watched him being led away like a sheep.

I returned to Manon's house at once, and to allay any suspicions
the servants might have, announced the minute I arrived that she
was not to expect M. de G... M... for supper; some business had arisen
that would detain him, in spite of himself, and he had asked me to
come and make her his apologies, then to stay for supper with her
myself, which I would consider a very great honour in the company
of so lovely a lady. She seconded my ruse very expertly. We sat down
at table. We assumed an air of gravity, so long as the footmen serving
us remained. At last, having dismissed them, we spent one of the
most enchanting evenings of our lives. I instructed Marcel in secret
to find a carriage and arrange for it to be outside the door by six
o'clock next morning. Towards midnight I pretended to take my
leave of Manon; then, returning quietly with Marcel's help, got
ready to occupy G... M...'s bed, just as I had filled his place at table. In
the meantime our evil genius was working to destroy us. We were in
an ecstasy of pleasure, while the sword hung suspended over our
heads. The thread that held it was about to break. But so that all the
circumstances of our ruin be more clearly understood, I must first
elucidate its cause.

At the moment when he was apprehended by the guardsman,
G... M... was being followed by his footman. This young fellow,
frightened by his master's misadventure, turned on his heel and fled
in the direction he had come from. Anxious, however, to do what he
could to help him, he went straight to old G... M... and informed
him of what had happened. Such a distressing piece of news could
not fail to alarm the old man greatly; he had only one son, and was
extremely quick-tempered for a man of his years. He first asked the
footman what his son had been doing that afternoon, if he had fallen
out with anyone, or been involved in a quarrel, or found himself in

some dubious establishment. The footman, believing his master to be in mortal danger, and thinking he should no longer withhold any information that might procure him assistance, revealed everything he knew about his love for Manon and the expenditure he had incurred on her account; the manner in which he had spent the afternoon with her at her house, his departure at around nine o'clock, and the misfortune he had met with on his return. This was enough to make the old man suspect that an affair of the heart was involved. Although it was at least half-past ten at night, he went straight to the Lieutenant-General of Police. He requested that special orders be given to all the patrols of the watch on duty that night; then, asking for another to accompany him, hurried off in the direction of the street where his son had been apprehended; he visited all the places in the city where he hoped to find him; and, uncovering no trace of him, finally asked to be taken to his mistress's house, where he supposed he might now have returned.

I was about to get into bed when he arrived. The bedroom door was shut, so that I did not hear him knock at the door to the street below; but he entered, followed by two constables, and having enquired in vain what had become of his son, suddenly took it into his head to ask to see his mistress, in case she could throw some light on the matter. He came up to the apartment, still accompanied by the two constables. We were on the point of getting into bed; he opened the door, and our blood froze at the sight of him. Oh God! I said to Manon, it's old G... M... I reached for my sword; unfortunately it was caught up in my belt. Seeing what I was about, the constables came at once and seized it from me. A man in his nightshirt is powerless to resist. They deprived me of every means of defending myself.

Disconcerted though he was by this sight, G... M... was not slow in recognizing me. He recalled Manon still more easily. Am I deluded, he enquired gravely, or do I not see before me the Chevalier Des Grieux and Manon Lescaut? I was so maddened with shame and grief that I made no reply. He appeared, for a while, to be turning over several ideas in his mind, then, as if they had suddenly combined to kindle his wrath, he rounded on me, crying: Ah, miserable wretch that you are! I am certain you have killed my son! This insult cut me to the quick. You old villain, I answered haughtily, if I had wanted to kill someone in your family, I would have started with you.

Hold him fast, he said to the constables; he has information about
my son which he must give to me. I will have him hanged tomorrow
if he does not tell me right away what he has done with him. You will
have me hanged? I retorted. You wretch! It is you and your kind that
are sent to the gallows. My blood, let me inform you, is nobler and
purer than yours.* And yes, I added, I do know what has happened to
your son; and if you vex me further, I will have him strangled before
another day dawns; after which, I promise you, the same fate will be
yours.

It was most unwise of me to confess to him that I knew where his
son was; but the strength of my anger had made me indiscreet. He
immediately summoned five or six other constables, who were waiting outside the door, and ordered them to seize every servant in the
house. So, Monsieur le Chevalier, he continued in a mocking tone,
you know where my son is do you, and you're going to have him
strangled? We will soon see about that, never fear. I realized at once
the mistake I had made. He went over to Manon, who was sitting on
the bed weeping; he addressed several ironical compliments to her
on the power she exercised over both father and son, and the good
use she made of it. The incontinent old monster then made as if to
take liberties with her. Dare to lay a finger on her, I cried, and
nothing, however sacred, will save you from my hand! He left the
room, ordering three of the constables to remain behind and to see to
it that we dressed quickly.

I do not know what at that moment he intended doing with us.
Perhaps if we had told him where his son was, we might have secured
our freedom. As I dressed, I wondered if this was not our best
course. But if he had been so inclined when he left the room, he had
certainly changed his mind by the time he returned. He had gone to
question Manon's servants, who were being held by the constables.
He could learn nothing from those that had been hired for her by his
son; but when he discovered that Marcel had been in our service for
some time previously, he decided to use threats to make him talk.

Marcel was a loyal young fellow, but simple-minded and uncouth.
The memory of the part he had played in Manon's escape from the
Hôpital, together with the terror G... M... now contrived to inspire in
him, made such an impression on his feeble brain that he imagined
himself on the point of being led away to the gallows or the wheel.
He promised to disclose everything he knew, provided his life was

spared. This was enough to convince G... M... that we were involved in something more serious and more criminal than he had previously had reason to suppose. He offered Marcel, in return for his confession, not only his life but a reward as well. The miserable fellow then revealed to him part of our plan, which, since it included him, we had not scrupled to discuss in his presence. It is true that he knew nothing about the changes we had made since arriving in Paris; but he had been informed, before leaving Chaillot, of the broad lines of the enterprise and the role he was to play in it. He therefore told G... M... that our aim was to dupe his son, and that Manon was about to receive, or had already received, ten thousand francs, which it was our intention should never revert to the heirs of the house of G... M...

Hearing this, the old man, beside himself with rage, marched straight back up to our room. He said not a word, but went into the dressing-room, where he had no difficulty in finding the money and jewels. He returned, his face inflamed, and, showing us what he pleased to call our plunder, started showering us with insults and recriminations. He dangled the pearl necklace and bracelets in front of Manon. Recognize these, do you? he asked her, with a mocking smile. But it was not the first time you'd seen them, was it? The selfsame ones, I do declare. To your taste were they, my pretty one? I can well believe it. Poor young things! he went on. Quite delightful, both of them; but a bit crooked. My heart was bursting with rage at this insulting speech. I would have given, to be free for just one second... Merciful Heavens! What would I not have given? At last I contained myself sufficiently to say to him, with a restraint that was merely a refinement of my fury: Let us have no more mockery and insolence, Monsieur. What precisely is the issue here? What do you intend doing with us? The issue, Monsieur le Chevalier, he replied, is you going this instant to the Châtelet.* Tomorrow is another day; we will see more clearly how our affair stands, and I hope you will be so good, at last, as to tell me where my son is.

I realized, without too much reflection, the terrible consequences of our being sent to the Châtelet. I saw already all the dangers of this, and trembled. Proud though I was, I knew I must bow beneath the weight of my destiny, and flatter my cruellest enemy, by my submission, in order to obtain something from him. I therefore begged him, respectfully, to listen for a moment. Allow me to explain myself,

Old G... M... shows Manon the jewels (Pasquier)

Monsieur, I said; I confess that my youth has led me to commit grave errors, and that you have been sufficiently injured by them to have grounds for complaint. But if you know the power of love, if you can judge how a young man must suffer who has had everything he holds dear taken from him, you will perhaps find it pardonable that I have sought the satisfaction of a little revenge, or at least think me punished enough by the insult I have just suffered. Neither prison nor torture are needed to force me to reveal to you where your son is. He is quite safe. It was never my intention either to harm him or to offend you. I am ready to name the place where he is spending the night in perfect peace and quiet, if you will do me the favour of granting us our freedom. The old tiger, far from being moved by my plea, turned his back on me, laughing. He said just a few words, enough to show that he knew all about our plan from start to finish. As for his son, he added brutally that, since he had not been murdered, he would find his own way home soon enough. Take them to the Petit-Châtelet, he said to the constables, and make sure the Chevalier doesn't give you the slip. He's a crafty devil, who has already escaped from Saint-Lazare.

He departed, leaving me in the state you can imagine. O Heaven! I cried, I will accept with submission any blow that is dealt me by your hand; but that a miserable scoundrel should be able to play the tyrant over me drives me to utter despair. The constables asked us not to keep them waiting any longer. They had a carriage at the door. I held out my hand to Manon to help her down the stairs. Come, dear queen, I said to her, come and submit to the full harshness of our destiny. Perhaps one day it will please Heaven to make us happier.

We set off in the same carriage. She crept into my arms. I had not heard her utter a single word since G... M... first arrived; but now, finding herself alone with me, she said a thousand tender things, reproaching herself continually for having been the cause of my misfortune. I assured her I would never complain of my lot so long as she did not stop loving me. It is not I who am to be pitied, I continued. A few months in prison hold no fears for me; and I will always prefer the Châtelet to Saint-Lazare. It is for you, dear soul, that my heart is anxious. What a fate for so enchanting a creature! How can Heaven treat so harshly the most perfect of its works? Why were we not born, both of us, with qualities consistent with our miserable lot? We have been given intelligence, feeling, taste. But alas, what a melancholy use we make of them, while so many baser souls, who deserve our fate, enjoy all the favours of fortune! These reflections filled me with grief; but this was nothing in comparison with that with which I contemplated the future; for I was consumed with fear for Manon. She had already been in the Hôpital, and even if she had left again by the proper route, I knew that a relapse of this kind could have extremely dangerous consequences. I should have liked to express my fears, but was afraid of exciting too many in her. I trembled for her, without daring to warn her of her danger; and sighing, I embraced her, to reassure her at least of my love, which was almost the only feeling I dared express. Manon, I said to her, tell me truly: will you always love me? She replied that she was very sad that I could even doubt it. In that case, I replied, I will doubt it no longer, and will brave all our enemies, armed with this assurance. I will use my family to get me released from the Châtelet; and all my blood will be worth nothing, if I do not rescue you in turn, the moment I am set free.

We arrived at the prison. They put us in separate places. This blow was the less severe for my having foreseen it. I recommended Manon to the gaoler, giving him to understand that I was a person of some consequence, and promising him a substantial reward. I embraced my beloved mistress before leaving her. I implored her not to distress herself unduly, and not to be afraid of anything so long as I still drew breath. I was not without money. I gave some of it to her, and from what remained paid the gaoler a month's full board in advance for each of us.*

My money had a very good effect. They gave me a decently furnished room, and assured me that Manon had been similarly treated. I immediately busied myself thinking up ways of hastening my release. It was clear that there was nothing positively criminal in my case, and even supposing that Marcel's deposition could be used to prove an intention to steal on our part, I knew very well that intention alone is an insufficient ground for punishment. I decided to write to my father at once, and ask him to come to Paris in person. As I have already said, I found it much less shaming to be in the Châtelet than in Saint-Lazare. Besides, although I continued to show every respect that is due to paternal authority, age and experience had greatly diminished my timidity. I wrote to him, therefore, and no objection was made in the Châtelet to my letter being sent out; but I could have spared myself this trouble, had I known that my father was to arrive in Paris the very next day.

He had received the letter I had written to him a week before.* It had been a source of extreme joy to him; but however much I had tried to flatter his hopes as to my conversion, he had thought it unwise to rely on my promises alone. Therefore he decided to come and judge with his own eyes the extent to which I had changed, and to regulate his own conduct according to the sincerity of my repentance. He arrived the day after my imprisonment. His first visit was to Tiberge, to whom I had asked him to address his reply. He could discover nothing from him about my present circumstances or whereabouts; all he was able to ascertain was the general course my affairs had taken since my escape from Saint-Sulpice. However, Tiberge spoke very favourably of the marked inclination I had shown, during our recent interview, for returning to the path of virtue. He added that he believed I no longer had any association with Manon, but that he was nevertheless surprised not to have heard from me during the past week. My father was no fool; he saw that there was more to this silence that Tiberge complained of than my friend realized, and was so diligent in uncovering my traces that, two days after his arrival, he discovered that I was in the Châtelet.

I had not expected his visit nearly so soon, but before he could make it, I received one from the Lieutenant-General of Police, or rather, to call things by their proper name, I underwent an interrogation.* Although he did not spare me, his reproaches were neither harsh nor unkind. He told me, gently, that he regretted my bad behaviour; that it had been most unwise of me to make an enemy of a man like M. de G... M...; that if the truth were told, it was easy to see that there was more imprudence and thoughtlessness than malice in what I had done; but that this was nevertheless the second time I had come before his judgement, and he had hoped that, having spent two or three months in Saint-Lazare learning my lesson, I might have acquired a little wisdom. Charmed to be dealing with so reasonable a judge, I explained myself to him in a manner so respectful and modest that he seemed entirely satisfied with my answers. He told me I should not give way to despondency too easily, and that he was inclined, in view of my youth and my birth, to do what he could for me. I ventured to recommend Manon to him, praising her for her good nature and the sweetness of her disposition. He replied, laughing, that he had not seen her yet, but that she was generally considered a dangerous young woman. This so aroused my tenderness on her behalf that I said a thousand impassioned things to him in defence of my poor mistress; nor could I suppress a few tears. He ordered me to be taken back to my room. Love, love! this grave official cried as he watched me go, will you never be reconciled with wisdom?

I was deep in contemplation of my own sad situation, and in reflecting on the conversation I had just had with the Lieutenant-General of Police, when I heard the door to my room open: it was my father. Although I should have been half-prepared for this visit, since I was expecting it in a few days' time, I was nevertheless so shocked at the sight of him, that if the earth had opened beneath my feet I would gladly have cast myself into its depths. Overcome with confusion, I went to embrace him. He sat down before either of us had said a word.

As I remained standing, eyes lowered and head uncovered, he at last said gravely: Sit down, Monsieur, sit down. Thanks to the scandal your dissolute ways and villainous tricks have caused, I have discovered where you are living. Merit of the kind you possess has at least the advantage of being hard to conceal. You are on the direct road to fame. I hope it will soon lead you to the Place de la Grève, where you will at last have the glory of finding yourself exposed to the wondering gaze of the whole world.*

I made no reply. At length he went on: How unhappy the father is who, tenderly loving his son, and sparing nothing in his efforts to make of him an honourable man, discovers he is nothing but a villain who brings shame upon him. When ordinary misfortunes assail us, we can nevertheless find consolation: time softens the blow, our grief grows less keen; but what remedy is there against an evil that grows from day to day; as do the dissipations of a depraved son, who has lost all sense of honour? You say nothing, wretch, he added. Look at his feigned modesty, his hypocritical air of meekness! Would you not take him for the most honourable man of his race?

Although I was forced to recognize that not all of these insults were unmerited, they seemed to me nevertheless to be carried to excess. I thought it not improper to respond with a degree of candour. I assure you, Monsieur, I said, that the air of modesty I assume in your presence is in no way affected, but is the natural demeanour of a well-bred son who is infinitely respectful of his father, more especially of a father whose displeasure he has incurred. Neither do I aspire to being thought the most upright of our race. I know how justly I deserve your reproaches; I beg you to temper them nevertheless with a little more kindness, and not to treat me as the most abominable of men. I do not deserve such harsh words. It is love, as you know, love alone—fatal passion!—that has caused all my errors. Alas! Have you never felt its force yourself? Can it be possible that your blood, from which mine flows, should never have burned with the same ardour? Love has made me too tender, too passionate, too faithful, and too ready, perhaps, to indulge the desires of a mistress who is all enchantment. These are my crimes. But is any of them so shameful as to bring you into dishonour? Surely, dear father, I added tenderly, you can spare a little compassion for a son who has always been filled with respect and affection for you, who has not, as you suppose, renounced all honour and duty, and who is a thousand times more to be pitied than you could imagine. With these last words, I let fall a few tears.

A father's heart is nature's finest work: she reigns there, so to speak, indulgently, and herself sets all its springs in motion. My own father—who was, moreover, a man of taste and understanding—was so touched by the felicitous turn I had given to my apology that he had not sufficient self-command to hide from me this change of feeling. My poor Chevalier, he said, come here and embrace me. I pity you, I do indeed. I embraced him. I could tell from the way he held me what was happening in his heart. But, he continued, how are we to get you out of here? Tell me exactly how your affairs stand, and be sure you hold nothing back. Since, after all, there was nothing in my conduct, taken as a whole, that could totally dishonour me, at least when compared with that prevailing in certain circles of young men, and since a mistress is not considered shameful in the century in which we live, any more than using a little art in persuading fortune to favour one at cards, I described to my father the life I had been leading frankly and in detail. Hoping to make my own faults seem less shameful, I was careful to add the example of some well-known person to each one I confessed. I am living with a mistress, I said to him, to whom I am not bound by formal ties of marriage: the Duc de... keeps two in full view of all Paris; M. de... has had one for ten years, whom he loves with a constancy he has never shown his

wife. Two-thirds of all Frenchmen of rank make it a point of honour
to have one. I have sometimes used trickery while playing cards: the
Marquis de... and the Comte de... have no other source of income;
while the Prince de... and the Duc de... are leaders of another band
of knights belonging to the same order. As for my designs on the
purse of G... M... and his son, here again I could have proved that I
was not without models; but I still had too much sense of honour not
to see that I myself would stand accused alongside those whose
example I cited, so that I begged my father instead to excuse this
frailty as the work of two violent passions I had been swayed by—
vengeance and love. He asked if I had any ideas to offer as to the
quickest way he could secure my release, in such a way as to avoid
any scandal. I told him of the leniency the Lieutenant-General of
Police had shown me. Any difficulties you encounter, I said, can only
come from M. de G... M... and his son; I think, therefore, it would
be as well if you were to take the trouble to see them. He promised he
would do so. I did not dare ask him to appeal to them on Manon's
behalf. This was not from want of courage, but rather from fear that
any request of this sort would outrage him and prompt him to take
some action fatal to her and me. I still wonder if this fear was not the
cause of my greatest misfortunes, preventing me, as it did, from
sounding out my father's inclinations, and from attempting to persuade him to look more favourably upon my unhappy mistress. Perhaps I could have moved him to pity a second time. I could have put
him on his guard against the adverse impressions he was about to
receive from old G... M..., and which he was all too ready to accept.
Who knows? Perhaps, in spite of all my efforts, my malign destiny
would have prevailed; but at least I would have had only fate and the
cruelty of my enemies to blame for my ill-fortune.

   Immediately on leaving me, my father went to visit M. de G... M...
He found him with his son, duly restored to freedom by the guardsman. I have never known the detail of their conversation; but it has
been easy enough to judge of it from its fatal effects. They went
together—the two fathers, that is—to see the Lieutenant-General of
Police, of whom they asked two favours: first, that I be released from
the Châtelet then and there; and secondly, that Manon should be
shut up for the rest of her days, or sent to America. They were just
beginning, at this time, to ship great numbers of undesirables to the
Mississippi. The Lieutenant-General of Police promised them he

would have Manon dispatched by the first boat. M. de G... M... and my father came at once to find me and give me the news of my release. M. de G... M... made a civil allusion to the past and, having congratulated me on my good fortune in having such a father, exhorted me to profit from his wisdom and example in future. My father ordered me to apologize for the supposed injury I had done him and his family, and to thank him for having contributed to my release. Then we left, the three of us together, without a word having been said about my mistress. I did not dare even to mention her to the prison guards in their presence. Alas! my poor recommendations would have been in vain. The order sealing her fate had arrived at the same moment as that granting me my freedom. An hour later the hapless girl was taken to the Hôpital, to join a group of other poor wretches condemned to suffer the same destiny. My father had insisted I go with him at once to the house where he was staying, so that it was almost six o'clock in the evening before I found an opportunity to escape his vigilance and return to the Châtelet. My sole purpose in doing so was to arrange for some food to be taken in to Manon, and to recommend her to her gaoler, for I did not flatter myself I would be given permission to see her. Nor, as yet, had I had time to reflect on the means of setting her free.

I asked to speak to the gaoler. Pleased with the mildness and the liberality I had previously shown him, he was already disposed to do whatever he could for me, and therefore spoke of Manon's fate as of a misfortune he greatly regretted because of the distress it must cause me. I did not know what he meant. We continued to talk for a few moments without understanding one another. At last, realizing that some explanation was necessary, he told me what it has already appalled me to have to tell you, and that does so now, when I am obliged to repeat it. No violent seizure ever produced a more sudden or more terrible effect. I fell to the ground, with so painful a palpitation of the heart that, as I lost consciousness, I believed I had escaped this life for ever. Something of this feeling stayed with me even after I came to myself. I fixed my gaze on every part of the room in turn, and at last on myself, so as to ascertain whether I still enjoyed the unfortunate distinction of being alive. Indeed, although I was simply obeying the natural impulse whereby we seek relief from suffering, nothing could have seemed to me sweeter than death, at this moment of despair and dismay. Religion itself could offer me no vision of eternal torment more intolerable than the cruel convulsions by which I was afflicted. In spite of which, by a miracle that love alone could have wrought, I had soon regained enough strength to thank Heaven for restoring me to reason and consciousness. My death would have benefited no one but myself. Manon needed me—and needed me alive—to save her, support her, avenge her. I swore to devote myself unsparingly to this.

The gaoler gave me all the assistance I could have hoped for from my closest friend. I accepted his services with heartfelt gratitude. Alas! I said to him, you at least are touched by my woes. Everyone has abandoned me. My father himself has, without a doubt, become one of my cruellest persecutors. No one pities me. You alone, in the place where harshness and barbarity dwell, are moved by compassion for the most miserable of men! He advised me not to show myself in the street until I had recovered from my distress a little. Let me be, I replied as I took my leave; I will see you again, and sooner than you think. Prepare your darkest dungeon for me; for I intend to deserve it.* And indeed, my initial resolve had been nothing less than to rid myself not only of the two G... M...s, but of the Lieutenant-General of Police as well, and then to descend by force of arms on the Hôpi-tal, flanked by all those I could enlist in my quarrel. My father himself would have met with scant consideration in a vengeance that seemed to me so just, for the gaoler had not concealed from me the fact that he and G... M... were the authors of my ruin. But after I had walked for a while in the street, and the air had cooled my blood and calmed my spirits a little, my rage gradually gave way to more reasonable feelings. The death of our enemies would have done nothing to help Manon, and would doubtless have risked depriving me of every means of assisting her. Besides, would I have resorted to a cowardly murder? What other route to vengeance could I take? But first I must free Manon, and I summoned all my strength and courage for this task, postponing everything else until after the success of this important undertaking. I was now short of money. Nevertheless, it was fundamental to my enterprise, and its acquisi-tion must be my first task. I could think of only three people from whom I could expect to receive any: M. de T..., my father, and Tiberge. It seemed unlikely I would obtain anything from the last two, and I was ashamed of wearying the first with importunate requests. But who observes such niceties when in despair? I went straight to the seminary at Saint-Sulpice, without even stopping to reflect that I might be recognized there. I asked for Tiberge. His first words made it clear that he knew nothing as yet about my most recent adventures. I had intended to appeal to his compassion, but, on seeing this, I changed my plan. Instead, I spoke in general terms of the pleasure it had given me to see my father again, then asked him to lend me some money, on the pretext of some debts I had to repay before leaving Paris, and which I preferred to keep secret. He at once handed me his purse. I took five hundred of the six hundred francs I found there. I offered him a promissory note; he was too generous to accept it.

Next I went to M. de T...'s house. I felt no constraint with him, but gave him a full account of my sorrows and misfortunes. He already knew them, down to the last detail, having followed young G... M...'s adventures. He listened nevertheless, and greatly pitied me. When I asked for advice as to how I might rescue Manon, he replied sadly that he could see so little prospect of this succeeding that, but for some extraordinary intervention on the part of Heaven, I had no choice but to abandon this idea; hearing of Manon's imprisonment, he had gone especially to the Hôpital, but not even he had been able to obtain permission to see her; the Lieutenant-General of Police's orders were of the utmost severity; and thanks to a final stroke of ill-fortune, the wretched little band she was to join was destined to leave in two days' time. I was so dismayed by what I heard, that he could have talked for another hour without my thinking of interrupting. He went on to tell me that he had not come to visit me in the Châtelet, so as to leave himself more freedom to work on my behalf than if he was suspected of having some connection with me; that ever since my release a few hours before he had endured the vexation of not knowing where I had taken refuge; that he had wanted to see me as quickly as possible, so as to give me the only advice that seemed to him to offer any chance of averting Manon's fate; but it was dangerous advice, and he begged me to conceal his part in it for all eternity: this was that I should find some gallant comrades, brave enough to attack Manon's guards once they were outside the city limits. He did not wait for me to mention my lack of money. Here is a hundred pistoles, he said, presenting me with a purse, which might be of use to you. You can repay me when fortune once more favours your affairs. He added that if his concern for his reputation had permitted him to undertake my mistress's rescue himself, he would at once have offered me his right arm and his sword.

I was moved to the point of tears by this extraordinary generosity. Summoning all the strength my afflicted state allowed, I expressed my gratitude to him. I asked if there was nothing to be hoped from interceding on her behalf with the Lieutenant-General of Police. He said he had thought of this; but he believed this stratagem to be pointless, since a pardon of this kind could not be requested without grounds being offered, and he did not see what grounds we could use that would persuade so weighty and powerful a person to intercede on her behalf; that if there was anything to be gained from that quarter, it could only be done by persuading M. de G... M... and my father to change their minds, and themselves ask the Lieutenant-General of Police to revoke his sentence. He offered to do what he could to win over young G... M..., although he thought he had cooled a little towards him, on account of certain suspicions he had concerning M. de T...'s involvement in our affair; and he exhorted me, for my part, to omit nothing that might soften my father's obduracy.

This was no small undertaking; not only because it was most unlikely that I would persuade my father, but for another reason too, which deterred me from even approaching him: I had slipped away from his lodgings against his orders and, since learning of Manon's sad fate, was firmly resolved never to go back there. I was afraid, and with reason, that he might detain me there by force, and oblige me to return to the country with him against my will. My older brother had already used this same method with me. It is true I was now older; but age counts for little against superior strength. At last, however, I thought of a way in which I could avoid this danger: which was, under an assumed name, to ask him to meet me in a public place. I immediately acted on this decision. M. de T... went off to G... M...'s house, I to the Jardin du Luxembourg, from where I sent a message informing my father that one of his gentlemen-in-attendance was waiting for him. It was beginning to get dark, and I was afraid he would find difficulty in coming. He appeared soon afterwards, however, followed by his footman. I proposed we take a walk along a path where we would be certain of being undisturbed. We continued for a hundred yards at least without exchanging a word. He no doubt imagined that so many careful preparations must indicate some serious intention on my part. He was waiting for me to speak; I was pondering what to say.

At last I broke my silence. Monsieur, I said to him, trembling, you are a good father. You have showered me with favours, and over-looked an infinite number of faults; and Heaven is my witness that I feel nothing for you but the greatest filial affection and respect. But your severity... or so it seems to me... Well then, my severity, my father interrupted, no doubt finding his patience sorely tried by this long-drawn-out speech. Ah Monsieur, I went on, it seems to me you have been excessively harsh on poor Manon. You have relied on what M. de G... M... has told you. He hates her, and has painted her in the blackest colours. You have formed the most terrible idea of her. And yet she is the sweetest and dearest creature that ever was. If only Heaven had inspired you with a wish to see her, even for a moment! I am as certain that she is enchanting as I am that you would have found her so. You would have taken her side, you would have detested G... M...'s wicked endeavours, you would have pitied her and me. Alas! I am certain of it. Your heart is not hard; you would have let yourself be moved. Seeing that I was speaking with an ardour that was unlikely soon to run its course, he interrupted me again. He enquired as to what conclusion so impassioned a speech was tending. To that of imploring you to spare my life, I replied for I cannot live a moment longer if Manon is sent to America for ever. No, no, he said sternly; I would rather see you deprived of life than of wisdom and honour. Let us go no further then! I cried, seizing him by the arm; take this hateful, this intolerable life from me now; for so deep is the despair you have plunged me into that death itself would seem to me a favour, a gift worthy of a father's hand.

It would be no more than you deserve, he retorted. I know many fathers who would not have waited nearly so long, before themselves becoming your judge and executioner; but what has ruined you is my excessive kindness.

I flung myself at his feet: Ah, if you have any such feeling left, I cried, clasping him about the knees, take pity on my tears. Consider that I am your son. Alas! Remember my mother. You loved her so tenderly! If someone had tried to tear her from your arms, what would you have done? You would have defended her to the death. Do not others have a heart, like you? Could anyone who knows what it is to love and to grieve be so barbarous?

Do not mention your mother again, he rejoined irascibly; her memory can only increase my indignation. If she had lived long enough to see your dissolute ways, she would have died of grief. Let us end this conversation, he said, it vexes me, and will not make me change my mind. I am going home now; I order you to follow me. I could tell from the curt and harsh tone with which he communicated this order that his heart was inflexible. Fearing he might take it into his head to seize me himself, I moved several steps away from him. Do not drive me even further to despair, I said, by forcing me to disobey you. I cannot follow you, any more than I can go on living, after you have dealt so harshly with me. Therefore I bid you farewell for ever. My death, which you will hear of soon enough, will perhaps rekindle the feelings of a father in you. I turned to leave. So you refuse to follow me, do you? he cried in a rage. Go then, go to your ruin. Farewell, ungrateful and rebellious son. Farewell, I answered, my fury equal to his own, farewell, barbarous and unnatural father.

I at once left the Jardin du Luxembourg. I walked, like one demented, through the streets to M. de T...'s house, casting my eyes to the heavens as I went, and raising my hands in invocation of all the celestial powers. O Heaven! I said, will you be as merciless as men are? Only you can help me now. M. de T... had not yet returned home, but he arrived a few minutes later. His errand had been no more successful than mine. With a downcast face, he told me what had happened. Young G... M..., although less angry with Manon and me than his father, had been unwilling to petition him on our behalf. He had excused himself on the grounds that he, too, had reason to fear this vindictive old man, who, beside himself with rage, had already reproached him for seeking an intimacy with Manon. The only course left open to me, then, was violence, such as M. de T... had outlined in his plan; I fixed all my hopes on this. They are very uncertain, I said to him, but the most solid of them—and the one from which I draw most comfort—is that I might at least perish in the enterprise. Whereupon, having asked for his good wishes in all my endeavours, I left him, and thought only of finding comrades to whom I could communicate at least some spark of my own courage and resolution.

The first to come to mind was the guardsman I had employed to apprehend G... M... I had anyway been proposing to go and spend the night in his room, having been too preoccupied during the afternoon to procure myself a lodging. I found him alone. He expressed joy at seeing me released from the Châtelet, and affectionately offered me his services. I explained to him what I had in mind. He had enough good sense to see the difficulties involved, but enough generosity to try and surmount them. We spent part of the night debating my plan. He mentioned the trio of soldiers from the guards he had employed on the previous occasion as three gallant comrades who were ready for anything. M. de T... had told me the exact number of constables that were to accompany Manon: he had assured me there would be no more than six. Five bold and resolute men would be enough to inspire mortal terror into these miserable wretches, who are anyway incapable of defending themselves honourably, if they can avoid the perils of combat by cowardly means. Seeing that I was not short of money, the guardsman advised me to spare no expense that might ensure the success of our attack. We will need horses, he told me, as well as pistols, and each of us our musket. I myself will undertake all these preparations tomorrow. We will also need three sets of ordinary clothes for our soldiers, who would never dare take part in an affair of this kind dressed in the regimental uniform. I handed over to him the hundred pistoles M. de T... had given me. The whole sum was used up, down to the very last sou, by the end of the following day. The three soldiers paraded in front of me. I encouraged them with grand promises and, so as to allay any doubts they might have about me, began by making each of them a present of ten pistoles. Early on the morning of the day we were to put my plan into action, I sent one of them to the Hôpital to ascertain with his own eyes the precise moment at which the constables would be setting out with their prey. Although only my excessive anxiety and circumspection could have prompted this precaution, it turned out to have been absolutely necessary. I had been relying on various pieces of false information I had been given about their route, and having concluded that this pitiable band was to be embarked at La Rochelle, had planned—pointlessly, as it would have turned out—to wait for them on the Orleans road. The report that the soldier from the guards brought back, however, made it clear that they were to take the Normandy road, and that it was from Le Havre-de-Grâce that they would set sail for America.

We set off at once for the Porte Saint-Honoré, taking care to go by different routes. We met again on the outskirts of the city. Our horses were fresh. We had soon caught up with the six guards and the two wretched wagons you saw at Pacy two years ago. The very sight of them almost deprived me of strength and consciousness. O Fortune! I cried, cruel Fortune! At least grant me either death or victory* here. We deliberated for a moment as to the best means of mounting our attack. The constables were scarcely more than four hundred yards ahead of us. We could easily intercept them, moreover, by cutting across a little field, which the main road skirted. The guardsman proposed we take this route and surprise them by a sudden onset. I approved this plan, and was the first to spur on my horse. But pitiless Fortune had rejected my plea. The constables, seeing five horsemen bearing down on them, were in no doubt that they were under attack. They prepared to defend themselves, making ready their bayonets and their rifles with a resolute enough air. This sight, which kindled new spirit in the guardsman and me, deprived our three cowardly companions, at a stroke, of all their courage. They stopped, as if by agreement, and, having exchanged a few words I could not catch, turned their horses' heads and set off at a gallop back along the road to Paris. God in heaven! said the guardsman, who seemed as bewildered as I was by this atrocious desertion, what are we going to do now? There are only the two of us left. Astonishment and rage had robbed me of all power of speech. I stopped, uncertain whether my first act of vengeance should not be to pursue and punish these cowards who were abandoning me. I watched them flee, then glanced in the other direction at the constables. If I had been able to divide myself into two I would have descended, at one fell swoop, on both these objects of my fury. I consumed them, meanwhile, with my gaze. The guardsman, seeing from my distracted looks how perplexed I was, asked if he could offer some advice. As there are only two of us, he said, it would be madness to attack six men, who are as well armed as we are and apparently ready to take us on in earnest. We must return to Paris, and hope for better luck next time in our choice of comrades. The constables won't make much progress in a day with two such heavy wagons; we will have no difficulty in catching up with them again tomorrow.

I reflected on this course of action for a moment, but seeing on all sides nothing but reasons for despair, came to a truly desperate decision. This was to thank my companion for his services, then, far from attacking the constables, to go and beg them humbly to admit me to their number, so that I might accompany Manon as far as Le Havre-de-Grâce, and from there set sail with her across the sea. Everyone persecutes or betrays me, I said to the guardsman. There is no longer anyone I can depend on. I can expect nothing further, either from Fortune or my fellow men. My misfortunes crowd in on me from every side: I have no choice left but to submit to them. I must shut my eyes to every hope. May Heaven reward you for your generous heart. Farewell, for I have decided to resist my evil destiny no longer, but to embrace it by going voluntarily to meet my ruin. He tried to persuade me to return to Paris, but in vain. I beseeched him to allow me to do as I had resolved, and to leave me right away, for fear the constables should go on thinking we were intending to attack them.

I advanced alone towards them, slowly and with such a despondent air that they cannot have found my approach at all intimidating. They remained on the defensive, nevertheless. There is no need for alarm, Messieurs, I said as I reached them; I have come, not to bring war but to beg a favour. I assured them that they could resume their journey with confidence, and explained, as we set off, the favour I hoped they would grant me. They debated among themselves how to respond to this approach. Their leader spoke on behalf of them all. He said that they were under the strictest orders concerning the watch that had to be kept on their prisoners; nevertheless I seemed to him such an agreeable young fellow, that he and his companions were prepared to be a little less zealous in the exercise of their duty; but that I must understand that this would necessarily cost me something. I had about fifteen pistoles left, which, I told him frankly, was the full extent of my resources. In that case, said the constable, we will give you generous terms. We will charge you only one écu an hour for conversing with whichever of our girls takes your fancy; this is the going rate in Paris. I had said nothing to them about Manon, thinking it better they should not know of my passion. At first they imagined it was simply a young man's caprice that had led me, by way of diversion, to seek out these poor creatures; but once they thought they had observed me to be in love, they increased the tribute they demanded of me so much that my purse was empty by the time we left Mantes, where we had broken our journey the day before we arrived in Pacy.

Manon sees Des Grieux from her wagon (Pasquier)

Shall I tell you how sorrowful my conversations with Manon were on this journey, or what effect the sight of her had on me, when at last I gained permission from the guards to approach her cart? Ah, words can only half express the movements of the heart! But picture my poor mistress, chained about the waist, seated on a few handfuls of straw, her head leaning languidly against the side of the wagon, her face pale and damp with the flow of tears that forced their way between her eyelids, even though her eyes were always closed. She had not been curious enough to open them even when she heard the noise the guards made when they thought they were under attack. Her clothes were dirty and dishevelled, her delicate hands exposed to the ravages of the air; in short, this creature composed of such enchantments that she could reduce the whole world to idolatry, seemed to be in a state of unutterable dejection and disarray. I spent some time observing her as I rode alongside the wagon. I was so little concerned for myself that several times I was in danger of falling. My sighs and frequent exclamations at last drew her eyes in my direction. She recognized me, and her first impulse, I saw, was to try and reach me by throwing herself from the cart. But, restrained by the chain that bound her, she fell back into her original position. I appealed to the constables, imploring them, out of compassion, to stop for a moment; out of greed, they consented. I got down from my horse, and went to sit beside her. She was so languid and enfeebled that for a long time she seemed robbed of the power of speech, and even of the capacity to move her hands. Meanwhile, I bathed these poor hands with my tears; but since I too was unable to utter a single word, our situation was the most melancholy that could be imagined. Our words, once we were able to speak, were no less so. Manon said little. It was as though shame and grief had impaired her organs of speech, and left her voice weak and trembling. She thanked me for not forgetting her and, with a sigh, for at least procuring her the happiness of seeing me once more, so that she could say her last farewell. But when I assured her that nothing could make me part from her, and that I was determined to follow her to the ends of the earth, to care for her, serve her, love her, and unite my miserable destiny inextricably to hers, the poor girl gave vent to such tender and sorrowful feelings that I began to fear for her life, so violent was her emotion. All the impulses of her soul seemed to meet in her eyes. She kept them fixed on me. Sometimes she opened her mouth, but could not find the strength to complete the few words she had begun. A few murmured expressions escaped her lips, nevertheless—of wonder at my love, of tender complaint at its excess, of doubt that she should be fortunate enough to have inspired in me so perfect a passion, of urgent entreaty that I should renounce my plan of following her and seek elsewhere the happiness I deserved, and which she said I could not hope to find with her.

Although mine was the cruellest of fates, I found felicity in her glance and in the certainty of being loved by her. It is true I had lost everything that other men prize; but I ruled Manon's heart, which was the only prize I cared about. In Europe, in America, what did it matter where I lived, so long as, living with my mistress, I was certain of being happy? Is not the whole universe home to two faithful lovers? Do they not find in one another father, mother, family, friends, wealth, and happiness? If anything caused me anxiety, it was the fear of seeing Manon exposed to indigence and want. I imagined myself alone with her, in a wilderness inhabited only by savages. I feel sure, I said to myself, that none of them could be as cruel as G... M... and my father. They will let us live in peace, at least. If the accounts we have of them are true, they follow the laws of nature.* They know neither the furies of avarice that possess G... M... nor the fantastical ideas of honour that have made my father my enemy. They will not trouble two lovers they see living with as much simplicity as they do themselves. I was easy, therefore, on that score. But I could form no such romantic notions concerning the ordinary requirements of life; I had learned by bitter experience that certain privations are intolerable, especially to a delicate girl who has been used to an existence of ease and plenty. I was in despair at having squandered the contents of my purse to such little effect, and at finding myself once more on the point of being deprived of the little money I had left by the rapaciousness of the constables. I reflected that even a small sum would have allowed me, not only to ward off poverty for a good while in America, where money was scarce, but even to make plans for some permanent establishment there. This last consideration gave me the idea of writing to Tiberge, whom I had always found so prompt in fulfilling the offices of friendship. I sent him a letter from the next town we came to. I gave no other motive for writing to him than the pressing need I anticipated I would be reduced to at Le Havre-de-Grâce, where

I confessed I had gone in order to accompany Manon. I asked him for a hundred pistoles. Arrange for the postmaster at Le Havre to hold them for me, I said. You will appreciate only too well, I am sure, that this is the last time I will take advantage of your affection for me; and that, since my unhappy mistress is being taken from me for ever, I cannot let her go without doing what little I can to alleviate her wretched lot and my own mortal anguish.

As soon as they discovered how violent my passion was, the constables became so inflexible in their dealings that, continually doubling the price they made me pay for the least of their favours, they soon reduced me to total penury. Nor did love allow me to use my purse sparingly. Forgetting everything else, I was at Manon's side from dawn till dusk; so that it was no longer by the hour that my payments were calculated, but by whole days. At last, my purse being by now entirely empty, I found myself at the mercy of the whims and brutality of six miserable wretches, who treated me with intolerable disdain. You saw this for yourself at Pacy. My meeting with you there was a moment of blessed respite, granted me by Fortune. The pity that filled you at the sight of my woes was the only recommendation your generous heart could have received on my behalf. The help you gave me so liberally enabled me to reach Le Havre, and the constables kept the promises they made to you more faithfully than I had feared.

We arrived in Le Havre. I went straight to the post office. Tiberge, it appeared, had not yet had time to respond to my letter. I enquired as to the precise day on which I could expect his reply. The earliest it could arrive was in two days' time, and by some strange twist in my malign fate, it so happened that our ship was to leave on the very morning of the day on which I might have hoped to receive it. My despair was beyond words. What! I cried. Already oppressed by ill-fortune, must I always be singled out for some new blow? Alas! Manon replied, does so wretched a life merit the care we take to preserve it? Let us die in Le Havre. Let death, at a stroke, put an end to all our woes! Why drag them with us to an unknown land, where doubtless we must suffer the most terrible extremities—for are they not intended as my punishment? Let us die, she repeated; or rather, let me die by your hand; then go and seek a different fate in the arms of some more fortunate mistress. No, no, I replied, for wretchedness itself, as long as I share it with you, is to me an enviable fate. Her words filled me with dread. I realized she was overwhelmed by her sufferings. I forced myself at once to assume an air of greater calm, so as to dispel these gloomy thoughts of death and despair. I resolved to follow this course in future; and was soon to discover that nothing inspires more courage in a woman than fearlessness in the man she loves.

Once I had abandoned all hope of receiving help from Tiberge, I sold my horse. The profit from this, together with what remained of the money you so generously gave me, made up a modest sum of seventeen pistoles. I devoted seven of these to purchasing various items that were essential to Manon's comfort; the remaining ten, which were to be the basis of our fortune and our hopes in America, I carefully put away. I had no difficulty in being taken on board ship. At that time they were looking for young men who were disposed to join the colony voluntarily. My passage and food were provided free of charge.* Since the post for Paris was due to leave the next day, I left a letter for Tiberge. It was touching, and must have been capable of moving him to the depths of his being, for it prompted a decision on his part that could only have come from an infinite fund of tenderness and generosity towards an unhappy friend.

We set sail. The wind was favourable throughout. I procured from the captain a place where Manon and I could be alone. He was kind enough to view us differently from the rest of our wretched associates. I had taken him aside on the first day and, hoping to gain some consideration in his eyes, related to him part of my misfortunes. I did not believe myself guilty of a shameful lie when I told him I was married to Manon. He pretended to believe me, and offered me his protection. We received evidence of this throughout the voyage; he saw to it that we were properly fed, and the regard he showed us helped to win the respect of our companions in affliction. All my efforts were devoted to protecting Manon from the least discomfort. She was well aware of this; and, together with her lively sense of the strange extremity I was reduced to for her sake, it made her so tender and passionate, so attentive to my smallest needs in her turn, that there was a perpetual contest between us as to who could lavish more care and love on the other. I felt no regret at leaving Europe. On the contrary, the closer we came to America, the more I felt my heart expand and grow calm. If I could have been confident of not

lacking the absolute necessities of life, I would have thanked Fortune
for arranging so favourable a turn in our destiny.

After two months at sea we at last reached the longed-for shore.
At first sight the countryside offered nothing very appealing. There
were only barren and uninhabited plains, with here and there some
sparse reeds and a few trees stripped bare by the wind. There was no
sign of men or animals. However, once the captain had ordered our
guns to be fired, it was not long before we saw a troop of citizens of
New Orleans coming towards us with gestures of joyful anticipation.
Not that we had caught sight of the town as yet. It is hidden, from
this side, by a little hill. We were welcomed as though we had been
dropped from Heaven. The poor townspeople plied us with a
thousand eager questions on the state of things in Paris, and the
various provinces where they had been born. They embraced us like
brothers, and like dear companions come to share their poverty and
solitude. We set off with them towards the town, but were surprised
to find, on coming nearer, that what we had always heard boasted of
as a fine town was nothing but a collection of a few mean cabins. Five
or six hundred people lived there. The Governor's house, because of
its elevation and superior situation, seemed to stand out a little from
the rest. It is protected by earthworks, around which there runs a
broad moat.*

We were presented to the Governor first of all. He had a long
conversation in private with the captain, then, rejoining us, he examined all the girls who had arrived with the ship, one after another.
There were about thirty in all, for another party had been waiting at
Le Havre, which had then joined ours. The Governor, having stud-
ied each of them carefully, summoned various young men from the
town, who had been longing for wives for some time now. The prettiest were give to the more prominent among them, and lots were
drawn for the rest.* He had not yet spoken to Manon; but when he
had ordered the others to withdraw, he asked us to remain behind. I
understand from the captain, he said, that you are married, and that
during the voyage he has found you to be people of merit and intelligence. I will not enquire into the reasons for your present misfortune; but if you are as well acquainted with society as your
appearance would seem to promise, I will spare no efforts in alleviat-
ing your lot, and you, for your part, will contribute to my finding
some pleasure in this wild and desolate place. I replied in the manner

I thought most likely to confirm the idea he had formed of us. He gave orders for lodgings to be prepared for us in the town, and meanwhile detained us to supper. I found him very refined, for the leader of a band of wretched exiles. He did not press us in public for a detailed account of our adventures. The conversation was general and, in spite of our dejection, Manon and I did everything we could to make it agreeable.

Later that evening we were taken to the lodgings they had prepared for us. We found a wretched cabin made of wood and mud, with two or three rooms on the ground floor and a loft above. Five or six chairs had been left there, along with a few basic necessities. Manon seemed horrified at the sight of so dreary a dwelling. She was distressed for me much more than for herself. As soon as we were alone, she sat down and began weeping bitterly. At first I tried to comfort her. But when I realized that her sorrow was solely on my account, and that the only thing about our common misfortune that grieved her was the suffering it must cause me, I put on a show of courage and even, in order to inspire similar feelings in her, of joy. What is there to complain of? I said. I have everything my heart desires. Do you not love me? What other happiness have I ever aspired to? Let us commend ourselves to Heaven's care. Not that I think our position so very desperate. The Governor is a decent man; he treats us with respect; he will not let us lack the necessities of life. As to the meanness of our cabin and the crudeness of our furniture, you will have noticed that there are very few people here who seem better housed than we are, or who have better furnishings; besides, you are an admirable alchemist, I added embracing her, you turn everything to gold.

In that case, she replied, you will be the richest man on earth; for, if there has never been a love like yours, so it is impossible to be loved more tenderly than you are. I must at least do myself this justice, she went on. I know very well that I have never deserved the extraordinary attachment you feel for me. I have grieved you in ways you could never have pardoned, but for your extreme goodness to me. I have been fickle and flighty; and in spite of loving you to distraction, as I have always done, I have been the most ungrateful of creatures. But you would not believe how much I have changed. The tears you have seen me shed so often since we left France have never once had my own misfortunes as their object. I stopped feeling those, the moment you began sharing them. I have wept solely out of tenderness and compassion for you. I am inconsolable at having occasioned you a single moment of grief; I never stop reproaching myself for my inconstancy, nor contemplating, with emotion and wonder, what love has made you capable of doing for a miserable wretch who is not worthy of it, and who could never repay you, even if she were to shed her whole life's blood, she added, weeping copiously, for even half the sorrow she has caused you.

Her tears, her words, her tone of voice, made so astounding an impression on me, that it was as though my soul had split in two. Take care, I cried, take care, dearest Manon! I am not strong enough to bear these ardent expressions of affection. I am not used to such extremes of joy. O God! I cried, I have nothing more to ask of you! I am assured of Manon's heart; it is all I wanted it to be in order to be happy: I will never stop being so now. My felicity is assured. It is, she replied, so long as you depend for it on me, just as I know where I can always count on finding mine. I went to bed, my head filled with such enchanting notions that they transformed my cabin into a palace fit for the first king on earth. America now seemed a place of delights. Anyone who wants to taste love in all its sweetness, I often said to Manon, should come to New Orleans. For only here can one love and be loved without self-interest, jealousy, or inconstancy. Our compatriots come looking for gold; they have no idea how much more precious are the treasures we have found here.

We cultivated the Governor's friendship assiduously. Several weeks after our arrival he was kind enough to offer me a modest position that had just fallen vacant in the fort. Although it was of no particular distinction in itself, I regarded it as a sign of Heaven's favour, and accepted. It enabled me to live without having to depend on anyone else. I took a valet for myself and a maid for Manon. Our fortunes, modest though they were, improved. I was steady in my conduct, Manon no less so. We let no opportunity pass of doing some good turn or service to our neighbours. Our willingness to oblige, and our mild-mannered ways, won us the trust and affection of the entire colony. We were soon so well regarded that we were considered the foremost people in the town, after the Governor himself.

The innocence of our pursuits, and the tranquillity of our daily lives, served to bring us back imperceptibly to thoughts of religion.

Manon had never been an impious girl. Nor was I one of those flagrant libertines who pride themselves on adding irreligion to licentiousness. Love and youth alone had led us into dissolute ways. What we lacked in age, however, we made up for in experience, which was beginning to give us a maturity beyond our years. Our conversations, which had always turned on serious matters, now led us almost imperceptibly to thoughts of a virtuous union. I was the first to suggest this change. I knew the principles that ruled Manon's heart. She was straightforward and natural in all her feelings, a quality that always predisposes to virtue. I intimated to her the one thing that was missing from our happiness: which is, I said, to have it approved by Heaven. Our souls are too noble and our hearts too upright to allow us to live in wilful neglect of our duty. It was one thing to have lived this way in France, where it was equally impossible either to stop loving one another or to satisfy our love by legitimate means; but in America, where we are answerable only to ourselves, where we need no longer submit to the arbitrary laws of rank and decorum, where we are believed, indeed, to be married already, who will prevent us from being so in fact, and from ennobling our love with vows that religion itself has sanctified? As for me, I added, although in offering you my heart and hand I am giving you nothing new, I am ready to renew this gift before an altar. She seemed overcome with joy at these words. Will you believe me if I tell you, she said, that since we came to America I have had this same thought myself a thousand times? Fearful of causing you displeasure, however, I have hidden it in my heart. I am not so presumptuous as to aspire to the honour of being your wife. Ah Manon! I replied, if by Heaven's grace I had been born with a crown, you would shortly be the wife of a king. Let us not delay a moment longer. There are no obstacles that need deter us. I will speak to the Governor this very day, and confess that we have been deceiving him up until now. Let ordinary lovers fear the indissoluble chains of matrimony, I added. They would not fear them if they were certain, as we are, of always being bound by those of love. I left Manon beside herself with joy at my decision.

I am convinced that there is no man of honour anywhere who would not have approved of the decision I made, in the situation in which I found myself: that is, fatally enslaved by a passion I could not conquer, and assailed by a remorse I ought not to suppress. But will anyone, equally, accuse me of injustice, if I complain of Heaven's harshness in rejecting a plan I had formed solely in order to satisfy its commands? Alas! Did I say 'reject it'? It was punished, as though it were a crime. As long as, in my blindness, I trod the path of vice, Heaven bore with me in patience; its cruellest persecutions were reserved for when I began to return to that of virtue. I fear my strength will fail me, before I can finish relating the most fateful event that ever was.

I went to see the Governor, as I had agreed with Manon, to ask his consent to the solemnization of our marriage. I would have been very careful not to mention it, either to him or to anyone else, if I could have been certain that his chaplain, who at the time was the only priest in the town, would perform this service without informing him; but not daring to hope he would agree to remaining silent, I decided to act openly. The Governor had a nephew called Synnelet, of whom he was extremely fond. He was a man of some thirty years, brave, but easily angered and prone to violence. He was not married. He had been struck by Manon's beauty from the first day of our arrival; and the innumerable opportunities he had had of seeing her during the nine or ten months that had intervened had so inflamed his passion that he was wasting away for her in secret. However, since he believed, like his uncle and the rest of the town, that she and I were married, he had mastered his passion to the point of letting no sign of it escape him; and had even, on several occasions, shown himself eager to do anything he could to oblige me. I found him with his uncle when I arrived at the fort. Since there was no reason for me to keep my plans secret from him, I did not scruple to explain, in his presence, what had brought me there. The Governor heard me with his usual kindness. I told him part of my story, which he listened to with pleasure; and when I invited him to attend the ceremony I was planning, he was generous enough to offer to bear the full cost of the accompanying celebrations. I went away well satisfied.

An hour later the chaplain arrived at my door. I assumed he had come with instructions about my wedding; but, after a cold greeting, he informed me brusquely that the Governor forbade me to think any more about it, and that he had other plans for Manon. Other plans for Manon! I cried, my heart seized with mortal anguish, what plans would those be, Monsieur? He replied that, as I very well knew, the Governor was master here; that Manon had been sent from France for the good of the colony, and that it was his duty to dispose of her as he thought fit; that he had not done so up until now, because he believed her to be married, but having learned from my own lips that she was not, he thought it proper instead to give her to M. Synnelet, who was in love with her. Forgetting the need for prudence, I gave way to anger. Haughtily, I ordered the chaplain to leave my house, swearing that the Governor, Synnelet, and the whole town together would not dare to lay hands on my wife, or, as it pleased them to call her, my mistress.

I informed Manon at once of the dreadful message I had just received. We supposed that, after I had left them, Synnelet, acting upon a scheme he had long had in mind, must have cajoled his uncle into changing his mind. They were the stronger party. In New Orleans, we were as if in the middle of the sea: that is to say, separated by immense distances from the rest of the world. Where could we flee to? Into an unknown region, unpeopled perhaps, or inhabited by ferocious beasts, and by savages who were no less barbarous? I was respected in the town; but I could not hope to be so successful in stirring up dissent among the people that they would offer me support in any way commensurate with the wrong I had suffered. That would have taken money; I was poor. Besides, a popular uprising was not certain to succeed; and if fortune failed us, the disaster would be irremediable. I kept turning these thoughts over in my mind. I communicated some of them to Manon. Without listening to her reply, I formed new ones. I reached a decision; I rejected it in favour of another. I talked to myself, I answered myself out loud: in short, I was in a state of agitation beyond comparison, since nothing has ever equalled it. Manon kept her eyes on me. She could tell from my distress how great our danger was; and more frightened for me than for herself, this tender-hearted girl did not dare even to open her mouth to voice her fears. After endless reflection, I at last arrived at a firm decision, which was that I must go and see the Governor, and try to move him by appealing to principles of honour, and by reminding him of my respect for him and his affection for me. Her eyes brimming with tears, Manon tried to prevent me from leaving. You are going to your death, she kept on saying. They will kill you. I will never see you again. I want to die before you do. It took a great deal of effort on my part, to persuade her of the absolute necessity of my going out and of her staying at home. I promised I would be back very soon. She did not know, any more than I did, that it was on her head that Heaven's wrath, and the fury of our enemies, was about to fall.

I went to the fort. The Governor was with his chaplain. I humbled myself before him; I displayed, in order to move him, a submissiveness that, had it had any other end in view, would have made me die of shame. I used all the persuasions that never fail to made an impression on anyone who has not the heart of a cruel and ferocious tiger. But, barbarian that he was, he dismissed all of my complaints with two replies, which he repeated a hundred times over: that Manon was his to dispose of; and that he had given his word to his nephew. I was determined to restrain myself to the very last. I contented myself with saying that I believed him too good a friend to desire my death, which I would consent to more readily than the loss of my mistress.

I was only too convinced, by the time I left him, that there was nothing to be hoped for from this obstinate old man, who would have seen himself damned a thousand times over for the sake of his nephew. Nevertheless, I persisted in my plan of maintaining an air of restraint to the last, resolved as I was, should I find myself the victim of extreme injustice, to offer America one of the bloodiest and most horrible scenes that love has ever produced. I was on my way home, musing on this idea, when fate, intent as ever on hastening my ruin, caused me to encounter Synnelet. He read in my eyes something of what I was thinking; and, as I have already said, he was brave. He approached me. Were you perhaps looking for me? he said. I know very well that I have plans that offend you, and I have always foreseen that there would come a time when we must fight it out. Let us find out now which of us is to be the happier man. I told him he was right, and that only my death could settle our differences. We walked on together until we reached a spot some hundred yards outside the town. We crossed swords; I wounded him and, at almost the same moment, disarmed him. He was so enraged at his ill-luck that he refused either to beg for his life or renounce Manon. Perhaps I would have been within my rights to have deprived him, with one stroke, of both; but noble blood never demeans itself. I threw him his sword. Let us begin again, I said, but this time remember, no quarter is to be given. He attacked me with indescribable fury. I possessed, I have to admit, no great proficiency in arms, having attended fencing-school for only three months in Paris. It was love that guided my sword. Synnelet was able to pierce me through my arm, but I caught him off his guard, and dealt him so powerful a blow that he fell motionless at my feet.

In spite of the joy that victory in mortal combat brings, I soon began to reflect on the consequences of Synnelet's death. I could hope neither for mercy nor even for any stay of execution. Knowing as I did the Governor's passion for his nephew, I was convinced that my own death would follow within an hour of the discovery of his. However pressing this fear was, it was not my greatest cause of anxiety. Manon, her needs, the danger she was in, the certainty that I would lose her, all of this so troubled me that darkness clouded my vision and I no longer knew where I was. I regretted Synnelet's untimely fate. Instant death seemed the only remedy for my sufferings. Nevertheless, it was this very thought that brought me back to my senses and made me capable of resolution once more. What! Wish to die, so as to end my own sufferings? I cried. Are there any I fear more than the loss of everything I love? Let us suffer even the cruellest extremities in order to save my mistress, and put off dying until we have suffered them in vain. I set off back towards town. I arrived home. I found Manon there, half-dead with anxiety and fear. My presence revived her. I could not hide from her the terrible event that had just happened. Hearing that Synnelet was dead, and that I was wounded, she fell senseless in my arms. It took me more than a quarter of an hour to restore her to consciousness.

I was myself half-dead. I could see no prospect of salvation either for her or me. What shall we do, Manon? I said, when she had regained a little strength. Alas! What are we to do? I have no choice but to flee. But what will you do: will you stay? Of course you must stay. You can still be happy here; as for me, I must leave you, must go far away and seek death among savages or between the claws of some wild beast. Weak though she was, she got to her feet and, taking me by the hand, led me to the door. Let us fly together, she said; and let us not lose a moment. Synnelet's body may already have been dis-covered, leaving us no time to escape. But where can we go, dearest Manon? I cried, utterly distraught. Is there anywhere left for us to turn to? Would it not be better for you to stay here and try to live without me, and for me to give myself up voluntarily to the Gov-ernor? This suggestion only fired still further her eagerness to depart. I had no choice but to follow. As we left, I still had enough presence of mind to snatch up some brandy I had in my room, and as many provisions as I could cram into my pockets. We told our servants, who were in the next room, that we were going out for our evening walk, as was our custom every day; and we set off out of town, more quickly than Manon's delicate state would seem to allow.

Although I was still undecided about where we should seek refuge, two possibilities seemed to hold out some hope, without which I would rather have suffered death itself than uncertainty as to what might happen to Manon. I had acquired enough knowledge of the country, during the almost ten months I had been in America, to have some idea of how to tame the ferocity of the natives. I knew that it was possible to entrust oneself to their care without inviting certain death. I had even acquainted myself, during my various encounters with them, with a few words of their language and with some of their customs. This was a melancholy resource indeed; another was offered by the English who, like us, have established themselves in the New World. But the vast expanses that lay between our lands and theirs terrified me. To reach their colonies we would have to traverse barren plains it would take several days to cross, and mountains so high and steep they would daunt the roughest and hardiest of men. Nevertheless, I flattered myself that we could call upon both of these resources: on the natives to guide us, and on the English to receive us into their settlements.*

We walked for as long as Manon's courage sustained her, that is, for about five miles; for my incomparable mistress steadfastly refused to stop any sooner. At last, overcome with weariness, she confessed she could go no further. It was already dark. We sat down in the middle of a vast plain, unable to find a single tree to give us shelter. Her first concern was to change the dressing on my wound, which she herself had bandaged before we left. I opposed her wishes in vain. It would have dealt her a final, mortal blow to have refused her the satisfaction of believing me to be comfortable and out of danger, before she thought of her own preservation. I submitted to her care for a few moments. I accepted her ministrations silently and with shame. But once her tender feelings had been assuaged, with what ardour I indulged my own! I stripped myself of my clothes, hoping to make the ground seem less hard by spreading them beneath her. I persuaded her, against her will, to let me use every means I could devise to lessen her discomfort. I warmed her hands with burning kisses and the ardour of my sighs. I spent the whole night watching over her, and imploring Heaven to grant her a sweet and peaceful sleep. How urgent and sincere, dear God, were my prayers! And how harshly must I have been judged, for you to disdain to answer them!

Forgive me, if I conclude in as few words as possible a story that kills me. The misfortune I am about to relate has no equal. I am destined to mourn it my whole life long. But although it is for ever present in my memory, my soul recoils in horror every time I try to put it into words.

We had passed part of the night peacefully. I believed my beloved mistress to be asleep, and scarcely dared even to breathe, for fear of disturbing her slumber. At daybreak I noticed, touching her hands, that they trembled and were cold. I drew them to my breast to warm them. She felt this movement and, trying to catch hold of my hands in turn, said in a faint voice that she thought her last hour had come. At first I took this for nothing more than a form of words common enough in moments of misfortune, and replied with simple expressions of consolation and love. But her frequent sighs, her silence when I questioned her, the pressure of her hands on mine, which she continued to hold, soon convinced me that the end of her sufferings was not far off. Do not ask me to describe my feelings, nor to repeat to you the last words that she spoke. I lost her; I received tokens of her love at the very moment she died; that is all I have the strength to say about this fatal and most lamentable event.

My soul did not follow hers. Heaven doubtless did not consider me sufficiently punished as yet. It has condemned me ever since to drag out a wretched and languishing existence. I renounce willingly and for ever any thought of a happier one.

I remained there for more than twenty-four hours,* my lips pressed to the face and hands of my beloved Manon. My intention was to die there; I reflected, however, at the start of the second day, that after my own death her body would be exposed to the ravages of wild beasts. I determined to bury her, and await death lying on her grave. Weakened as I was by fasting and grief, I was already so close to my end that I had to make a supreme effort even to remain upright. I was obliged to resort to the brandy I had brought. It gave me the strength I needed for the sad office I was about to perform. It was not

The burial scene (Pasquier)

difficult to open up the earth in a region covered largely by sand. I
broke my sword so that I could dig with it; but found it less useful
than my hands. I dug a large grave; in it I placed the idol of my heart,
having first wrapped her carefully in all my clothes, to prevent the
sand from touching her. I placed her thus only after embracing her a
thousand times, with all the ardour of the most perfect love. I sat
down beside her again. I gazed at her for a long time. I could not
bring myself to fill in the grave. At last, feeling my strength begin to
fail, and fearing I might lose it entirely before I had completed my
task, I buried for ever, in the bosom of the earth, the most perfect
and the loveliest thing it had ever brought forth. Then I lay down
on the grave, my face turned towards the sand; and closing my
eyes, with the intention of never opening them again, implored
Heaven's assistance and waited impatiently for death. You will find
this hard to believe, but during the whole of my performance of
these doleful rites not a tear escaped my eyes, nor a sigh my lips. My
deep dismay and resolute determination to die had stemmed the flow
of my grief and despair. Nor did I remain for long in the position I
had taken up on the grave, before losing what little consciousness
and feeling I had left.

After what you have just heard, the ending of my story is of so
little importance that it scarcely merits the attention you are so kind
as to devote to it. Synnelet's body was carried back to town and his
wounds tended with care; it soon became evident, not only that he
was not dead, but that he had not even been dangerously wounded.
He told his uncle everything that had passed between us; further-
more, impelled by nobility of soul, he at once made public the role
my own magnanimity had played in our encounter. They sent someone to look for me. My absence, as well as Manon's, made them
suspect I had decided to flee. It was too late for them to mount a
search that day, but they spent the next two following my traces.
They found me lying, with no apparent sign of life, on Manon's
grave; and those who discovered me in this state, almost naked, and
bleeding from my wound, were in no doubt that I had been robbed
and murdered. They carried me back to town. Their movements as
they transported me brought me back to my senses. My sighs on
opening my eyes, and my groans at finding myself once more among
the living, were indication enough that my condition was not so
desperate as to be beyond help. The help they gave me was only too

successful. Nevertheless, I was held in a closely guarded prison throughout this time; I was brought before the court; and, since there was no sign of Manon, was accused of having done away with her in a fit of jealousy and rage. I told my pitiable tale exactly as it had happened. Synnelet, although transported with grief at what I had to relate, was generous enough to plead for clemency on my behalf. He obtained it. I was so weak that they were obliged to take me straight from prison to my bed, to which I was confined for three months by a violent illness. My hatred for life did not diminish. I called on death continually, and for a long time persisted in refusing all remedies. But Heaven, after chastizing me so severely, intended that I should benefit from my punishments and misfortunes. It lightened my darkness, and reawakened in me ideas worthy of my birth and education.* Since a certain calm had also been restored to my soul, this change led almost at once to my recovery. Resolved in future to follow the dictates of honour alone, I returned to my modest employment at the fort while waiting for the ships that visit this part of America once a year to arrive from France. I was resolved to return to my native land, and to rectify, by a wise and well-ordered life, the scandal of my past conduct. Synnelet had assumed the task of transporting my beloved mistress's body to an honourable resting-place.

About six weeks after my recovery, walking alone one day along the shore, I saw a vessel arrive, brought by some business or commerce to New Orleans. I watched attentively as the ship's company disembarked. Among those who were making their way towards town I was amazed to see Tiberge. My faithful friend recognized me from afar, in spite of the changes sorrow had wrought on my face. He told me that the only motive for his journey had been the desire to see me and persuade me to return to France; that, having received the letter I had written to him from Le Havre, he had gone there in person to bring me the help I requested; that he had felt the keenest distress on discovering I had already departed, and would have followed me there and then, if a vessel had been ready to set sail; that he had spent several months searching for one in various ports, then, finding one at last in Saint-Malo that was weighing anchor for Martinique, had embarked in the hope of finding, when he arrived there, an easy passage onwards to New Orleans; that the vessel from Saint-Malo had been captured on its way by Spanish pirates, and taken to one of their islands; that he had managed, by cunning, to escape; and after various further detours, had taken advantage of the small craft that had just arrived to reach me safely at last.

My gratitude towards so generous and constant a friend was beyond anything words could express. I took him to my house. I made him master of everything I owned. I told him all that had happened to me since I left France; and, hoping to afford him a joy he was not expecting, declared that the seeds of virtue he had long ago sown in my heart were beginning to bear fruits that I thought would give him satisfaction. He protested that so sweet an assurance was compensation for all the hardships of his journey.

We remained together for two more months in New Orleans, waiting for a ship to arrive that would take us back to France, and, having put to sea at last, landed two weeks ago at Le Havre-de-Grâce. I wrote to my family as soon as I arrived. From my older brother's reply I learned the melancholy news of my father's death, to which I fear, with only too much cause, my errors have contributed. The wind was favourable for Calais; I therefore re-embarked at once, with the intention of making my way to the house of a gentleman-in-waiting to my parents, only a few miles outside the town, where my brother writes he will await my arrival.

END OF THE SECOND PART

EXPLANATORY NOTES

3 *presented separately*: the story we now know as *Manon Lescaut*, but whose full title is *The Story of the Chevalier Des Grieux and Manon Lescaut*, first appeared in 1731 as the seventh and final volume of Prévost's fictional *Memoirs of a Man of Quality*. The narrator of all seven volumes of Prévost's memoir-novel, the Marquis de Renoncour, justifies in this Foreword to his last volume the inclusion within his own memoirs of a lengthy episode narrated to but not lived by him, and its anachronistic position as a sort of addition or annex to his own story.

Ut jam . . . omittat: 'he [the poet] should at once say what ought to be said at once; and the rest he should postpone and leave aside until later', from *The Art of Poetry* (43–4), by the Roman poet Horace (65 BC–8 BC).

4 *to instruct while entertaining them*: another precept of Horace's, much repeated by apologists for literature from the Renaissance onwards, and fundamental to Renoncour's whole argument in this Foreword, was that poetry and fiction should combine entertainment with instruction.

pleasing features: see Horace, *Satires*, II. vi. 72–6; and *Épître* vi. 153–8, by the French poet Nicolas Boileau (1636–1711).

7 *short journeys . . . as possible*: the earlier volumes of the *Memoirs of a Man of Quality* record in full the events alluded to here: Renoncour's retreat, after the death of his wife, to an abbey near Paris, his efforts on behalf of his daughter, and his emergence from retirement to accompany on his travels a young pupil, the Marquis d..., who makes a brief appearance in the pages of *Manon Lescaut*. The evidence of these earlier volumes also allows us to date this first meeting between Renoncour and Des Grieux as taking place in the first half of 1715, since they make it clear that Renoncour learns of the death of Louis XIV, which took place in September 1715, just after arriving in Spain. For further discussion of the chronology of *Manon Lescaut*, see the Introduction, pp. xii–xiii.

the parlement: the *parlements*, of which there were sixteen under the *ancien régime*, were courts of law.

8 *off to America*: contemporary records, as well as eyewitness accounts, document the deportation of prostitutes and other undesirables to the French colonies of the New World from the last quarter of the seventeenth century onwards, and to Louisiana, for a short period, during 1719 and 1720. They include reports of armed attacks on the convoys, and bear witness, too, to many of the poignant details Prévost includes both here and later in the novel. Saint-Simon, for example, describes not only the privations that the women suffered but also the sympathy elicited by their plight, which 'excited pity and indignation' (Deloffre–Picard, p. 11, n. 2).

8 *the Hôpital*: the Hôpital de la Salpêtrière in Paris was one of a number of general hospitals throughout France that served not only to house the incurably sick and the aged, but also to detain beggars, vagrants, and women condemned for immorality. It was from these hospitals that the women destined for deportation were taken. The Hôpital in Paris was notorious, not only because of the supposed moral degeneracy of many of its inmates, but also for the brutality of its regime.

10 *four louis d'or . . . noticing*: under Louis XIV the basic unit of money was the franc or livre. A louis d'or was worth 24 francs or livres in 1715, the pistole was worth 10 francs, and the écu 3 francs. Here, as so often in the novel, social realities are communicated in terms of money: it is a sign of M. de Renoncour's quality that he deals in louis d'or, as it is also of the rapaciousness of Manon's guards that they ask for this form of payment.

11 *I had met in Pacy*: according to the time scheme set out in the *Memoirs* (vol. 5), this second encounter must take place in June 1716, on Renoncour's return from London. Needless to say, since the story of Des Grieux and Manon is, as it were, inserted in 1731 into the chronology of the earlier volumes, there is no mention there of either meeting.

12 *Chevalier Des Grieux*: as a younger son, Des Grieux is destined for a career in the Order of Malta. The Knights of Malta or, more properly, Knights of Saint John, were a religious and military order, who took vows of obedience and celibacy. They were famous for their successful defence, against the Turks, of the island of Malta, which they ruled from 1530 to 1798. Their wealth came from estates they owned in various of the richer countries of Catholic Europe, and it was from among the sons of the nobility in these countries that their ranks were formed. Des Grieux is presumably typical of such recruits. But before beginning his military career he must complete his education, which, having graduated from the Jesuit college in Amiens, he can now expect to do by spending two years at the Académie in Paris, learning physical and social accomplishments.

examples of Antiquity: of which the best-known example, and the most relevant one, perhaps, to Des Grieux's own story, is that of Orestes and his faithful friend Pylades. Des Grieux would have known the story of Pylades' friendship for the doomed Orestes—pursued by the Furies in return for his crimes—from classical sources, but also, as an ardent theatregoer, from Racine's *Andromaque*. (See below, notes to pp. 94 and 120.)

14 *evil star . . . my reply*: for the theme of astrological determinism in *Manon Lescaut*, see the Introduction, pp. xxi–xxii.

15 *Argus had now rejoined us*: Argus, having a hundred eyes, was the classical example par excellence of the watchful servant. See Ovid, *Metamorphoses*, i. 625 ff.

humble birth herself: in the 1731 version of the novel Manon is described at this point as being 'not a person of quality, although of quite good birth'. By 1753 she has sunk much lower down the social scale. Prévost is perhaps responding to criticism of his 1731 version—that it portrayed people of standing as behaving unworthily—by reducing Manon (even though she is not quite 'quality' even in 1731) to a level of society where vicious behaviour is only to be expected. At the same time, by widening the social gulf between Des Grieux and his mistress, Prévost presents himself with a further difficulty to be overcome: how to present as worthy of a noble passion like Des Grieux's a girl who is not only faithless but, socially, beneath contempt.

17 *if this is possible*: Des Grieux is accurate, a few lines earlier, in identifying this little phrase as an 'equivocation', suggesting as it does one thing to Tiberge, who thinks it likely the interview will take place, and another to Des Grieux, who knows it cannot. It not only successfully deceives Tiberge, but has the added advantage of absolving Des Grieux from telling an outright lie. English writers, no less than French, are quick to attribute such specious devices to the teaching of the Jesuits, whose pupil Des Grieux has been in Amiens: 'You won't tell a downright fib for the world, but for equivocation! No Jesuit ever went beyond you.' (Richardson, *Pamela*, 1741).

18 *M. de B..., the well-known tax-farmer*: in the seventeenth and eighteenth centuries novels were often presented in the guise of authentic memoirs. This convention served to defend the novel, which was not a classical genre and had none of the authority of tragedy and epic, from accusations of frivolity, even immorality, and untruth. The memoir-novel of which *Manon Lescaut* originally formed the last volume is of this type; both of its 'real' narrators, Des Grieux and the Marquis de Renoncour, are scrupulous therefore in suppressing the names of prominent and wealthy men, like, for example, M. de B..., who could have been embarrassed by the revelations it contained. Hence the use of initials to conceal the 'true' identity of many of the character of this story.

As a farmer-general, or tax-farmer, M. de B... is certainly both wealthy and prominent, one of a small group of men to whom, in eighteenth-century France, was 'farmed out' the collection of indirect taxes. Although often immensely powerful, they were *nouveaux riches* rather than aristocrats. Thus, though Manon and her servant may be impressed by M. de B...'s aristocratic pretensions, he remains, for Des Grieux père, plain M. B... (see below, pp. 23–4).

without his consent: a minor seeking to marry without parental permission in Paris at this period had first to fulfil a residence requirement of six months; and would automatically have been disinherited.

19 *our apartment*: an apartment is a suite of rooms, usually the private rooms used by the masters of a wealthy household.

24 *how to consolidate your conquests*: an allusion to a famous comment on the great general Hannibal, which the Roman historian Livy puts into the mouth of a fellow Carthaginian: 'vincere scis, sed victoria uti nescis' (Livy, *History of Rome*, xxii. 51).

27 *faithful Dido deserved*: Book IV of Virgil's *Aeneid* narrates the passion of Dido, Queen of Carthage, for Aeneas, and her suicide when, destined to found Rome, he abandons her.

a contempt that has no equal: Tiberge, a model pupil of the Jesuits, describes his conversion to true piety in terms his masters would have approved of: as a contest, that is, in which worldly temptations are overcome by a combination of reason, reflection, and the exercise of the will, aided by divine grace. The optimistic view of human nature that such a spiritual journey implies is in stark contrast to Jansenist teaching (for which see note to p. 65). We learn from this passage, too, something that Des Grieux suggests later on—while turning it to his own advantage: that piety, although desirable in a cleric, was not considered essential.

29 *solitude . . . with Manon*: descriptions of the pleasures of the life of virtuous retirement from the world are a classical commonplace, much repeated in literature of this period.

a considerable benefice: after two years at the seminary in Amiens, Tiberge will be able to complete his studies for the priesthood at the seminary of Saint-Sulpice in Paris thanks to a benefice or vacant living. The incumbent of such a living benefited from the revenue provided by a parish or monastic estate without being required to reside there. Des Grieux receives a similar promise in the next paragraph.

33 *Dear Manon . . . your glances*: Des Grieux's mingling of sacred and profane language, which he himself concedes here, as well as his manipulation of sacred language to exonerate a profane and indeed illicit passion, are later to shock Tiberge (pp. 63–4). They are not, however, confined to the moments of high drama in the novel, but occur throughout. For the colouring that the use of theological and biblical language gives to Des Grieux's narrative as a whole, see Introduction, pp. xxi–xxii.

36 *the assembly . . . Chaillot*: it was de rigueur during this period for people of fortune and fashion to hold an assembly after the theatre. On these occasions they opened their houses to members of their own social circle and provided various forms of entertainment, dancing, for example, and, in particular, gambling.

a guardsman: Lescaut is a member of the *garde du corps*, four companies of guards whose function it was to protect the king. They enjoyed a number of privileges, including immunity from prosecution. Notorious for their loose-living and violence, they also, as in this novel, acted as hired men who would commit any crime for gain.

39 *favours of a girl like Manon*: this circumlocution replaces the more candid hope expressed in the 1731 version, that the nobleman will pay liberally to 'spend the night with a girl like Manon'. This change is consistent with a general move in the 1753 version towards greater decorum and elevation of tone (see the Note on the Text).

40 *the League*: i.e. the association of card-sharpers, for which see note to p. 44.

44 *the Hôtel de Transylvanie*: the rage for gambling in this period was such that, not only were the assemblies largely given over to this pursuit, but a number of fashionable gaming-houses were opened in order to cater for this taste. The Hôtel de Transylvanie, where Des Grieux is to practise, is a celebrated, and historical, example. The house belonged to the exiled Prince of Transylvania, a military ally of Louis XIV, whose officers carried on a lucrative business in all forms of gambling. Cheating in such places took place on a large and organized scale. The ironically named League or Order of the Chevaliers of Industry was an 'association' or 'confederation' of practised card-sharpers, who plied their profession in the gaming-houses. Training for this profession was no less organized: 'academies' were formed for this purpose, complete with 'professors', 'associates', and 'novices'. Des Grieux, abandoning the Order of Malta, his noviciate at Saint-Sulpice, and the Académie where he was to have completed his education, is to prove an apt pupil in the card-sharping circles that parody these honourable institutions.

53 *making little shrines*: Catholic children were encouraged, especially at the time of the feast of Corpus Christi, to express their piety by making models of shrines or altars out of simple materials, and decorating them with flowers. Lescaut hopes by this reference, susceptible of course of a number of ironical interpretations, to persuade G... M... of Des Grieux's piety and naivety.

a little more of society: an untranslatable pun in the original, depending on two senses of the French *du monde*, meaning, first, social graces, which Lescaut says Des Grieux lacks, and secondly, people in general, which is the sense in which Des Grieux pretends to understand him.

55 *arrested . . . as downright libertines*: M. de G... M... has evidently obtained a *lettre de cachet*, a letter, that is, under the king's seal, authorizing the arrest and imprisonment of the lovers.

56 *appals me even to name*: Des Grieux, as so often, keeps his audience in suspense; but we are about to learn that it is to the Hôpital that Manon has been sent. As we already know, it is from this same prison that she is eventually dispatched to America (see above, note to p. 8). During this first incarceration, however, and in spite of Des Grieux's fears for her, Manon is held in the wing dedicated to the 'correction' of women from good families, where the regime was less harsh than in other parts of the same prison.

No indignities . . . I said to him: Saint-Lazare was a reformatory for the sons of good family but irregular conduct. Floggings were sometimes administered there, but Des Grieux, we learn, is to be spared such indignities by virtue of his noble birth.

64 *monstrous libertinism*: a libertine is someone who allows himself—or, more rarely, herself—freedom to the point of licence in either his spiritual life or his sexual conduct. Des Grieux is accused at various times of being a libertine in both senses; but although he rejects in particular the charge

of religious libertinism, passages like the present one, where he uses religious language and indeed religious doctrines to plead the cause of human passion, exploit to the full the ambiguity of the word.

65 *our Jansenists*: Jansenism, an influential and highly controversial doctrine among late seventeenth- and early eighteenth-century Catholics, insists, after St Augustine, on the powerlessness of humankind since the Fall to resist the evil inherent in its own nature and, except by God's grace, to do good. Neither grace nor salvation can be earned or merited by human effort, but are the gratuitous gift of a God who has elected, from all eternity, those who are to be saved. In explaining his inability to resist Manon as the powerlessness of one who is, by contrast, deprived of God's grace, Des Grieux invites Tiberge's accusation of Jansenism. But Des Grieux, as we have already seen, is equally ready to exploit Jesuit teachings.

76 *the night-watch*: each of the patrols of the night-watch consisted of a sergeant, a corporal, and five common soldiers.

78 *the strangest adventure . . . destiny*: this remark seems to look beyond the interpolated episode of the Italian prince (see note to p. 83) to the affair with young G... M... and its consequences.

80 *at the Académie*: see note to p. 12.

83 *the first few weeks*: the twelve paragraphs that follow comprise what has come to be known as 'the episode of the Italian prince', and are the only addition of any length that Prévost made to the 1731 version of *Manon* when he revised it in 1753. His own note to the Foreword of the 1753 edition (p. 5) justifies this additional episode as 'necessary for the fuller portrayal of one of the principal characters', usually taken to mean Manon; and it does indeed enrich her character by showing her to be witty and inventive (manipulative even), as well as in love with Des Grieux, and capable of loyalty in a way that anticipates and makes more plausible her conversion to fidelity in the New World. The episode functions, indeed, as a Parisian parallel to the idyll the lovers will enjoy in the New World; for whereas in the 1731 version young G... M... appears on the scene on the very day of the lovers' return to Chaillot, here they first enjoy several weeks of contented domesticity and even respectability. Once G... M... has put in an appearance, however, the reader may well look back on this episode as fulfilling a rather more ambiguous role: since no sooner is Manon's fidelity established, it seems, than it is undermined by her ready accommodation of one wealthy young suitor when she has just rejected another.

94 *from Racine*: as devotees of the theatre, Des Grieux and Manon are able to quote and even to parody lines from Racine. The passage in question is from Racine's *Iphigénie* (II. v. 674–6 and 681–2):

> Moi? Vous me soupçonnez de cette perfidie?
> Moi, j'aimerais, Madame, un vainqueur furieux,
> Qui toujours tout sanglant se présente à mes yeux...

> Ces morts, cette Lesbos, ces cendres, cette flame,
> Sont les traits dont l'amour l'a gravé dans votre âme.

In the first of these speeches, Ériphile denies what Iphigénie, correctly, suspects: that she is her rival for the affections of Achille. To Ériphile's argument that she could not possibly love the bloody conqueror of her native Lesbos, Iphigénie, more shrewd than Des Grieux, replies—in the second speech— that it is these violent memories themselves that have seduced Ériphile. The lovers' application of Racine's lines to their own situation seems to depend partly on a pun on the many meanings in French of the noun *trait* (a detail of a scene, a feature of a face, a shaft or dart).

108 *even the wad of a pistol*: G... M..., a commoner and hence, in Des Grieux's eyes, a coward, fears anything a pistol might contain, even the wad of fabric that holds in place the charge and ball.

110 *to the gallows . . . purer than yours*: in the event of his being condemned to death, Des Grieux, as an aristocrat, would enjoy the privilege of being beheaded, whereas G... M..., a commoner, would suffer the ignominy of being sent to the gallows.

111 *to the Châtelet*: the Petit-Châtelet was a prison reserved for debtors and relatively minor offenders. But since the sentences there were immediate and without right of appeal, and since Manon, as a reoffender, was likely to be treated harshly, Des Grieux, as we see in the next paragraph, shows alarm at the very mention of the name.

114 *full board . . . for each of us*: an ordinance of 1676 had forbidden gaolers to accept payment from prisoners or their families in return for improved conditions. The practice nevertheless continued.

115 *a week before*: in spite of the care which Prévost devoted to other aspects of his revision of the 1731 text, he has here neglected to correct the errors in chronology that the episode of the Italian prince introduces into the rest of his story. Since this letter pre-dates the lovers' return to Chaillot, and since, we are told, they spent several weeks there, it must have been written longer ago than 'a week before'.

I underwent an interrogation: the Lieutenant-General of Police's personal intervention in Des Grieux's case, and indeed his leniency, are clear signs of the deference an aristocratic family could expect from the authorities. As we are about to see, Manon, as a woman of no standing and less reputation, enjoys no such favours. Indeed, her case is hopeless unless someone of the age and rank of Des Grieux's father takes it upon himself to intercede directly with the Lieutenant-General of Police (see p. 122).

116 *Place de la Grève . . . whole world*: the Place de la Grève was where public executions were carried out.

120 *I intend to deserve it*: a reminiscence, perhaps, of Orestes' defiant challenge to the gods in Racine's *Andromaque* (III. i): 'Let us merit their anger; let us justify their hate.'

126 *either death or victory*: the prayer for death or victory was a classical commonplace, repeated, for example, by the Knights of Malta on the eve of battle, and also, in Aphra Behn's *Oroonoko* (*c.*1688), by the enslaved noble savages in their fight for freedom. In spite of obvious differences in tone and style, there are a number of interesting parallels between *Oroonoko* and *Manon*. Not only do the burial scenes in the two stories have aspects in common, but Oroonoko, like Des Grieux, speaks 'with the best grace in the world'.

130 *follow the laws of nature*: Des Grieux may have in mind here the propaganda put out by the Mississippi Company, which, in a series of articles in the government-controlled newspaper the *Mercure de France* in 1717–19, offered an optimistic account of the friendliness of the indigenous people of America. Des Grieux could also be relying on the many descriptions of the New World Indians published by Jesuit missionaries from the middle of the seventeenth century onwards, or indeed on the contemporary cult of the 'noble savage'. His hopes and fears concerning the Indians seem, however, to owe more to his state of mind at any particular moment than to anything he has read.

132 *free of charge*: the *Compagnie du Mississippi* or *Compagnie des Indes*, founded in 1717 to exploit the wealth of Louisiana, not only advertised the attractions of life there ('an eternal spring reigns ...'), but also offered material inducements to prospective settlers.

133 *We set off ... a broad moat*: Prévost's account of the environs of New Orleans bears little relation to reality. The settlement, founded in 1718, was built not on the sea, which is some 60 miles distant, but on the Mississippi, and not on sandy but on marshy terrain. As described by Prévost, it bears more resemblance to Biloxi, the port of embarkation at the time for New Orleans, than to New Orleans itself. His sombre description of the settlement, by contrast, with its Governor's house and rows of adobe huts, is rather more accurate, more so certainly than the Mississippi Company's propaganda of a pleasant and bustling town. In other words, Prévost's account is shaped more by the psychological and emotional requirements of his story than by any strict realism.

The prettiest ... for the rest: the role of the Governor in allotting the prostitutes newly arrived from France to the male settlers is well attested. The drawing of lots, however, although irresistible to writers of contemporary fiction, seems to have been practised only in exceptional circumstances.

141 *into their settlements*: it is presumably Charlestown in Carolina that Des Grieux has in mind as a possible safe haven, a town some 800 miles distant from New Orleans—in order to reach it, the lovers would have had to cross two deserts, the Appalachian mountains, and miles of dense forest.

142 *more than twenty-four hours*: in the 1731 version Des Grieux spends 'two days and two nights' prostrate on Manon's body.

145 *my birth and education*: the change of heart and mind that Des Grieux announces to Tiberge on his arrival in New Orleans is, in the original version, that of a Christian conversion: 'Heaven shone the light of its grace upon me, and inspired in me the intention of returning to it by the path of penitence. I gave myself over entirely to the practice of piety.' In the present text this conversion, although not without religious reson-ance, becomes a more secular one, a return to class and family, in other words, without any reference to grace, penitence, or piety. Whatever else may be said about it, this change assures Des Grieux a much greater consistency of character than in the earlier version. After all, he does not, as narrator, greatly distance himself from his younger rebellious self, but still seeks on the one hand to defend a sinful passion and on the other to reproach Heaven for its harshness towards him. Too sudden a conversion on the part of such a character would risk shocking the reader's aesthetic sense and in doing so alienate the sympathy Des Grieux is bent on gaining.

American Literature

British and Irish Literature

Children's Literature

Classics and Ancient Literature

Colonial Literature

Eastern Literature

European Literature

Gothic Literature

History

Medieval Literature

Oxford English Drama

Poetry

Philosophy

Politics

Religion

The Oxford Shakespeare

A complete list of Oxford World's Classics, including Authors in Context, Oxford English Drama, and the Oxford Shakespeare, is available in the UK from the Marketing Services Department, Oxford University Press, Great Clarendon Street, Oxford OX2 6DP, or visit the website at www.oup.com/uk/worldsclassics.

In the USA, visit www.oup.com/us/owc for a complete title list.

Oxford World's Classics are available from all good bookshops. In case of difficulty, customers in the UK should contact Oxford University Press Bookshop, 116 High Street, Oxford OX1 4BR.

Six French Poets of the Nineteenth
Century

HONORÉ DE BALZAC **Cousin Bette**
Eugénie Grandet
Père Goriot

CHARLES BAUDELAIRE **The Flowers of Evil**
The Prose Poems and **Fanfarlo**

BENJAMIN CONSTANT **Adolphe**

DENIS DIDEROT **Jacques the Fatalist**

ALEXANDRE DUMAS (PÈRE) **The Black Tulip**
The Count of Monte Cristo
Louise de la Vallière
The Man in the Iron Mask
La Reine Margot
The Three Musketeers
Twenty Years After
The Vicomte de Bragelonne

ALEXANDRE DUMAS (FILS) **La Dame aux Camélias**

GUSTAVE FLAUBERT **Madame Bovary**
A Sentimental Education
Three Tales

VICTOR HUGO **Notre-Dame de Paris**

J.-K. HUYSMANS **Against Nature**

PIERRE CHODERLOS **Les Liaisons dangereuses**
DE LACLOS

MME DE LAFAYETTE **The Princesse de Clèves**

GUILLAUME DU LORRIS **The Romance of the Rose**
and JEAN DE MEUN

	Eirik the Red and Other Icelandic Sagas
	The German-Jewish Dialogue
	The Kalevala
	The Poetic Edda
LUDOVICO ARIOSTO	Orlando Furioso
GIOVANNI BOCCACCIO	The Decameron
GEORG BÜCHNER	Danton's Death, Leonce and Lena, and Woyzeck
LUIS VAZ DE CAMÕES	The Lusiads
MIGUEL DE CERVANTES	Don Quixote Exemplary Stories
CARLO COLLODI	The Adventures of Pinocchio
DANTE ALIGHIERI	The Divine Comedy Vita Nuova
LOPE DE VEGA	Three Major Plays
J. W. VON GOETHE	Elective Affinities Erotic Poems Faust: Part One and Part Two The Flight to Italy
E. T. A. HOFFMANN	The Golden Pot and Other Tales
HENRIK IBSEN	An Enemy of the People, The Wild Duck, Rosmersholm Four Major Plays Peer Gynt
LEONARDO DA VINCI	Selections from the Notebooks
FEDERICO GARCIA LORCA	Four Major Plays
MICHELANGELO BUONARROTI	Life, Letters, and Poetry

GEORGE ELIOT	Daniel Deronda
	The Lifted Veil and Brother Jacob
	Middlemarch
	The Mill on the Floss
	Silas Marner
SUSAN FERRIER	Marriage
ELIZABETH GASKELL	Cranford
	The Life of Charlotte Brontë
	Mary Barton
	North and South
	Wives and Daughters
GEORGE GISSING	New Grub Street
	The Odd Woman
THOMAS HARDY	Far from the Madding Crowd
	Jude the Obscure
	The Mayor of Casterbridge
	The Return of the Native
	Tess of the d'Urbervilles
	The Woodlanders
WILLIAM HAZLITT	Selected Writings
JAMES HOGG	The Private Memoirs and Confessions of a Justified Sinner
JOHN KEATS	The Major Works
	Selected Letters
CHARLES MATURIN	Melmoth the Wanderer
WALTER SCOTT	The Antiquary
	Ivanhoe
	Rob Roy
MARY SHELLEY	Frankenstein
	The Last Man

Women's Writing 1778–1838

JAMES BOSWELL	Life of Johnson
FRANCES BURNEY	Cecilia Evelina
JOHN CLELAND	Memoirs of a Woman of Pleasure
DANIEL DEFOE	A Journal of the Plague Year Moll Flanders Robinson Crusoe
HENRY FIELDING	Joseph Andrews and Shamela Tom Jones
WILLIAM GODWIN	Caleb Williams
OLIVER GOLDSMITH	The Vicar of Wakefield
ELIZABETH INCHBALD	A Simple Story
SAMUEL JOHNSON	The History of Rasselas
ANN RADCLIFFE	The Italian The Mysteries of Udolpho
SAMUEL RICHARDSON	Pamela
TOBIAS SMOLLETT	The Adventures of Roderick Random The Expedition of Humphry Clinker
LAURENCE STERNE	The Life and Opinions of Tristram Shandy, Gentleman A Sentimental Journey
JONATHAN SWIFT	Gulliver's Travels A Tale of a Tub and Other Works
HORACE WALPOLE	The Castle of Otranto
MARY WOLLSTONECRAFT	Mary and The Wrongs of Woman A Vindication of the Rights of Woman